THE
BORROWED
HILLS

A NOVEL

SCOTT PRESTON

Scribner

New York   London   Toronto   Sydney   New Delhi

Scribner

An Imprint of Simon & Schuster, LLC

1230 Avenue of the Americas

New York, NY 10020

First Scribner hardcover edition June 2024

SCRIBNER and design are registered trademarks of Simon & Schuster, LLC.

Simon & Schuster: Celebrating 100 Years of Publishing in 2024

For information about special discounts for bulk purchases, please contact Simon & Schuster Special Sales at 1-866-506-1949 or business@simonandschuster.com.

The Simon & Schuster Speakers Bureau can bring authors to your live event. For more information or to book an event, contact the Simon & Schuster Speakers Bureau at 1-866-248-3049 or visit our website at www.simonspeakers.com.

Manufactured in the United States of America

1 3 5 7 9 10 8 6 4 2

Library of Congress Cataloging-in-Publication Data has been applied for.

ISBN 978-1-6680-5067-5
ISBN 978-1-6680-5069-9 (ebook)

THE
BORROWED
HILLS

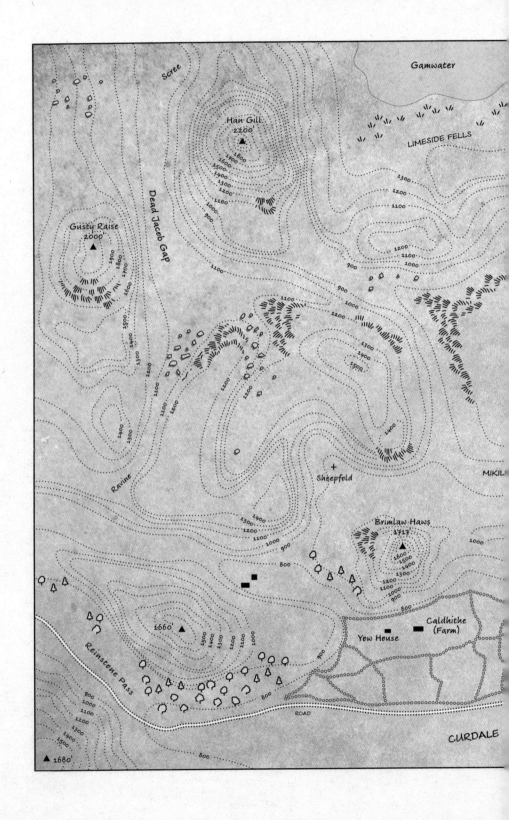

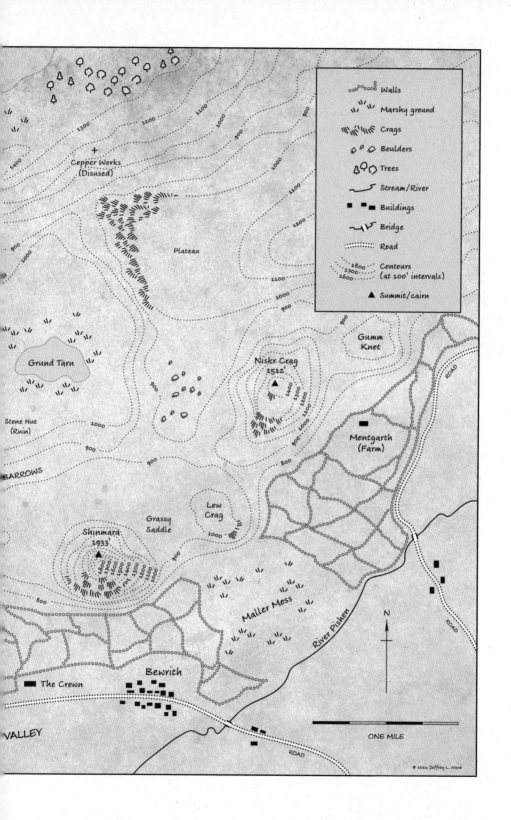

Walls

Marshy ground

Crags

Boulders

Trees

Stream/River

Buildings

Bridge

Road

1800
1700   Contours
1600   (at 100' intervals)

▲ Summit/cairn

Copper Works
(Disused)

1300

1200

1100

1000

900

1400

900

1000

Plateau

1100

1200

1100

1000

Gumm
Knot

900

Niskr Crag
1512
▲

1400
1300
1200
1100

1000

900

Grund Tarn

Stone Hut
(Ruin)

1000

900

BARROWS

900

Montgarth
(Farm)

800

Low
Crag

Grassy
Saddle

1000

900

Shinmara
1933
▲
1800
1700
1600
1500
1400
1300
1200
1100

800

Maller Moss

River Pishon

N

ROAD

ROAD

Bewrith

The Crown

VALLEY

ROAD

ONE MILE

© 2024 Jeffrey L. Ward

PART I

An Empty Country

Yan

The farm was in one of the fourteen green-purple wet deserts, in a dent six miles wide with its shoulders covered in scree and a rainy season that lasts twelve months a year. Always acid in the water, always vinegar in the ground. It's a hanging land known for its lakes but we live in its hills. Cloud-eaten mountains named fells. None of it is tall but all of it is steep and the slopes are topped with dwarf grass and soil thin as tea stains.

We raise our flocks on the sides of cliffs and teach each sheep to clear its plate—took them five thousand years, but they did it. Left nowt but bare rock, soaked black, and learnt to love the taste of moss. Everything fell down to the floor of Curdale Valley, back when meadows had wildflowers, and there it was flat enough to sell your sheep. Some folk decided to stay and build a village called Bewrith. It was a market at first, then they got at the coal under the fells and then the slate, and when that was gone, it was where offcomers came to eat ham and chips on their way through to postcard country.

It's all in Cumbria. The valley and the village and the farm. A made-up county with the border of England and Scotland to its north, though fitting into neither so well. Yorkshire and Northumberland to its east with the ridge of the Pennines keeping us safe from their inbred eyes. The Irish Sea to the west and the Isle of Man if you're wanting a swim. Then to the south there's the South and that's never far enough away.

People in the fells are as friendly as any that can be found. So friendly, they'll spot your house up by a rock face and make sure theirs is built far enough away you can't spot them back.

Miles of nowt makes thick walls.

I don't get into the village much now, and less back then, some thirty years ago. It never changes. It's got two wet-dash pubs, one painted white and the other yellow, and that's one pub for every twenty houses, and the homes are built of slate, jagged to look at, and the bricks are green on dry days and grey every other. The people in Bewrith, all two hundred-odd, they'd tell you all they had was the view and that was fine by them. All that's needed to keep going would take care of itself since folk watched out for each other. Take your washing in if it starts mizzling, get the sandbags stacked when it's flooding, keep an eye on your nan or your kids or your bloody wife. Keep their eye on you. More than one way to watch out for someone. Got to know when they're ready to boil over so you can keep your boots dry.

That's my way of introducing you to William Herne. The only one of us anyone wants to hear about. A sheep farmer. When people get talking about him—it's always what a mad old bastard he was, like we saw him walking about with thieving and killing in him and just took shy at asking him to stop. But that wasn't the William I knew, and I did know him, for longer than anyone still living and, since he's dead now, I suppose for longer than anyone will get to. When I tell you he'd been a good sort for the most part, that's because I think it's the truth.

He was a farmer, a shepherd, better than some but no more special than most. The son of a farmer and the dad of a farmer and the husband of a farmer. He was quiet so we thought him principled—when he did speak it was to the point as if he read the paper too much. Kept to himself or his family as he could. He was house proud yet never cleaned. Near the same age as me but you'd not know it. First hairs that grew out his chin were grey, and he never aged while always being bloody old. He wore this wax coat for the last seven years of his life and it fell dress-length. He buttoned it all the way up, so he looked like a man of God. His wife, Helen, she'd not let him keep it in the house, the coat, it stunk so bad of muck and wild mustard.

Like a lot of the hill people, the village didn't see too much of him. Knew he was out there doing his work and you might run into him if you got lost in the fells or kept an eye on his stool at The Crown. He was well liked, though, respected even—was always a man you never wanted to bother with owt, but knew you could if it was needed. Took his role as a tourist attraction a touch serious. Would find more than a few offcomers talking of a farmer they could swear was staring them down a field away, or else they found him pointing to signs he kept about the place reading, *Dogs off leash will be shot*. If they laughed, he'd start barking at them like a dog himself.

Which is to say he'd always been some sort of mad bastard. To tell the truth we all are. Only thing in our heads is what's about us. The sheep, the dogs, the fields. And when there's only emptiness about, then I guess you'd call us empty-headed.

I'll start with telling you about foot and mouth. Most won't talk about it, worrying if they do that'll make it come back. But without it, all you've got is what William did and not what made him do it. It began early spring in 2001. For us here in Cumbria anyroad. I gather it all started months before with some pillock in Northumberland feeding his pigs up on bits of other pigs from parts of the world where folk don't look after animals. They say pigs will eat owt, sickness and all.

At the time I was back living on my dad's farm. Montgarth it was called, a small place that peeled back from the road, scarce a thumbprint on the valley. The house we lived in and the storehouse next to it were forever sinking, inch by inch, year by year, pushing out the draining soil till the land pushed back and formed a banking all about it. From the way he kept it, my dad, you'd be forgiven for thinking it'd been left empty till you walked near and heard his dog yapping. The field walls were left to fall in on themselves and the gaps shod over with wood pallets and rolls of wire.

I'd been there maybe six months at that point, helping him out. He'd got so weak with it all that it made me forget why I left. Like everything he did he got weak in his own way. Was heading for his late sixties, what he'd call his eighties in workingman years. Could about lift a ewe above his head but was ten minutes getting up the stairs to take a piss. Three fingers on his right hand curled inward for good and he could still work a pair of shears with nowt save his knuckles and thumb. He never asked for help, then you'd find yourself getting yelled at for not giving any. I tell you how it was with him. I'd been away for years as a driver. Working crop fields in sowing season, trailing clouds of lime the length of the east coast. Ground so flat you'd go for ten miles and still see the dust settling from that morning. Busy with all that, and he gave me a call, no clue how he'd got the number, and said, "When you coming home?"

"I've no plans to," I told him. "I'll be getting a place of my own soon, earning some cash. You ever heard of that? Making a life for myself like you always talked about."

"Doesn't sound like it."

"You going deaf?"

"Less than you might think," he said.

I was back in my old room the week after.

We were waiting for the new year to bloom when we started hearing about it. Not on the local news. Radio even. But whispering, *foot and mouth's back*. For people who spend all day with nowt but sheep for company we don't half get some gossiping done.

Foot and mouth. Only folk old as my dad remembered what it was.

A letter turned up. Sat on the floor all morning before we gave in to take a look. It was full of pictures, a catalogue of raw-mouthed stock showing us what to watch out for. The sheep getting lazy, getting skinny. Lying like their bones are nests. Legs not moving, head and eyes not moving. Blisters on their feet, feet white, feet rotten. Blisters in their mouths, on their gums or tongues. Hot and cooked all over. Lambs born dead like they're smarter than the rest. All that and it said to keep our flock indoors, or as close to that as we could fix. Keep it from spreading across the fells. My dad looked at the letter and told it to eff off. "I'm not doing that."

"Sounds like that's what they're asking for. Doing nowt."

"None of it, then. I'll let the flock go where it wants. Sheep can make up their own minds."

"Says they'll die if they get it."

"Aye, and to stop some of them from dying they'll all be fit for being killed. Make any sort of sense to you?"

"More to it than that."

He told me to eff off.

For the bigger places, the farms needing maps to find the toilet and barns that tunnel the length of a field, they could have indoor sheep. Night lights to calm the lambs and slam gates crossed to make hotel rooms for every gimmer, gummer, tup, and wether. Take them for daily walks on leashes through their feedlots and less crowding to be found about the bed straw than at a post office. That wasn't us. If we called Montgarth a smallholding, then others called it a hobby plot. Only two hundred sheep left in the flock then. You'd think that'd make it easier, but we were headed into lambing. You couldn't ask the mams to hold their bellies a few months while we locked them together in the two fields close to the house.

Our flock was living wild on the open fells a thousand feet atop the valley. We left them to wander the slopes and crags beyond the last stone walls—ones built to keep back the mountain fog. They made their dinner of what curled about rocks and lumped trees, skins of lichen on the faces of outcrops, some of it glowing greener than what spills out Sellafield. Sedges, whipping grass, string-stem ferns hid in the cracks of boulders, and winter heather that sprouts pink and reddens with the cold. My dad was being maungy and locked himself indoors in place of the stock, watching telly and swelling his chilblains on the hot lamp heater, with the only dog we had by his side.

I set off while it was still night. The sheep slept higher than where the flycatchers and doves roosted in cragfolds, and higher than where falcons nested watching their dinner below, and they'd lie on bare ground with steep rims at their backs, pressing their ears to the floor, listening for tumbling rocks. No place for quad bikes and if you're talking sense, no place for people. I climbed over the pasture gates as practice for what was to come and there were two domes of rock that let you know you'd left the grasslands of Montgarth. The first slope past them is what we called *eating your crusts.* Wind stuck to it like a river, and you knew the end was close when you were rubbing grit out your eyes. Once you'd crawled over that, you came to a wide crest that made every gale fresh and there was a slow ridge along its back to the top of Gum Knott. I kept one foot in scree and the other on spongy turf. Walking steady. Before day comes over, you don't know how alone you are out there. There's no edge to the ground and any bump could be a bluff and there are boulders big enough to mistake for the sky, but it's not so hard going when the only trail is the one your family's spent sixty years treading out.

I saw the flock when my torch caught one of their eyes on a wide ledge of bracken. Lying in a pile to make windbreakers of themselves and taking turns as blankets. Had to wake them. Yelled loud enough to taste my throat and heard their bleating back. Waited as the lot of them clambered over, counting sheep on sheep dropping down the ledge, yan, taen, tedderte, medderte, pimp. Trick of moving a herd is to get them on a leader, on a bellwether, so the rest will follow. We call them sheep for a reason. In normal times, that leader would be me and they'd walk close enough that if I took a plunge off a cliff, they'd go down with me. But it was my dad they were used to, and a bucketful of pellets only kept their minds for so long. Left me the bloody dog work. Clapping under their chests so they skipped through my arms, shouting so they learnt the words, stick slid across their ribs shunting them like their mams once did. Held my crook in both hands to collar the jumpers and steer them off the mountain. Ewes in lamb are as keen for listening as any pregnant lass. By the time we were back at the domes of rock, I was wearing one of the bastards over my shoulders.

Cooping them up in the two fields was only the start. If you know Cumbria, then you know it likes to rain. If you don't know it, then some days it's so green it makes your eyes hurt and it's not got that way on blue skies. Rains fit for bursting that week and with two hundred sheep topping and tailing in a field made for fifty, the ground turned itself to slurry. Each animal trotting in the stuff all day—getting up their sides and gumming their fleeces. The muck looked thicker every time I went back. Got so that the bigger ewes, pregnant springers with bellies dragging, would sit all day in the one spot as bother moving.

After three days, my dad came to look at them, first time he'd been out. "It's nine inches deep," he said, standing in the mess. "Feel stuck in my wellies just looking at it. We can't leave them out here, Steve."

"You want them inside with you? You've woke up to worse."

"Piss off."

"You know there's nowhere else for them."

"If a lamb plops into that it'll not be getting out."

"I'll keep an eye on them, then. Keep it cleared as much as I can."

"Keep an eye on all sixty springers at once? Got Bible passages written for less."

"We'll take it in shifts."

"Shifts, aye? Tell you what. You take the first one and I'll come let you know when I'm ready for mine." I heard him call me a bloody idiot as he walked off.

They were strong sheep and good birthers but lambs drown even in dry years. Herdwicks were all we had on the farm. They don't keep them elsewhere in the world and we took that as something to be proud of. Not as a warning. They're bred for living on fellside where rain comes in sideways or slantways or shoots up from the ground. If you'd asked me before that disease, I'd have said they could live through owt. Tougher than mountain goats and would look at you funny if you made a face in bad weather. White heads shaped like bricks, squarer and thicker than the slabs filling up the walls about them. We kept them fell-worn and as wild as a flock's let to be for months on end. When they came back from winter, they'd have grown out wobbling coats twice as big as their naked bodies. Patches of grey wool mashed together with blue and red rutting paint and weeks of dried old shit.

All I could do was watch them day and night, ready for the first drop. I built a map in my head of the ewes closest to birthing and did laps of the flock to check them in turn. Tried to muck out the field so much I could've hit brimstone and scrambled for my footing where the sheep needed a hand to move. Made duckboards of up-turned troughs. Stamped out beds of woodchip. Nodded off in the Land Rover when I stopped or lay down by the walls like one of the flock when standing got too much. On the fourth night of wading through the bottomless mud, our biggest lass was ready, stopped eating, day of fasting before she staggered off to a corner on her own with her hips sunk and her udders puffed out.

My dad turned up like he knew it was time. Wore a slop-brimmed fishing hat halfway down his ears and sat aside me with a thermos of tea. "Good night for it."

"Would be saying the same if I'd been kipping all day," I said.

"Not one to waste a lie-down." He started drinking from the canister. "Y'know, this was your mam's favourite time of year. The lambing. Don't think she got much sleep through it either."

"I remember."

"Course you do."

"What would she make of this?"

"We've had it worse. You'll be too young to think back on it but there was a year the flock got sick, real baddish, and we lost half the lambs. Come out zigzagged and their mams were walking into walls with milky eyes."

"They're not doing so rough now, all things considered."

"Should think not. I know you're like the rest of them. See me as a daft bugger for letting the flock get so small but every one of them's worth ten from any other farm."

"That'll be why you're getting ten times for them."

"Should be if they had any sense."

"Cheap at half the price."

"Don't talk soft." He stood up to pull one of the shearlings over. "Tell me she's not the most beautiful ewe you've ever seen." Started running his hands over her back to show how straight it was. Squeezing the muscling in her shoulders and hips, pulling her lips back, teeth sitting straight atop each other. "There's three hundred years of sheep in some of them. All children of Admiral Rust. Wrote books about him." He let the shearling go back to the flock. "You don't see it, do you?" he said, laughing to himself. "Never could."

I sat quiet like I always did when he was like that.

"That's something my own dad was forever yammering on about, *You've to give them your all*. Feels truer every time I think about it. It's supposed to be the sheep that end up feeding us but it's the bits of you that don't come back that need costing. Each year you heal less than the one before and it's only once you've offered most of it up that you feel it missing and know the deal you made."

"So, what now?" I asked him.

"They'll let us know."

That big lass, she found the only dry grass we had left and lay till daylight, then burst her water bag. Head resting in the dirt. She shook her ribs as if to bowk, squeezing sideways for an hour. Her black lamb cleared its own sack and she turned to lick the gunk out its nose and eyes till it could blink. Another ewe went off to lay itself down. A humpback lass with a curved smile. Three lambs shot out of her like links of sausages and the mam gobbled the birth skin off before I could get in. That set the rest of them off. Huffing on their sides or bowing down, tucking their legs under, and some on their feet or walking, birthing lambs with both eyes held open, no time to strain, no time to shudder.

My dad was back after that night, with me all through the last lambing—working like I'd not seen before. A sheep's head under each arm, and his face red from cold and redder from sweat. He took their kicks and barges front-on, slipping back, back on his boots, then his toes, then his hands and his knees so he was dragging the ewes to the mud with him. Only his cheeks puffing let you know it was him in all the muck. "Slow down," I said to him. "You want a heart attack?" Told me it'd been under attack since the Second World War. That got me following the same pace, working to remember what the snot in my nose was for. Not letting up to drink for fear my body would take it as a sign of stopping. It was as if we put everything in, they'd not be able to take it from us.

There was this one ewe with bunny ears and a twinter fleece near red as toadstool. She was ready for it but was lying with all the fussing out of her—would go to squeeze but only coughed. Smelled like a bin that needed taking out. She'd got her lamb's two front feet sticking out and she kept trying to stand or squat back and I'd to roll her sideways, lean on her, first milk spraying up my shirt. Got in there. Her with four legs in the air and me with my hand up inside her, putting it delicately. Tied the lamb's legs together with some twine and wiggled them for some space. Trying to start the whole thing all over again.

The lamb came out steaming, and I wafted it away to check he was moving on his own. Looked up at her but each of her breaths was shorter than the one before, and I was stuck giving him a shake till he was able to do it on his own. Then she was dead. "That lamb needs naming," my dad said over my shoulder.

"Since when did you start naming sheep? A ram at that."

"I'm getting touchy feely in my old age."

"Thought feelings was why you never let us do it."

"Just never had a head for names."

"Aye, well," I said to him, looking down at it. "How about Rusty?"

"Big boots to fill with a name like that."

"Just how old are you now?"

Gave himself another laugh at that and scooped the mam up in his arms to take her away.

With the lambing taking all my time, I never heard much in the way of news, and my dad was avoiding the phone like it could spread disease.

Saying we were on our own meant more than usual. Nobody was risking coming up to farms. They'd send us food. Meat-and-potato pies and fruitcake packed up and sent down rivers of disinfectant to reach us. Soon that got too close for them. Could carry the disease up your nose and in your hair, in the wet of your eyes—looking at a farm was a danger. Not even offcomers were daft enough to visit.

Wasn't till the slaughterman came to pick up the dead ewe that I got a sense for it. Could scarce get him round, he was so busy. "It was a normal death," I told him. "Way it should be."

"I believe you," he said, tying a chain about the ewe's leg and reeling her to his van.

"It was from lambing. Tough old bird as well."

"Always the way."

"Got a lot more today?"

"This is my dinner break."

He'd not look me in the eyes before he drove off.

You couldn't help finding signs of it in the flock. The lambs had come out safe, but it felt different—some had less pluck than their mams. Heads dragging with necks like too much string. My dad looked at them. "It's the mud that's still to clear up, that's what's slowing them." When they'd not quickened, he found other reasons. Said it was cold that year. Snow stuck on the flats. Open buckets of chemicals. Fumes on the wind. The swoop of buzzards. Bony crows on the fence. The great hum of the fells. Stress in our hands. Turned patches of snakeroot, pokeweed, arrowgrass. A loose mongrel dog. No lamb's blood on the door. Milk fever. Bluetongue. Scrapie. Soremouth. Blackleg. Lungworm. Scab. Bighead. Bottle jaw.

Every day it was another theory. No hint of me asking. Foot and mouth. Got sick of saying the bloody words.

The vet came for a visit. Robbie Slater was his name—a good lad and a local one at that. Made himself known over the cattle grid and stepped out his car dressed as a white rubber spaceman. I went to say how do, and he spoke like he'd never met me before. Could smell hospital bleach on him where it should've been cow muck.

I took him to the field where the ewes were staying. Sat single file against a wall. Walked one of the sheep over to him with my hand under its neck like I was presenting at a show. He pulled her up and plonked her down on her arse. Ran a gloved thumb about her teeth and waggled her leg to get a good eyeful, then let her run off. Told me to get the next sheep and the next till he'd looked at four or five. "Bit slow, aren't they?" he said.

"What you expect? Turning bone idle stuck down here."

"You've been doing it, then, isolating them?"

"Course I have, you lot told me to."

"You'd be surprised round here." He went over to pick up one of the lambs but didn't spend long checking before he let it go. Stood watching them lie back down. "You had a look at them recently?"

"I'm not out here with my eyes closed each day."

"In their mouths, Steve."

"What about their mouths?"

"A few of them have lesions on their gums."

"Lesions? Course they got lesions in their mouth. Like to see you gum up half the bloody fellside without any cuts between your teeth."

16

"They're lesions."

"That mean they've got it?"

"Hard to say."

"Well, how many others have you seen with it?"

"It's hard to say."

"Try starting with what's easy. How many of the ones you've tested have come back positive?"

"We're not doing tests at the moment."

"You're going to kill them without any testing?"

"If it's within three miles of an outbreak they're getting done and they're not messing about. I'm only here to see how far it's got."

"Out from where?"

"Caldhithe. William Herne's place."

A van turned up and another aback it. They spilled out the back—squaddies on our farm dressed in white suits and holding brooms and buckets and guns. Shoved their boots on the bumper of the van and sprayed them down with antiseptic.

Knocked on our door. Polite. Gentle. Giving orders. The one in charge, she knew how to get things done. "We need a hose point. We need them ready out here. Where are your loading banks?" Got all the fellas she brought unpacked. Lined up. "What do you mean, you've not got any?" Shook her head. "We'll make do." Said that a few times. "We'll make do." She was being kindly with it all. Reminding us about purchasing orders and putting nowt in her voice I could get hurt on.

I walked out to that field, walked among our animals, and any sickness in them found a place to hide. They gathered at my boots and followed my hands as they swung at my side. Our dog, Molly, was stalking low from wall to wall and watching me closer than the Herdwicks. Pressed a whistle to my lips. "Walk on. Walk on." She brought the flock together and kept them steady to the dry-lot as they funnelled through the gate. The squaddies stood watching in their killing clothes. Hands at their backs, gloves over their sleeves, condoms on their feet. They'd set up a trailer as a butcher box. Wanted to get each sheep shot clean where they'd not move, then laid out to make a pile. Wanted the standing boards kept clear for each coming animal. And they'd soak the dead in disinfectant and hold them fresh till they could burn.

First kills went fine, far as killing goes, one pop, one thud, sometimes a bleat, and the sheepdog waiting by their side to keep them still. Rifle muzzles placed between their ears and the bullets lined along their backs, so each bang stayed inside their heads. Guns weren't to blame for what happened. The mess started on the boards, slicked with muck, leaking pissholes, sorry-spilled blood, and it got on the ramp, a wooden one, and if we didn't steady the sheep, they tumbled off, fell on their necks or jumped up to get back in the field. We didn't own a sheepfold big enough and when one sheep broke the herd, two did, and then all of them, leaping and shoving, shoulder to shoulder. No stopping without getting trampled. The rams at the front butted a wall till the copestones rattled and the gimmers aback them started pushing, mounting the others, using them as steps. One wriggled high enough to slice her belly on the wire and fell to the other side, knocking a gap out for the rest to have a run. "In here," I yelled for Molly. She tried barking at the head of them, turning them about. "In here." She got a hoof to the eye and ran off herself. Curled about the rootstock of a hawthorn, caught her fur on brambles and cotton grass, shitting down her legs.

You'd think the squaddies would have more sense than the sheep. But they went mad and all. Chasing on foot and shooting them where they stood against walls or feed troughs or other bodies. Pouncing on the backs of ewes with knives to bleed through, pulling two-handed when they got stuck, jamming rods in their skulls, using the rams' horns as handles. Riding out the death spurts between their legs, then getting on their boots to run down more.

I bloody ran. Bolted over the gate and took through the field, made like I was going to grab the hoppers, and got my hands about one ewe's front legs. Dropped her. Other gimmers dived to the ground when I got near. I kept running. Heard the squaddies yelling. "Get the farmer in here. Calm them down." Half the flock was dead or brained, shot holes forming slow through their heavy fleeces, and the soldiers backed a smaller group to the barn. The sheep made a stand there—swinging their heads to make room to charge and pouncing like foxes at anyone stepping close. A tall squaddie got sent on his arse, chest stomped, and he shot the ewe who did it from the floor. Worked their way through using three or four bullets to bring each one down. "Where is the bastard?" The lass in charge saw me in the field. "You need to keep them in." I couldn't think who she was talking to. She swore ugly and went to the dog, picked her up and waited for me to come back. "Take her and get inside."

"You don't need me?"

"You chose to be out here."

"They're my sheep."

"Get inside."

Had to pin Molly to keep her still. Barking in my ear and her soft claws scratching me. Shoved her face into my neck, and I felt her ribs. I remember she smelled of biscuits. She'd not get off me in the house—I'd to roll her on her back and slide her into bed. I went in the kitchen, boiling the kettle again and again with an empty mug in front of me. Not sure I could look at a sheep without seeing blood pouring out a hole in its head. I got the telly on, watched for hours like I was the poorly one. Could hear shots no matter how loud I put the volume but the gaps between each bang got longer till they stopped.

Another knock on the door. That lass was back telling me they were ready to head off. "When you going to burn them?" I asked her.

"It's a small farm this," she said. "Caldhithe up the road's going to lose a thousand. Maybe more. Could be tomorrow. Could be next week or one after."

"Can you not move them? So they're not in the lot?"

"You can. I wouldn't recommend it."

"We can see them from out the kitchen window. From the bloody toilet window if we look out."

"I wouldn't recommend doing that either," she said. So I kept the curtains closed.

For all her talk, they had the bodies shipped up the next day and headed for a trench they'd set into the valley two miles away. By all accounts that was quick. Some farms had them in the fields long enough to taste wool in their water. Only sign they'd been in Montgarth was the blood spilling along the road on their way out.

Taen

The morning after they'd taken them, I got the first lie-in of my life, or whatever it's called when it's five a.m. and you've spent so long looking at the shapes about your bed you can see in the dark. I got up and put my wellies on, trying to feel useful. Thinking I'd know what to do when I was back in the fields.

I was among the fells—feeling small as owt I could see on the horizon. The pasture more torn up with mud than before and it was quiet. You're no doubt thinking it's always quiet where people come to get away from it all. But I've learnt what quiet is. It's finding the ringing in your ears you didn't know you had. It's what you don't hear. Jackdaws and rooks and crows keep silent when death smells clean.

I was looking at our empty fields, planning how we'd start again. I'd heard of fellas growing apples for cider and that—done all right with it. Don't need to take an apple to the knacker's yard. Strawberries. Make a go of them. Could plant them in lumps of dogshit and they'd be right. Not that any would grow bigger than a gooseberry out here. Cabbages. No bugger could tell if they'd gone rotten or not.

I was stood in the place we birthed the lambs, thinking all those lies, and I heard a voice.

How. How. How.

Each word cut up, juttering and holding long in my ears. *How.*

Out there, sound can carry like nowt else. I looked to see if my dad was about. Nobody. It would stop and start, the voice, muffled. Like it was stuffed in a tin someplace in my brain. Smacked my head to loosen it and spun about to see it wasn't hiding between my shoulders. Thought I might've gone mad. That should've worried me more than it did.

It grew louder or softer when I moved. Stepped aimless, dowsing for sound, and I did the polite thing—talked back. *How what? How bloody what?*

All it had to say was *How*.

Walked to where it was loudest and stayed still when the noise stopped. Nowt but mud at my feet and even now I can't shut the idea that it was another person talking to me.

The mud moved. A quivering I couldn't place. *How*, it said.

I headed closer. *Give over. How do I what?*

It was a bleating. A lamb's bleating. I knew that's what it must've been. Young Herdwicks are black as soot, even their eyes are black, so I got on my knees to look, and pulled apart the pats of mud. Kept crawling till I saw where the little bastard was moving. Breathing with his whole body and holding more soil on his back than meat. Started digging. Pulling up cold clods. Saw that reddish brown tint in its fleece. Saw it was Rusty. Rubbed him down with my coat some way to clean and swaddled him in waterproofs.

The house couldn't warm him. My dad didn't keep it heated— said it was only for sleeping in. Had to run a bath and top it with three trips to the kettle. Thawed out some colostrum and held the lamb's throat with two fingers to get a tube down to his stomach and not his lungs. His eyes twitched and then his shoulders and his knees. Came more alive with every shiver. I wrapped him in a blanket and he sat with me on the sofa as we watched telly. He was in good fettle not long after, feeding on owt I put near his face and happily shitting on the carpet. Couldn't stop myself looking in his mouth—see if he'd any lesions forming. I sat there, holding that lamb long enough it got dark out again. All that was left of the farm sleeping on my knee.

We were one of the first to get culled, at Montgarth, and I'd say we got off lighter than most since we didn't have so far to fall. I grew up hearing stories about Westmorland from my dad and granddad and other farmers. Before Cumbria existed and as you might talk about old stamps and steam trains, they'd talk about what cut each farm down. The way soldiers remember wars and want to go back to them. It was disease that got us, that was our story, but I couldn't help thinking foot and mouth wasn't its name. There was one thing filling up my head, same space the bleating had done. *William Herne. William bloody Herne.*

I'd known William all my life. We grew up as neighbours who couldn't see each other for the hills between us. Caldhithe, where he lived, was one of the last of what's known as the great farms of Westmorland and big enough that it's on maps of Curdale. If I say it was home to a thousand sheep that might not sound much but it was seen as a lot and Caldhithe was his. All of it.

Most farmers work tenancies. Renting. When one tells you to get off his land or he'll shoot you, he's telling half-truths. That's something you need to get about life in the fells. It's never about the money. Only reason to make it out here is so you can be the tallest man for five square miles. Owning means something. Every gorge, beck, fall, cliff, bog, dale, and weathered white boulder is yours. The dogrose and gorse in the roadside ditches and the road itself. The alder tree with a field of its own and the birch seeds in the stomachs of wagtails and warblers. If people walk across your land it's because you let them. If they spend a day looking out on the mountains and valleys, it's your view they're borrowing. Fell country is empty country so you'll be forgiven for not seeing it as an empire but that's how it felt to us and none more so than William.

Owned the ground under him and seemed to think that stayed true anywhere he stood. All of us had a story about him. Selling things he'd no right to—tubs of red diesel or dropped trolleys from the slate mines. Using the types of feed on stock that would make a prizefighter bowk. Meant his lambs came out finished with extra helpings of meat, bone, and fat. You'd find his sheep wandering the wrong side of Bletter Pike, his rams sniffing your lasses, and he'd call it a compliment. Tell him to piss off and he'd tell you to take it up with your landlord.

None of it bothered me. If you can't do what you want out here, there's no place you can. As long as he left me alone, I'd do the same back.

It'd been a week since my dad's flock had got executed. With no work to keep busy, I'd get sick of watching telly, and try sitting in the kitchen, sitting with my thoughts, and they made me sicker than the telly, so I switched the radio on. I wanted to hear someone talking. Put the news on like I didn't know what it would say. Every bastard farm in Curdale had been culled and those up in Ullswater and in all of Eden and not a sheep or cow was left this side of the River Pishon. Every farm except one, that is. They were having problems at Caldhithe, had been for days. William Herne's place. "What if I

went to speak to him?" I said to my dad while he buttered his toast. "To William?"

"What for?"

"Find out what's going on. Get him to listen to sense if any's on offer."

"When's talking ever fixed owt?"

"What good's sitting here gonna do?"

"Richest fellas I know get paid to sit on their arses all day. Must be something to it."

I heard a cawing under the table. Lamb was there nipping at my britches. Teaching himself to walk, stottering about, with those eyes so black you'd think him blind. Picked him up and laid him across my lap. "I'll bring him Rusty."

"What's he want a bottle lamb for?"

"A ram's no good without a flock. And William's the only fella left who's got one."

"Not for long by the sounds of it."

"I want that bastard to look at what he's done to us."

I stood up with Rusty tucked under my arm and searched for my keys.

"Is that it?" my dad said, looking small in his chair. "You off right now?"

"I'm done waiting."

Caldhithe was four miles on foot but driving took half an hour, through country roads that are one-way depending on the way you're going. William's farmhouse was at the lowest dip of the valley, so any direction you came from you sank deeper and deeper into it—the hills and roads you came from curling to cliffs in the rearview. More pheasants on the roads than cars that day. When I

looked about me, there was something I couldn't place. I was driving on a snakeback lane, walls tight on my sides as ever, windward slopes falling flat across my eyes. It was all there. Only a mountain was missing. That's how it felt. Not an animal to be seen, y'know, not a sheep. I'd say it was all dead on the fells, but the smokestacks made it seem alive as I'd never known it.

There was one roadside entrance to Caldhithe and, a trick of the land where no matter how far or close you were, you'd not see it till it near smacked you in the face. That day I couldn't miss it for all the cars parked about. Three or four Rovers waiting wonky, one aback the other, and this army van blocking the lane, built as a cattlebox for squaddies. At the front was a police wagon, resting to the side, flashing the road white and blue. Soldiers were there, young lads with fresh-shaved heads and polished shitkickers, sat up on bonnets looking wormy, passing about fags and sausage rolls. They'd not move to let me through.

I pulled up, facing them down, and they stared at me when I got out, eyes bored and bloody hungry. There was one familiar face. A copper stood over a map. Taller than the rest by more than a foot. Stood with his hands tucked into a flak jacket, hair past his ears and it was so orange you'd smell satsumas looking at him. Was known to us lot as Simply Red. For years, he'd been Big Red—a fat bastard. Pub kitchens opened late if he turned up, but his wife had got him on the Weight Watchers and it stuck, unlike his name. "What's all this?" I said to him, walking on the road.

"Sorry, sir, access to this area's restricted at the moment," he told me. "You'll need to turn back and go Saddlesby way if you want to carry on."

"Don't remember getting knighted. What's this sir business?"

"Look, Steve, it's not a good time, can you go the other way?"

"Not heading on, want to speak to the boss man himself."

"To William?"

"If it were you I was after, I'd have called ahead."

"He asked you to come?"

"Near enough did, aye." I looked at the fellas who were crowding about me with their hands at their belts. "What you lot waiting out here for?"

"He won't let us in."

"Have you tried the gate?"

"He got tetchy when we went up yesterday. Was leaning on his rifle and said he'd take care of it."

"Not been cleaned up here yet?"

"Not yet."

"So that's it, you're scared he'll shoot all of you?"

"You didn't see him. We don't take chances in situations like this. At least one of them is armed and that makes us outgunned as far as the law's concerned." I stood looking at the farm's slanting pastures. "What you doing here, Steve? Shouldn't you be looking after Montgarth?"

"Not much of it left."

"They got you lot, then?"

"Aye."

"Can't have taken long."

"Took them sixty years by my dad's count."

"You've seen nothing compared to some of the others out here."

"So, you in with the MAFF lot?" I asked. That's what they called themselves then, the government fellas in charge of farms and fresh air. MAFF. Changed their name to DEFRA soon as everyone saw what they'd done up here.

"I'm in with the police if that's what you mean," Red told me. "It's my job."

"Have I to sort William out for you?"

"I can't let you do that."

"But you'll not stop me?"

"He's got someone watching us," he said, pointing up to the farm. "Up on the wall there, been waiting for hours." I squinted till I saw a dark figure sat scarecrow at the edge of the field.

"No doubt he'll watch me walk up, then."

I went to my car and leaned over the lamb with my coat spread, stuffed it arse-first into my pocket lining, twisting it close about my belly like some hernia. Crooked my arm about him from the outside and kept low as I walked past the squaddies, keeping on the grass verge.

At the gate to the farm, there was this estate car parked up the other side. Wedged against the wooden slats so you'd not get the bastard open. Had a lock on the steering wheel and a paper sign in the windscreen. *Gone for petrol.* Zipped my coat tight and launched myself over one-handed, dented the bonnet with my knees and slid on my wet boots, clawed with my right hand to slow my fall but fell all the same. Heard laughing from the road. There were wheel lines run in the ground, trailing from the road to the farmhouse, and I followed them, keeping my eyes on the fella atop the wall.

The lowland field I made my way through was empty and so were all the ones branching off it. There was all this scratched-off wool, drifting, clumping into balls that grew as they rolled. I couldn't see the mountains. The sky aback the house was a bone smoke, getting greyer and darker as it rose. Closer I got, the more the air thickened up from a distant burning, and owt sat still had a layer of ash on it.

The farm buildings were resting on a roll of hill with something moving over them. Men shouting, running with dogs, and boxing in a line of sheep that kept coming on. Hundreds of them made single file from a dale below—Herdwicks and Swaledales and fat-fleece Roughfells left plodding at the back.

I got through that one field and was into the next, where I was facing the fella on the wall. Not such a big lad the nearer I got. Smoke pulled back on the wind and I could see it was William's son, Danny Herne. He was worn out, soot about his face, wearing a man's shirt rolled back to let his hands free and a collar pulled up to his chin, his hair cut back, chopped wild, to keep it out his eyes. He was looking at me through binoculars on a string about his neck, a dainty pair you might see at a horse race. He started speaking into his walkie-talkie when I got to the ridge he was guarding. "Who're you?" Danny called down.

"A farmer," I told him. "Steve Elliman."

"Where you from?"

I pointed to over the hill. To Montgarth. "They think you're wanting to shoot them down there," I said.

"Can think what they want."

"What are you doing?"

"Nowt," he said. "Watching. I'm on lookout and you're the first person who's showed up in hours." Then he remembered what being a lookout meant. "What you doing here?"

"Need a word with your dad."

"You're not the only one."

"What's going on?"

"We're burning our sick sheep like we're supposed to."

"Just the sick ones?"

"My dad says we're doing all that's asked of us."

"You don't want their help getting it done?"

"We're not signing owt. Our bloody sheep and we'll look after them ourselves."

"How're you going to do that?"

He looked away and didn't answer me. Had a long stick across his lap that he rested his arms on as he thought. Got on his walkie and kept catching my eye till he was done chatting. He held the thing out for me then. "He wants to talk to you."

I walked up and took it off him. "Who does?"

"The man on the other end."

Put my ear to it. Sounded like somebody was rubbing gravel across the speaker and William's voice cut through. "What you want, Steve?"

"I need to set things straight."

"You not see we're busy?"

"It's about this."

"About this? Well, there's not much that needs saying. We're not letting them go. Heard what they did at your place and that might suit you. Far as I can tell, just about owt does at Montgarth."

"Not this."

"Not this?"

"How're you planning to stop them?" I looked about the fields trying to spot him. "It'll not be long before they're more scared of what you're doing than they are of you."

"We're sending the strong ones out to the fells," he told me with no shame in it. "Then we'll take care of the rest ourselves."

"Not much good hiding them if you're telling people you're doing it."

"Not people, just you."

"What you telling me for?"

"Because you're going to help."

"Am I now?"

"If you want to talk to me, you'll help."

"What if I want to talk to the small army camped on the road?"

"Then I'll know. And you can be sure of this, Steve. When I set things straight I don't do any talking." The gravel sound got louder again. "Put Danny back on," he told me. Did as I was told and heard the lad saying *all right* before he got down from the wall.

"You can help us or not," Danny said to me. "But if my dad says this needs doing, then it's getting done."

He was barely a teenager then, and I stood there as the lad collected his things. Followed his lead to the farmhouse, and he held the gate open for me into the yard. It was a big place where William lived. Two long barns, a wide-set drylot, old horse shed, outdoor shitter full of tools, tanks of oil and molasses and water, one working tractor in the garage, a long row of tillers, mowers, tedders, and spreaders. Each building was set wall-to-wall in a square about the yard to leave as much pasture free as possible. No way in but the two gates. The farmhouse rose tallest. It'd been built by William's granddad with limestone and slate he'd taken from two flooded cottages. It felt homemade. There was concrete in patches over the ground, ripped up and washed out, gaps filled in with stomped gravel, and that's how he kept the place. No glass in the windows except those in the house the family slept in, roof tiles sitting under slabs of corrugated iron, and algae on everything, up the sides of the barn and over the slurry spinner, letting the buildings go free range. "This way," Danny said to me. "We're keeping them in here."

Kept leading me on to one of the barns, doors lashed with thick chains and the lights off. I could hear animal coughs and bleats trapped inside. There were maybe ninety sheep in there. Mix of gimmers, hoggs, and rams with their white heads cutting through the dark and their backs painted red and white. Good-looking sheep. Couldn't accuse William of getting that wrong. "These the chosen few?" I asked.

"Something like that."

"You done owt like this before?"

"Herded sheep?"

"Aye."

"Not on my own."

"If a shepherd finds themselves out there on their own, they've done something wrong."

Now, them sheep were part of a fell flock so they're born heafed. Means the hills are part of who they are, and they know from a rock pinch to a bed of scree where's good to wander. Can leave them on the mountains with not so much as a fence between them and you'll not have trouble finding them. When all eyes were off Caldhithe, William would bring them down, stuff them inside, and breed the herd back out next year. The rest of the sheep being held back at the farm, ones destined for the fat any end—their cooked skins would be offered up as proof of job done. "What the hell you got in your coat?" Danny said, looking at me mad like. "You not check your dinner's dead before you eat it?"

I opened my coat up and held Rusty out to him. "It's the last of my flock."

"What's it here for?"

"Same as any of us."

"Dad told me some of you lot were weird," he said. "You can give him to my mam to look after."

"Helen?"

"She's in the house."

Danny got his quad bike geared up, green body of the machine browned from the sun and the plastic stirrups cracked in two or three. Dirt dried on its sides was older than him. "You ready?" I asked him.

"More ready than you."

If the smoke in the air about us got any thicker, I'd have needed a splitting axe to cut my way out. When I could open my eyes in it, I couldn't see much. Needed to look straight up to find the shape of the fells—smooth orange lines above the soot clouds, like a hundred sunsets stacked atop each other.

Danny went to the barn, worked the padlocks, and wrapped the chains about his hands. Pulled them down so the doors clacked open—smacked the heads of the first sheep running. Some of them animals would've never been inside a building since birth. Mustering themselves. Kicking up dust and straw and splints of wood. Twanging the metal walls for all the valley to hear. He kicked off on his bike to keep up with them and was soon gone into the hills aback his flock.

I walked up to the house, smoke hiding the door from me. Let myself in and closed it firm like it could keep the air fresh. The whole building was dimmed, and I was in a hallway with slate floors and the walls lined with boxes of papers. Was shunting them out the way when I heard a voice come from the kitchen. "I'm in here."

I headed over to where Helen was sat scribbling away. Marking the paper she wrote on hard enough to write double through to the kitchen table. Didn't look up while I stood there. I coughed and she still didn't look. "Danny says I'm to leave him with you."

"What?" she said, blinking at me. "What you doing here?"

"Dropping this lamb off."

"That's not an answer," she said. "William doesn't usually let you lot in the house."

"Didn't this time either."

"I can see that." She stood and put the kettle on, leaned back, still looking at me. "You've not been in the fells for a while, Steve."

"Six months now."

"What went wrong?"

"My dad needed helping."

"And now you're here to help us, that it?"

"It's looking that way."

I always liked Helen. Knew her from our school days and she was good to me when she'd no reason to be. She was better-looking than you'd guess. Was big in the way only a woman can be—five foot four for standing but could blank your thoughts like a field of sun when you close your eyes. "You ever think this is how we'd end up?" she asked me.

"In the fells?" I said. "Were you thinking we wouldn't?"

"Not many of us left."

"Doesn't matter. So long as there's one fella still going, that's enough."

"We'll see how that ends up."

She went to the window like there was a view worth seeing, and I looked over the papers on the table, lists of deadweight numbers, lost stock, land-use payments. She still did the maths by hand. I felt that lamb wriggling in my arms. Kicking at me. "Whose idea was all of this?" I asked her. "Hiding his bloody sheep."

"Been about three days since it would've made a difference who thought it up."

"You not helping?"

"I'm doing the only bit that matters."

"Best get back to work, then."

"What's this lamb?"

I handed over Rusty and she held him to her chest, his neck resting against hers till he shut his eyes and settled. "He's on the bottle," I told her. "Not to be seen by anyone. Not to be touched by anyone but me, and you, I suppose."

She dragged a rug over with her foot and laid the lamb on it. "There's bags of powdered ewe milk that'll be going to waste this year," she said. "He may as well have them."

"He'll be a good ram, that one."

"He'll be better off not waking up."

As we talked, we started hearing bangs, a long way off they were, and through the walls they sounded like fizzing or cracking, but they echoed the way only gunshots can. We kept talking like we couldn't hear them, and Helen had made me a brew without asking. The kitchen door opened, and a dog pushed its way in, an old collie, walked without bending its legs. Stood over Rusty and watched the sleeping lamb. Sniffed him, then walked to the window ledge, rose on its back legs and waited for the next bang, barked like it could catch the sounds and stood barking away till the gunshots stopped a long while after.

I was washing up my own mug when I heard some clattering

outside, heard talking, close this time, from people in the yard. "If you want a word with William," Helen told me. "Now's the time."

Four men were out the front of the house, one sat on this up-turned bin, and the others stood about. The three on their feet were farmhands. Grease on their faces made them look ancient but they were all lads, wheezing and twitching, one with a fag in his mouth like he couldn't get enough ash down him. Their coats were bloodied and piled at their feet. The fella sat down was William Herne. Just out his thirties then, and he'd not taken to wearing his wax coat yet. There was a handprint of grime across his balding head and a tea towel tied about his throat and his britches shoved into his boots. His farm lads were taking turns drinking out the end of a hose. Holding their thumbs over the spray to wet their heads and squeezing dirt out their hair.

They all turned to see me walk out the house. William put his gloves in his back pocket, took the hose to fill up a tin mug and offered me it. "I hear you've been wanting a word."

"Two come to mind."

"That's what you came here for? Tell me to piss off?"

"I came to show you Rusty. What's left of Montgarth."

"Who?"

"The lamb that's in with Helen."

"You expecting me to off that one as well?"

"What's one more after what you did?"

"What'd that be?"

I eyed up the three lads, stood nervy they were, and all a step too close. William saw my fists turning white and told them to eff off back to work so we could talk. They shook themselves dry and spat themselves thirsty and walked away, leaving the pile of clothes. When it was just me and him, he said again, "So, what'd that be?"

"It's your lot that spread it," I said. "I heard you're not keeping them in like was needed."

"Could've been," he said to me, shrugging the idea off. "What were you doing in Montgarth anyroad? Before all this."

"Getting by."

"Just a matter of time, then."

"Still, it was our time."

"Y'know, nearly a week cooped up with these smelly bastards and I've forgot what talking's for. You've come here to show me what you lost and feeling sorry I've not done the same. They say there's sickness in them that's fit for spreading but I've not seen any face of it. If it's blood they want, then I suppose they'll get it but if I'm to make a sacrifice of myself, then it's me who has to make it."

I went to say my piece and he hissed me quiet.

"Now, let me finish. You want your time back, and I get that, but it's not how this works. Only choice we've got is how to send it all off. You can come with me, and I'll thank you for the hand but there's not much speaking left in me these days."

"I'd not be here at all if it wasn't for what you've done."

"I didn't make this sickness and I didn't ask to be the cure for it either."

"For a fella who's no idea what he's doing, you're certainly sure of it."

"I know it just fine," he said and got up. "It's you that needs to make up his mind. Far as I can see, not taking a side is the same as taking theirs. And doing nowt when there's a gun in your face is the same as killing yourself." He helped himself to more water out the hose and looked to the sky, what was left of it to be seen. "It's been going slower than I wanted. Fire's a mess," he said to me. "These lads haven't got the bottle for it. They don't reckon they're paid enough for the job. But I'd not be paying you owt to help get it done. So that's how it is. Your choice if you're up for it."

He was done. Put his cap on his head and walked off aside the farmhouse where a sticky breeze lapped over him, wore itself on his face as a mask, and with each step it grew stronger till a gust of the stuff took him under and he was gone. That's when I started following William Herne.

Tedderte

That wind blew mad about the farmhouse. It stuffed my ears and blew without sound, the air sinking, filling up my boots, and it carried with it this reddened grit. I'd step out its way and it would feel about to find me, turn me round, suck the sweat from off my head. I walked in circles, came out cockeyed—stood in an empty pasture with William waiting on ahead.

He kept going. Led through a field of sprouting peas and through empty pasture with the grass still yellow from wintersleep and the gates tied open to their posts with twine. We walked a path of new-turned mud. Carried on for half a mile and reached a field so long and wide its far wall was hid aback a roll of meadow grass. Across its middle stood two metal mangers. Crisscrossed to make steel feeding cages with dripping troughs set underneath. Each could fodder fifty ewes at once or a hundred in a scrum. William told me they'd fed them all—not letting half a season of lambing hay go all to waste. More and more they gave them, so they never stopped their eating. Mouths grew sore before their stomachs did. They're messy eaters, those nervish sheep, but not a stalk of clover or wisp of hay was left. And looking out, I could see that plume of smoke and the field it rose from.

William stopped at a wall and rested on its kissing gate. "We've got them through here," he said when I caught up. "And you'll be needing these." Handed me some padded gloves.

"What's left to do?"

"The cleaning up."

It was a dirt field, a mud field, never seen it dry out, never seen it with a spot of green, and it had these wide slabs of rock all over, curved and terraced like baby cliffs, sitting aside soupy pits of clay. Nowt would grow there without buying in a thousand ton of seeding soil and the field was used for a washing tub, so it had puddles of grey water, and it was used for a rubbish heap, so it had old machines buried in it, waiting to be fixed—fridges, short motors, and tractor seats set firmer than the stone. You don't often know a field so well, and I'll not go there now if it can be helped.

They were stacked along the wall nearest me.

For two hundred yards they went on, few hundred dead ewes and rams, lambs born and not born, laying atop each other so you couldn't tell whose head was whose, one deep fleece with a thousand legs, each animal stretched out four ways as if leaping, bodies piled to the height of copestones, their backs and necks raddled in patches of green or blue or yellow, bright colours like warnings of poison. Each killed clean and proper, so their brains stayed in them or else they rested on fresh crowns of blood. I remember their tongues all hung out. Not long dead and too swollen to stay in their mouths.

I walked to where the farm lads were gathered downwind. For all the mess, it was a piddly thing, their fire. Flames no bigger than what they burned. It was being fed on crap from about the farm and the endless black was made by tyres and feed buckets, garden chairs and fireproof doors. Looked to be all the rubbish they'd owned getting torched. One of the lads was standing to it like fire was in short supply and poking it with a stick that pulled back melted rubber.

Wanted the smoke big enough to make cover for Danny, cover the whole fells, but they couldn't get it hot enough. Brown coal they were using. Secondhand from the power plant. Smoked more than a Frenchman, but you could still near pick up a chunk after an hour of cooking.

Waited for William to tell us what to do. "We'll get them moved closer," he said. "Make a new pile and get the bodies going. Can't wait any longer." He headed up to the fire as if he might walk into it. "Now like."

A Herdwick ram weighs as much as a man and the ewes aren't skinny either. We'd only one back each to carry them and that meant dragging near enough. With a choice of an arse in your face or brains dribbling down your shirt, I took to carting them by their middle. The three lads were more shy with them, thinking the looser they held them, the less dead they'd be. Between us, it'd not take so long to move them, but I felt every pound of them bastards. Worked silently. Nowt to say that day, and I wanted my mouth kept shut to stop flies or dirt or worse getting in. We moved them ready to burn but kept them back from the heat. Waiting.

Each of us had a knife to hand. Their guts would biggen on evil gas and needed cutting open before you could move them. William always had a knife on his belt. Made of iron from what I remember, as he was forever drying it on himself. He'd sharpened the Sheffield clean off over the years so that it looked to be made of thin air and he'd use it to point at things like his finger was too crooked for the job.

We kept dragging and dragging. I tried not looking at the lads, not being friendly like. We weren't in this together, what we did that day we'd carry alone. But I'd not help looking, catching their eyes.

Each time I did their faces were more tired, not from lack of sleep, though I doubt they'd slept a night between them—they'd soot filling their wrinkles, aged them thirty years, and they'd shadows on their cheeks with no light about to cast them.

I'd lost count of the sheep I'd hauled, when I heard a tumble, then a yelling from the floor. "Bollocks. Bollocks. Bollocks." It was the shorter farmhand—a lad from Patterdale. Got his foot hooked in a clay sink and fell down on his arse. The ewe he was bonehugging had fallen with him, resting on his chest, eye to eye, upside down, all six of their legs stuck up in the air. His mate ran in and took the body off, but that lad didn't stir from off the ground. Shirt was pulled up to his shoulders, and he'd got sheep's blood on his belly. Seemed to think if he didn't move, it might dry up, clear off on its own. He tried haggling with his thoughts. Crawling instead of standing so he'd not be looking down, stayed on his knees, wiped his face red, cleaned it with one sleeve and uncleaned it with the other, took his time, crawling and crawling. Only got up at the gate, where he propped himself up on the other side. Drained a pop bottle filled with water. William went over for a word. "That whisky you supping?" he said. "What's taking you so long?"

"It's only water."

"Getting thirsty's good for you. Means you're working hard enough."

"I can't."

"You can't?"

"I need a break today."

"Then you've to go home."

"Home?"

"Not here anyroad."

"I've been living at Caldhithe for months."

"The house is for people who work the farm."

"When you gonna pay me?"

"What for?"

"What you mean, what for? For the bloody work."

"You'll get what's owed to you."

I got the feeling the lad would've argued the point more if winning didn't mean getting back to work. He grabbed his stuff and did his best to run off without picking up his legs. Soon after, the other lads dropped the ewes they'd been hauling, dropped their gloves, and dropped their knives in the turf. Walked off with not a nod and nowt to say.

William picked up one of their fallen sheep, finished lugging it, launched it by its two back legs onto the fire. Chucked on the other and then two more and that doused the whole bonefire into hungry smoke. "We'll start again," he said, stopping me. "Don't know why I let them go at it like this."

Fair to say none of us knew what we were doing at the start. I'd burned stuff before like everyone has, storm-torn logs and sofas on Bonefire Night and piles of what maybe shouldn't have been for burning. But this was hundreds of sheep. Tons of meat and bone. Skin fit for making leather. Cremating one takes more heat than you know.

We couldn't stack them on the clap cold ground. Fire would snuff itself out. So we built a pyre, one great towering bastard, one more light dancing in the valley. William rode a tipping trailer across his lowland fields, filled the back with railroad sleepers, hedgerow, buckthorn, bedframes, bookshelves and each sodding book, with log piles made of fence posts, rolled and wrapped in rasper wire. Got to stacking, laid the wood in slats, in squares, in heaps, leaning like pyr-amids of beer mats, and when your flock's ate every tree there's only one thing good for kindling. One sheep, two sheep, three sheep, sitting safely, wedged in with their bedding straw. The pyre stood near tall as us and we'd to build it further up, slab by slab. Another layer, we'd doors and crates, we'd shipping palettes, fresh bags of coal, the glass-black stuff, so shiny it looked wet. We squashed their stomachs and folded up their legs, turned the ewes to bony bricks, the tups to flinted slate, close together, rubbing, rooing off their hair. Once William had offered everything save the shirt from off his back, he burned his breath and fattened up the glowing ash. Get a fire hot enough and you'll teach the sun to candle, but those sickly sheep, bloody stupid and bloody stubborn—catch owt but flames. Singed the wool and blackened up the meat, and still no fire was getting in, we found metal poles, two giant pokers, and beat their backs, spanking them like rugs. "Get on. Get on." Soaked the next lot with paraffin, with diesel oil, now that really got them going, went in heavy, squirting petrol at the coldly burning base, flames shot twice as high and took our eyebrows up to heaven. I waited as it roared and popped, *rip rap, rip rap*, shifted with loud bangs as if each spent bullet had come alive. We pulled rags across our mouths to taste the air less badly. Took swigs of water from melted soup flasks and spat on our thumbs and hands, tried rubbing the wetness back inside our eyes. Tried batting at the floating ash, stop it landing on our sleeves—and it landed all the same, turned to grease about our necks so we grew a second skin. I'd take dizzy, swimming in my head, both hands on my poker to keep standing, and William would slam against me, working side by side, my shoulder held up, no place to fall, and I'd thank him for the break. Sundown turned the far horizon red and with the smoke spilling up it looked as if we'd set all Cumbria afire.

I was back at the farmhouse after the first day while it boiled down, scrubbing at my face with hose water. From where I was stood in the lot, I could see down a trail to the big road. There were colours in the air, white then blue, casting over the smoke—I thought of Christmas, and through the mess, I could see the lights of a police car flooding the valley floor. A group of fellas walked up. Squaddies. More of them this time, and their heads and bodies wrapped in those white rubber suits that squeaked against their thighs. Simply Red leading at the front, looking jumpy, his flak jacket still across his chest.

I didn't shake myself dry. Didn't put my shirt back on. Half cleaned, still dripping as I walked to meet them, a fresh farmer's tan, my arms and face and neck near grey as pigeon meat. "You here for the invasion?" I asked when Red got close.

"We're here to see what he's up to."

"You're not worried he's going to gun you down?"

"We stopped Michael on the way out, he said it wasn't like that."

"Stopped who?"

"Michael, one of William's farmhands."

"Soft-looking bastard?"

"You've had long enough now."

"It's been done."

"It's been done, has it?"

I pointed to the smoke.

"We need to check, see that William's got all of them."

"I can show you what's left."

"Can we look about on our own?"

I walked them to the compound and banged on the kitchen window, let Helen know she'd got guests. They asked her if there was owt hiding in the buildings. She didn't get the question. "The animals," they asked. "The livestock, are there any left?"

"They've all bloody left," she told them.

The squaddies paired up and each searched a different building, the barns, the sheds, the store huts. Kept their torches off and hooked themselves quick about each doorway to surprise empty rooms. "Clear." Found black-wrapped bales of sileage. "Clear." Found the engine of a mower and the scoop from off a digger. "Clear." Found a wall of pricking hooks. Some fellas took off higher, walking to this outcrop atop a bankside field, checked the land about them to spot if there was owt left to kill. Simply Red stayed by me, so I asked him, "What they thinking they'll find?"

"It's procedure."

"You need to see where the action really is, Red," I told him. "To get what's going on here."

"We've people to do this for William. The culling. Do it properly."

"I've seen your best at work."

I walked with Red for half a mile, waving my torch at his feet and telling him there was no point washing them with disinfectant till he left. Carried on to the field and he about tripped over the corpses still resting at the wall, waiting their turn. "I'm not here for this bit," he said.

"Seems like you are to me."

William was stood by the fire, heat from it making the air about him look scared. He was pacing with his stick. Smacking up the bodies and chucking on what seemed whole trees to keep it going.

He turned to face us so we could only see his outline for the dark, and I called out to him, "They're searching the farm, William."

"Nowt better to do?" he said. "You'll want to be careful, Red."

"What for?"

"I hear they're burning pigs as well."

The copper almost laughed at that.

"Let's go," Red said to me. "I've seen enough."

"That easy?"

"If you made it any easier for yourselves, you'd be jumping in the fire."

Red and me took our time getting back. He asked about my dad and how we found the winter. Talked about death like it was the weather. The squaddies were sat on the ground outside with a mug of tea each from Helen and a tin of biscuits passed about. Red didn't ask if they'd found owt—told them to pack up and move on. He turned to me as he was leaving. "What you in with him for?"

"Because he asked."

"Doesn't take much for you, then, aye?"

"I'm a simple lad."

"Will be if you keep breathing down them fumes," he said. "We've too much shite to deal with to worry about this any longer."

They went, taking all the light from the road with them.

I sat on the cobbles where they'd been, none of me wanting to get back up and all the strength in me so gone I couldn't feel how weak my body was. My hands wouldn't stop trying to grip. I'd to stretch out my fingers to keep them from curling. I nodded off, cross-legged, head bowed. No idea how long I was out, but it was night when I woke, cold as owt. William had given one of my boots a kick. "Sitting down's a mistake," he said.

"Why stand when you can sit?"

"Harder to get a kicking on your feet."

"We stopping for the night?"

"It's the fire doing the work," he said. "Helen's made you some tea."

I went in and heard the telly on, so that's where I headed. The side table had been pulled up to the sofa, tea towel laid across it for a tablecloth, and a plate of baked spuds waiting for me. Some game show was on and there was Helen, other side of that sofa, watching it. Her legs up on the cushions, still pink from out her bath, still bare, don't know how she had such hot baths, and she pulled her feet back enough for me to sit down. I suppose you're not supposed to talk about a lass's legs so much. "How long did you leave me out there?" I asked William as he stood in the doorway.

"Thought you'd gone home."

"You didn't see me on the ground?"

"None of my business what you were doing on the ground."

He went back down the hall to the kitchen and was clattering in the cupboards. Sounded as if he needed to get every dish and cup out to find what he was after. There was all this babbling and beeping coming from the telly, and I tried watching—not sure when the ads had come on. Helen spoke to me. "You not eating?"

Didn't think I wanted to, but my ears were popping soon as I took a bite, like I'd come from underwater, and I was hungrier by the time I finished but I felt better. I looked over at her and started chatting. "You still going with the shop, Helen?"

"It's not going anywhere, but there's not much in opening."

"Empty?"

"No one's buying place mats of the fells right now."

"Any with Herdwicks on will be limited edition soon."

William came back with a tin of blood-warm ale and sat in his chair, flicking the lid.

"Couldn't you sell owt else?" I asked her.

"Like tinderboxes and quicklime?"

"I don't know. Makeup or frocks or something."

"You'd look handsome with a bit of lippy on, Steve."

"This about the bloody shop?" William said. "Can't we just watch telly tonight?"

The shop was Helen's and from what I remember she did well with it. In the early years, she worked the farm but a place in the village opened after Mrs. Harrison died and Helen went for it. It was the sort of place that sold keyrings with your name on or fudge with pictures of Buttermere on the box. All of it tat but that's what sold. Might've been the only thing making any profit on Caldhithe. "How's Danny doing?" I asked him instead.

"He likes camping."

"On his own?"

"You think he's better off here?"

"Don't think any of us are."

"First sensible thing I've heard you say."

I sank in my chair and William finished his ale before the foam could drip down his fingers. Breathed deep so we could all hear him, filled his chest and stored the air, and once his show was over, he stood up. "I'm headed back."

"Now?"

"You can rest up, Steve."

"You sure?"

"Don't need you falling asleep on me again," he said. "Might put out the fire."

What little I did sleep was on the sofa. Couldn't think of leaving yet and might've not gone if I'd been told to. Didn't want my dad seeing the state I'd got into.

I was woken by William rattling in the kitchen. Guzzling ale and clearing out the fridge. It was reaching morning, and I pulled my bedsheet off the floor and tucked myself in up to my neck. William came in and sat in his chair, looking out the window. "I can smell you in my dreams," I told him.

"Good to know you still have some."

"How many sheep left?"

"A day or two. Maybe three."

"We'll get through it."

He'd another drink with him and was as keen to sink it.

"Can I ask you something?" I said.

He didn't speak so I did.

"How're you walking through the smoke with your eyes open?"

"You what?"

"I saw you at it a few hours ago. Your eyes were all red, but you'd got them open. I can hardly keep them open now thinking about it."

"I don't remember that, but I'll tell you what, I'm more scared of that fire than the smoke."

"I swear down. I saw you."

"You go back to sleep," he said.

"You sure you don't need a hand?"

"I'd tell you if I did."

We burned animals for days, well into the night when all we could see was what we were burning, till the poles we used to push them down couldn't ever be cleaned and our hands smelled of butane and our bodies smelled of bonefire. That's how it was till early on the third morning when the fire couldn't keep itself going and the piles of the burning and the dead were all together. We'd been alone in that field for days, but it was the first time it meant owt. "That'll do," he said. Three days I've spent more time thinking about than I spent living.

We went back to the house, and I soaked myself with the hose again, down to my boots. No matter how much I scrubbed, I kept pulling crap out my scalp with my nails. Everything spilled off me grey into a puddle.

William came out with two tins of bitter and handed me one—I don't know how he drank the stuff. Was like supping the copper off a penny. I got through it so he wasn't drinking alone. "What now?" I asked him.

"Bed for me."

"Good an answer as any I can think of."

We both sat on upturned bins, and I had another drink with him. Then another, and then I lost count. Weirdest thing it was. Stayed out longer than we meant to, gulping down pints like the cups had holes in the bottom, but we never got drunk. He didn't say much but he listened to me talk about what might happen to Montgarth and how fat our dogs would get and how fat we'd get. Heading inside didn't feel right. Not yet. Needed to stop feeling like animals ourselves.

Sat till the ale could no longer keep us warm and then I stayed another night on their sofa. Even with all of what was going on, I liked being there. Helen was good to talk to and I wanted to be near someone like her for a while.

Early the next day, I was still on the sofa when William came in to eat his breakfast. His eyes more red than white from bloodshot and if he'd slept it didn't show. From the way Helen looked at me when she came in, I must've looked a ship's rat and all. She'd been talking on the phone in the kitchen, and I could hear the sound of her voice down the hall. She hung up and came into the room, sat on the armrest. "That was Simply Red."

"What's he want now?" William said.

"Didn't say. Just wanted to let us know he was coming by."

"Can't find a copper when you need one. Now they'll not piss off."

"You want me to stick around?" I said.

"You part of this?"

"For now."

"You can stay if you like. You've earned that much," he said. "But I've work to be getting on with."

"What work?"

"Got a farm to run." He stood up and left a rough bowl of breakfast to cement—headed outside.

"What you think he wants?" I asked Helen. "Simply Red?"

"Not a clue. But I'll tell you this much, he sounded right pleased with himself."

She followed William out not long after with his boots and came back to do paperwork in the kitchen. I waited on the sofa for a while like it was my own. When I got outside, I could hear him in the barn. He'd a tap running and was chucking buckets of water to the ground. Soapy air came out to the lot, almost harder to stomach than the smoke, and when I looked in, he was on his knees scrubbing the floor where the sheep had been. "What you cleaning the barn for?"

"Needs doing."

"Needs doing?"

"Never heard of a spring clean?"

Well, I bloody took a brush and got scrubbing. Getting the hardstuck dirt from out the flagstones so they were dark as the day they were put down. Sweeping everything that was left and setting it for rubbish. Mucking out was a way of life and we were finding out what the end of that looked like. Helen came by when the floor was close to sparkling. "He's here," she said. "In the house. Wants to talk there."

"I'll be in," William said, and made no effort to stop. Squaring up pools of thick brown water and shunting them outside. He'd a way of sweeping wide with his arms so that he was reaching a quarter of the floor with one go. Leaned against the door and started talking to me. "I didn't always want to be a farmer," he said.

"You've always been one."

"I know that," he said.

"This where you tell me you wanted to be a ballet dancer?"

"I didn't want to be much of owt. And I don't mean that in any lazy way. I thought I was working on my dad's farm till he got sick enough to sell it and that would be it. Raising up each lot of sheep so they were stronger than the last. Had to be a point where they couldn't get any more muscle on them or be more sound than they were."

"Then what?"

"It never hit me that it all keeps going and you're there for it. I didn't think I'd be dead but maybe not much more than that. When he snuffed it like he did, my dad, all of sudden like. I never had to think about all that, what I wanted. Till now."

"You going to sell?"

"Sell?" he said. "I told you I didn't always want to be a farmer. Thought of owt else makes me sick now."

"Plenty of practice with sick things."

"Aye, we have," he said. "I need to go speak to this fella. Be good to have you in there."

Helen was sat on the sofa and Simply Red was in William's chair. Plate of crumbs on his knees and what looked to be his second brew of the evening. "You're here, lads," Red said. "Starting to think you'd got lost."

"Not with you keeping us safe, Red," I said to him before sitting by Helen. William was stood in the hallway, one shoulder against the wall.

"Take a seat, Will," he said.

"I'll stand."

"You'll grow roots if you keep this up."

"What you want?" William said.

"I've got some questions about Caldhithe."

"I know a little about that."

"Part of the problem of being a copper out here is that it's hard to know where anything is. Who owns what. Any rock bigger than my head has got its own name. So I was wondering if you know where Caldhithe ends. Where the boundary is."

"Map's what you're after," William said. "It ends where it ends, far as I know."

"Fair enough. How about this?" he said. "There's a spot maybe three miles out from here. Flat as a pancake. Rough slopes every side of it and it's mad to see somewhere so flat so high up. Can't really miss it with a great heap of stones on one end. Would that be a bit of your land?"

"Could be if it's so close but stones I can't help you with. Heaps of stone everywhere I look."

"The thing is, William, it's important that we get all the live-stock."

"Very."

"Maybe more important than you know, and it's easy to over-look a few animals here and there. Just this afternoon we found ninety sheep in the upper fells in that very spot. Some idiot must've left them out and forgotten. Can you imagine?"

"Never been one for forgetfulness."

I didn't know what Red was getting at being so roundabout—if it was to get William fired up, he didn't have to try. I stirred in my seat to make sure my legs could move, and the copper got jumpy like he'd forgot I was there. Gripped his armrest, ready to spring. But he kept talking. "First time I heard about you, William, I think it was in '95 when I started on here. Peter Wilson, if you remember him, was talking to me. Wasn't going to be in the country show for the first time because you were entering. Wasn't worth wasting the entry fee, he said. You only came out every few years and said nothing when you did but you won first prize every time."

"Doesn't surprise me. Talking was about all Pete was good at."

"True at that. Weren't wrong, though. Best sheep in the valley."

"Good news, then. Shouldn't be much competition this year."

"I was thinking about what Peter had told me today. I was riding in a helicopter, don't get to do that much. Was over that spot, the flat one with the rocks, when we saw these sheep. Beautiful animals. Could see that from the air. Had to keep the chopper nearly flush to the ground as we shot them. Never think you have to do that sort of thing after training."

"Big day for you." William stopped leaning. Whale eyes under the big light.

"One last check, then," Red told him. "To see that you haven't any sheep left."

"If you head out to that smouldering field again, you'll have seen the before and after."

"If you say that's all of them, William, I believe you."

"That's handy for me."

"To tell the truth, the main reason I came by was to drop off some forms. So you can make claims for the stock you've lost."

William took a step toward him, swaying instead of leaning. "I'm not interested in any of your bloody schemes."

"Be the first time you've made any money on Caldhithe far as I can tell."

There was a large envelope on the side table, a chunky one, and Red reached over to get it, then stood to pissing height—squared off against William. Pressed the parcel to his chest and made him take the forms. Thought he might smack the copper round the head, but he stepped away, held the stack in two fists like a chicken's neck and tore it clean in half. Don't know how the bugger did it. A hundred pages ripped in two and dropped down to the floor. "You're good at cleaning messes up," he said. "So you can take that rubbish with you when you leave."

"I could take you in if I wanted."

"I doubt that very much."

Red looked about and found he was trapped, only rips of wallpaper to his back. Grabbed his belt and felt his cuffs and balled his hands. Calmed down and took a knee, picked up those papers and caught my eyes, then Helen's. "You'll be wanting a new set of these," he said to William. "I'll give them to your wife next time."

"You think I'm a bastard, Red," he said. "I'm nowt compared to her."

Simply Red was gone without another word, and William stayed where he was. Could hear his teeth grating as he turned to me. "You can piss off. You've done enough."

"You're telling me."

I left like he told me to and walked home for fear if I sat too long in the car, I might not find a reason to move again.

We'd burned through everything, even what we'd no right to, rubbed out the stars and hid the moon, and if the night sky wasn't already black, we'd have had a good go at making it. I was wandering in that dark and kept touching the wall on my right, couldn't get lost with that penning me in, five hundred years of shepherds guiding me. Same wall would take you all the way to Montgarth. I knew I was on Maller Moss Bog when I felt it in my socks and that meant I was halfway home. I took my coat off and pulled my shirtsleeves back to my armpits to get as much breeze on my skin as I could. Something about night air that feels fatter and fresher, and I wanted to get drunk on the stuff to clean all of me.

I had to get out. Not just Caldhithe but Cumbria. At the time I thought maybe forever. Before I got as rotten as the next few months were shaping up to be. If my legs would've taken it, I'd have stepped over the sides of the valley and kept going.

At the point where you step from Caldhithe into my old farm you've to walk on either side of a crack in the earth that lasts half a mile. I was avoiding it when I saw Danny walking switchback not far off. Thin torch beam swinging as he moved, a backpack on him that was bigger than he was, tent half stuffed in it. I called out to him. "You back, then?" I asked.

"I need to talk to Dad."

"He's home."

"They got them."

"I know."

"There were all these men in a Mountain Rescue helicopter," he said. "I hid when I heard them coming. They were shooting not long after."

"You did what you had to."

I gave him some water and didn't say owt about his whimpering or the snot drying on his arms. "I didn't look back," he said to me. "To see if there were any left."

"Don't think your dad's ever looked back on a thing he's done."

"Will he be mad?"

"Not at you."

His legs were stringy from scrambling, and he looked fit to collapse. I'd have offered to shoulder him back, but he'd not have said yes. I let him keep the bottle and sent him on his way.

My dad's home wasn't much further. The light from the toilet was always on to save him pissing on his feet, and I could see it a mile off. I felt out the copestones of the walls, running my hands chalky till I found the edge of a gate and pulled the latch open. From there it was only grassland. The turf left uneaten, firm, soft, made me feel like taking my boots off.

When I got close to the house, I sat where we'd planted a length of ryegrass and waited for morning. Started nibbling on the growth coming through, tasted sweet and bitter at the same time and it made me jealous of the sheep.

If I think back, that was the last time I saw the house while it was still ours.

PART II

Lamb on the Throne

Medderte

A couple of days later, and I was out of Cumbria. My dad didn't ask where I'd been or how a chat with the neighbours had lasted a week. Couldn't stop my eyes squinting and my fingers were stuck grey and the whole valley stunk so the ash in my chest was nowt to him.

Only thing I did was sleep. In a bed for a change, from morning till dark again, and when I woke I couldn't move my body, pinned down with aches in parts that only exist to ache and needed to unclench my jaw with a knife to get it working. Turned to the side where it hurt less and kept sleeping. Lost a day and learnt to walk again to take a piss that lasted half an hour, found out what banisters were built for, and sat in the kitchen drinking a pot of tea to myself. My dad came in looking scrubbed up, his hair combed and his nails clipped, wearing a suit jacket, holding himself straight in his seat to prove he could. We talked like we'd not in a while, about him spotting a goshawk and a henge of river boulders he'd found. When I finished my third mug of tea he said, "I expect you'll be going now."

"Where to?"

"I don't bloody know, wherever you were before you came back."

"So now you don't need me here?"

"Nowt for you to do."

"How you going to get on alone?"

"Pension will come in. Don't worry about that."

"You can barely hold your mug."

"I'm holding it fine." He gripped it tight with one hand for a change. "I'm not blind to the state I'm in. But for now, I'm okay, and I don't want you getting sick of me for when I do need you. I'll let you know when the time comes."

There was no bickering. No talking. Once he'd made up his mind, he'd my bags packed by the door and gave me the keys to his Rover. It sat waiting for me with its bonnet pointed to the road. If I tried saying owt other than goodbye, all I got was, *I thought you'd already left.*

Got in the driver's seat and slid the chair back, twisted the mirror, and started flattening my dad's grooves. Started riding away, and the smaller Montgarth got in the rearview, the better I felt. It looks different when you're leaving a place. Y'know, leaving for good. Running away. Make a stranger of yourself—you see it as a stranger. Weather turns perfect and everything you hated makes itself hidden. And when the sun's out in the fells it's like nowt else. See it beaming through shipwrecked clouds and the ground that looked dead catches it and you see mountains made of gold.

I took the long way out of Cumbria, down Copeland, to avoid seeing Caldhithe again. Made a stop by one of the lakes, a place where the kids would go swimming called Slodder Ground. My feet were feeling veiny, and I stuck them in the water. It was bloody cold and clouded with swan shit, but it was enough. Went there as a lad myself, rode my bike out when I wasn't up for school or a day in the fields. Back then, it seemed the lakes carried on for as long as you cared to look, had a way of filling your head and your eyes so you felt like you were floating in them, even when you were just riding past. I thought all sorts of things must've lived in them and sometimes

I'd be right. A fisherman would pull a pike out that even two men struggled to carry. You'd feel like telling them to throw it back, like it wasn't fair because the lake was showing them something they're not supposed to talk about.

That was the last stop I made for six hours save filling up on petrol. Took a zigzag through England and stopped at a roadside hotel outside Lincoln, got a room with a bed so big you could do six sausage rolls and not fall out. Had a holiday. Two weeks of thinking I'd sort it out tomorrow, what came next. Eating crisps in bed or in the bath and getting a headache from all the salt. Daytime telly on as if it can keep you warm—the kind that lets you know there's worse things than death. There's nowt so dangerous as a room with no view. Started seeing things in the popcorn ceiling. Every sad bastard thought come to life, stretching near forty years, and they went on and on, filling the room like a leaking oven, finding a gap under the door and flooding out till my head felt the size of the world.

I started driving lorries again. Only two things I knew was driving and sheep. And not enough to keep sheep alive. It's not a hard job, driving, just a thousand easy things to get done and you've to be awake to do them all, for hours on end, for days even, so you're wobbling inside like a bust exhaust pipe when you get to sleeping with the lights of the car park always on, the same flip-flop showers and piss troughs again and again for a hundred miles down the big road. Started off thinking it'd not last me long. I was hauling as much as I could, going back-to-back on jobs that family men didn't want, but I kept my eye out for a place to stop, to live in, long-term like. Saw most of the country from an eight-foot box, and I was glad I wasn't getting paid to sightsee.

65

At first, I was moving junk for shops. Enough crates of chemical bread to sop up the River Trent and boxes of screws that rattled on all the potholes. Town to town. Filling each Woolworths with tins of Coke and stuffed animals. Did the Channel run once a fortnight and made a game of seeing how far I could get without stopping for nine hours.

One day, I was in a lorry park by King's Lynn, finishing a haul and waiting my turn for the next. This sweaty bastard called Gary came up to me, smacked the side of my lorry till I got out. He smelled of the earth and had a sun-split face that made me hungry for pork pies. "You got experience with stock, haven't you?" he said to me.

"Doubt anyone would pay me to drive empty lorries for long."

"No, livestock. Cows and pigs."

"How can you tell?"

He looked me over. "How could I not?"

I was shy of crowds in an empty waiting room, walked at a dog's pace, and had a wet-finger whistle loud enough to split logs. I was easier to read than a copy of *Razzle*. He set me up driving animals for him. Cattle mostly, in four-deckers chained out with a trailer to double the haul. I knew nowt about cows but there was only so much that needed learning. One end has the udders, and if not, watch out for its horns. If the worst happens and they make to trample you, don't run from them, take a pop with one of your fists, hit a muzzle or two and show them you're not scared—hold your ribs close if that's not working.

I'd one rule, I wasn't going to Cumbria. Not to it, not through it. "You can always say no to a job," Gary told me. And that was good enough.

This bit I'm telling you about, the driving and the roving, it's because it's not something we talk about. I'm guilty of it and all. Acting like there's not a world outside the fells and dales. I'm sick of it. It's all I hear. If we're the only ones, only caring about us, then we're asking to be special and they've every right to ignore us. I saw how it was, from the deep end of Scotland to the wine sippers down south, same ocean whether you looked out to the Long Forties or the Strait of Dover. It was a disease that ate at everyone, foot-and-mouth, killed the animals with split hooves first but then it killed the farms and the farmers killed themselves, came for the country shows and the auctions next, and all that made a living from that. Just the offcomers left, and they didn't want to look till the soil settled. No doubt we had it worse than most, in Cumbria, but it wasn't right to say we were alone. Knowing there's a bastard in the bunker next to yours, still living, that's something.

I started driving livestock not long after the last sick creatures were chopped up and burned off or melted quicklime into soil, and I could still feel it in the countryside. I was bringing calves and lambs and piglets back to where there was nowt else and there was some joy in that, but I was going about these farms in oilskins like they'd ploughed their fields radioactive. I'd haul a trailer every few weeks that was stripped clean to dull metal but still stinking of dead bodies. Never went away, that smell, and it was fierce enough to make a bull sob when you caged one in it. My boss, Gary, once said something to me after he'd dealt with a starter who couldn't hack it. "That's why I like you farm lads. Know what it is to raise something to be killed."

I've driven all over this island but England's the only bit I know. Skelmersdale, Thurrock, Thetford, Giggleswick, Molton. Mud flats,

moors, fens, sunken cliffs, sealess beaches, and the scabby grey door-
stops of any city worth knowing. More days in Immingham than any
bastard should have to spend and fewer days in Falmouth than I'd
have liked. And wherever you go, they've got their own way of doing
things. There's the great wool farms of the south coast with Bluefaced
and Corriedale sheep like balls of lint rolled the length of the country
where the stock gets lost in corn mazes and they teach their animals
to walk in heels so their fleeces won't run mucky or rough. The bog-
foot farmers in the corner pocket, living off petting zoos and market
gardens, tomatoes grown on English sun, taste it in their juice—folk
there had me scooping up goats with ribbons in their beards and
haircuts neater than mine. One lass gave each cow a hug and kissed
them on the gums before she let them go and called the slaughter-
house to see they killed out well. Now, the fluffy western grasslands, a
weird lot if you ask me, spend too long looking in cows' arseholes and
drinking milk that coats your tongue with fat. The dairy yakkas talk
of clover and maize like snotterclouts talk of thick rich wine, would
stick handfuls of pearl millet in their gobs and say it tastes of cherry
or gold or butter, everything but bloody millet, each crop fed to milk-
ers with different jobs in mind, canola for cheddar, oats for Wens-
leydale, and I heard twice of an Italian ryegrass that was good as ice
cream. The clay country across the Midlands is home to the barbers
of England, scything rows of wheat that grow quicker than you can
cut them down and red cattle with cheeseburger written across their
topside, shape of them like a steak itself, long dewlaps hanging from
their necks as if they'd swallowed boulders and big enough bastards
to have done it. For the gut fat cows carrying muscles you can't fit
your hands about, bodybuilders with the evil eye and moos louder
and deeper and more fearful than a lass birthing triplets, you need to

head east where there's barley you can chew on unhulled like sweets, and Shorthorns and Herefords that can hardly stand under the thick sirloin they breed in them. Up north, up bloody north, there's sand and silt pretending like it's soil, sugar beets they grow in peat, and I know they're only foothills, the stunted mountains, but they're the tallest that we've got and for five thousand years those feral people have slept in bedsheets spun from dishcloth sheep.

I found a lot of home in the places I went. Families standing fast with all they had left and folk who thought *sticking it out* meant waiting to rot. And for all the people I met, I could go a week, two weeks, without talking. No words but *thanks, goodbye, how do.* You'd think living in that outside place, a driver in a box seat, you'd feel small and you'd feel empty, but there was so much of me inside myself that all I felt was crowded.

Late at night on country roads, all you can see is fifty yards in front, that's fifty yards of chipseal splitting away from the greenside verge. Fifty yards of lit-up trees or dirt or scrub. Till you see another pair of headlights in the distance, coming down on you. Can take a quarter of an hour between spotting them and scraping past, but for them fifteen minutes, I didn't feel so alone.

Anytime I tried meeting someone new, a pal for drinking with or a lass for drinking and more, it went to shite. Met this one lass, well, saw her about I suppose—right good-looking lass she was. Wore a party frock a hundred miles from the nearest dance floor and had a belt about her hips wider than a wrestler's though it had nowt to keep up. Each time I saw her legs, bare in the rain, I followed them all the way to the ground like a fella jumping off the

Humber Bridge. I felt an idiot for staring, biting my hands to stay conscious, just like she wanted. She left nowt to the imagination and that worked for me since I never had much for that sort of thing.

I saw her at services and rest stops all through the middle of the country, waiting for drivers at Telford, Derby, Northampton. I don't know how she got about but she was there more often than not, grinning at me. She'd tap on the window of my lorry and remember who I was. "Steve." Made it sound foreign. I'd send her away. "Not today, love." But I got friendly with her, would buy her a coffee when she looked bored, and we'd have a chat. More in common than you'd think. Both of us grew up on farms and took drinks without sugar and thought sandwiches cost too much. I'd start to look forward to jobs in that part of the country just to hear her say my name.

One time, I was sheltering near Peterborough to keep clear of a fresh gale—wind strong enough to top the rig on the big road if I kept driving. Could see her lipstick in the dark. I was one of the only lorries there that night and she'd knocked on the other drivers' windows only to be told to piss off. Heard her tapping on mine. Didn't have the heart to send her into a hurricane and, she said, for me, it'd only be ten quid for ten minutes. So up she came, and I held her hand for all three steps. She looked small and there was no hiding under the cabin light. Goose pimples the size of fleabites and the wind had loosened the powder on her face—she wasn't much younger than me. "How's this work?" I asked her.

"Up to you."

"It'd take me ten minutes just to think of something." I bumped the heating up, so at least it wasn't silent. "How's that?"

She put her hands over the vent.

"Let's start with your name, then," I said. "All the times I've seen you around, I still don't know it."

"Yelena," she said.

I didn't hear her right. "Your name's Helen?"

"No difference. Call me Helen if you want."

Thought of doing that made me sadder than owt else. She put her hand on my leg. "So, what you want?"

"What is it you always say when you come knocking? I'm after some company."

"That all?"

"My money, and I like talking," I said. "Tell me what you're planning to do after this."

She showed me the mouthwash in her handbag.

"No, not like that. How long you planning to keep doing this work?"

"As long as they pay me." She started warming the cigarette lighter and took out a fag. "Or I have money to buy a place back home."

"You planning on doing that alone?"

"You want to come with me?"

"I get worried seeing you out here all the time."

"I worry about you. But I like it. Being alone. You tell me what to do, you pay me."

She told me about the fellas she met and how big her house was going to be. What her home country was like and the family she didn't talk to anymore—had that in common too. "What about your home?" she asked me.

"It's up the top of the country."

"Scotland?"

"No, just looking up at it through the border. They're the only hills worth seeing in all of England."

"I heard of it. It's beautiful?"

"Being beautiful isn't all it's sold as."

She rolled her eyes. "If you took me, where would we go?"

"No need to take you anywhere. Once you're there, that's it. I don't know what to tell you about it—some folk find it scary because it's empty of trees and it's mostly rocks on top of bigger rocks. Never stops raining but the ground is almost purple and with your right head on, it could be a painting anywhere you look."

"You miss it?"

"To tell the truth, I don't know what that'd feel like. I'm still there in my head."

She looked at the time on the dashboard and then at me. "Don't worry," I told her. "I can pay you for the whole night."

"You don't need to."

"Happy to. You can go to sleep if you want, I'll keep the heat on." She said okay and took her shoes off, rested her legs on my lap. I liked having her there. It felt calming. But seeing her sleeping, the smooth outline of her face and her body—I woke her up. Wish I'd not. Wish I'd let her kip through to morning and asked for nowt more than a handshake. After it was done, I gave her all the cash I had in the lorry and asked her to leave. She hugged her elbows looking into the dark, wind making it hard to get the door open. She kissed me on the cheek and got out, and I felt homesick for the first time. Never had her tapping on my window again.

You'll be wanting to know how I got back to Cumbria, back to living here. It's William you want to know about, not me.

Like the first time I returned, it was because of my dad. I'd tried keeping in touch, but he was harder to talk to than God. When he did pick up the phone, he always started with "What you want?" If I didn't have a good answer, he'd hang up.

Last chat I had with him was at a park up near Worcester. I'd been driving this open trailer, coverless, sixty foot of tin pipes strapped to my back, and at fifty miles an hour the air sucked through all five hundred of them, a bagpipe on wheels, felt the hum in my teeth. I got a call, saw it was my dad. About the only thing that would've got me to stop. Pulled up. He rang again. "You all right, Steve?"

"Just working."

"So what's happening?"

"I don't know, Dad. You called me."

"I did, didn't I?" he said. "I thought you should know. I've not been well."

"What's the problem?"

"Doctor doesn't bother telling me."

"That can't be right."

"Lass who comes to see me twice a week gives me magnesium. Same as we did with lambs that got staggers. You remember that?"

"I never knew what we were pumping them with."

"You should see what else they've got me on."

"I can get there next week," I said to him.

"Now, you've not to come back. I've someone looking after me."

"I'll see you Monday morning."

"No, Steve. You're out now. That's how it should be."

That was him done with it. Done with everything.

I remember every word of that call and how his voice wasn't working and how his breath wasn't working. Remember him repeating himself, told me twice he was dying. *I've not been well.* He was never sick. He got worn out and he got angry. Sadness and sickness and weakness were all the same. I never know how to think about my dad. You're meant to understand them better as you get older, same age as they got to be, climbed the same hills they did, stopped dreaming of lasses and started dreaming of where's good to take a piss, but the older I get, the further away he feels. Maybe that's it. Maybe there's the view up and the view down.

I could tell you a story twice as long as this just about him. Eric with the Ears, my bloody dad, named for the swollen cauliflowers on the sides of his head. Dug two hundred sheep out the side of Brimlaw in the hundred-year winter with only his billhook, laid all the hedgerow from here to Towthwaite, tossed Bald Tom by his last hair out a backhold ring, was in the merchant navy for five years with a fella named Uncle Lanty, did something near Cyprus they didn't talk about. All that I could tell you—but it wasn't who he was. If I said I didn't get on with him, that would be saying he was somebody you could get on with. He was a man of opposites. He talked forever of family but it was always his house. Told me to make something of my life and was the first to laugh if I combed my hair. Nowt he wouldn't do for his wife, for his son, unless it was something he didn't fancy doing. Down the pub, he'd talk the sun down from the sky, but at home, he only talked if he felt like an argument, and he always won them—won that last argument and all because he was dead of heart attack before I could get to him.

Got another call from his phone the day before I was to go up. Was a fella I didn't know asking what needed doing with his body.

I went back to Cumbria all the same. Still had the old man's Rover and I drove past the last Burger King out of Lancashire, last motorway watchtower, and I saw pastures, real pastures, and I felt sleepy, and my stomach felt full, though I'd not eaten since morning, and it was like I'd come to the end of a drive that lasted too long. And ten miles in I saw mountains again.

I was there for Montgarth. It'd not ever really been ours, the farmhouse, the farm, we'd just lived there as long as anyone can remember. The place had three owners in my time but the same tenants. Us. My dad, my mam, and me. Then my dad and me. Then my dad. I'd to clear the place before the end of the month, to give them time to turn it into holiday homes. Two of them, side by side, called them The Barns and they filled the mud trails with golden gravel and grew summer flowers in the feeding troughs. Didn't take me long to get the house emptied—spent more time loading up the car with all his stuff. My dad had put about everything but his blankets into boxes in the hall. Four with *Charity* written on and two with *Bin*.

And I was there to bury the bastard. Being put in the ground was the first time he'd ever owned a handful of dirt for himself.

It rained on the day of my dad's funeral. Folk here are born with waterproof skin and a double set of eyelids like a trout. But I've seen nowt like it before. Wherever the ground dipped it turned to a puddle, and wherever there was a puddle it turned to a lake and the lakes turned to seas and every road became a river and the fields became swimming baths and the sheep became swimmers and the village of Bewrith became Venice and every window was now a door and every car was now a stepping stone and after three hundred years of standing, Bewrith Bridge was torn out its banks and villagers came to wave it off down the River Pishon like the launch of some royal ship only they drank from bottles of whisky instead of smashing them.

Nowt much else to say about the day. Only thing I asked for was a coffin big enough for all the rolling in his grave he was like to do. Just me and my two aunts there, near seventy-odd themselves. One had made a life in County Durham and the other in Stirling. I didn't have a suit to hand, so I'd got myself a shirt and shoes from a charity shop on my way through Kendal, but my aunts had no excuses. None of us looked a bit smart and we were lucky it was wet enough to wear our coats to hide the fact. I said I wasn't up for talking and they thought it was from all the mourning. Couldn't bloody stand them. Didn't know my dad had sisters till I was an adult, and it didn't take long to find out why I'd not met them.

It wasn't the church in Bewrith village that we buried him at. The one with cherry trees that makes it glow pink through spring and the benches with names on. It's further out. In the cut of a forked road with only scrubland for a view and a chapel made of the same stone Montgarth had been and it doesn't hold service save Christmas and Easter and no one turns up when it does. We put him in the uncut grass with gravestones swollen out wonky. The vicar took sad at us being the only ones there, stood under hell water that fell in flat sheets like guillotines. "You still want me to go through with it?" the vicar asked. "The whole service?"

I told him to hurry it along and stick to the main bits—enough to see he was done right by. He talked about Jesus and was proud of himself for spotting they were both shepherds. His Bible got so wet he couldn't turn the pages. He was still talking a few minutes later when this tractor started roaring up the lane next to us, clattering away loud as owt, more tarmac in its engine than under its wheels, and it brought with it this almighty whiff of cow shit. Smelled beautiful to me.

Pimp

A pint of mild. That was my dad's drink. Ale black as the throat it's going down. It's sweet, so you lap it up quick and after the first two pints the spit in your mouth gets bitterer than the beer and you forget you're drinking it.

I was sat in The Crown on my third mild after the funeral. It was the only pub we had left in Bewrith, The Crown. Y'know, the only pub where you'd really go for a drink. Course, there were other pubs, we're still in England, and it used to be the Putney Arms was the place for something special after someone had died or got married or won big on the dogs, but it'd got itself a facelift with deer heads and pickaxes on the walls like we were still hunters or miners. So we had The Crown, with its white plastered walls and sticky red floor and you weren't sure if you were in the toilet because it all felt the same and you'd scrape your head on the ceiling to order from the bar.

I was keen to see the pub clean up after me, see Cumbria drunk dry, sloppy in my seat, holding my pint like it could anchor me. Heard a sloshing when I stood. I told them to give me a job washing pots, and they took one look and said I wasn't qualified. Up and down to take a piss, broke the seal, tried corking my bladder with more grog. Was struggling with a bag of crisps when I felt a jabbing in my shoulder, rocked me forward, and I turned my head— William Herne was stood there. His coat so long I couldn't tell where the floor began. "Get off my stool," he said. I moved over one and he took his seat. Started pulling pound coins out his pockets like he wasn't sure how deep they went. Lined them up in front of him and handed them over, pound by pound, ordering half pints of strong bitter. Talking to me without taking his eyes off his glass. "Your daddy's dead, eh?"

"You heard?"

"Who you think was looking after the old fella?"

"Can't picture you playing at being a nurse."

"Not me," he said. "You're lucky Helen's a good woman."

"Why didn't you come see him off?"

"Saw enough when I carried what was left of him out his bed."

"You're lucky you're a good bastard."

Farmers don't get days off, but William sat with me that whole evening. Found more and more coins in his pocket and he kept us both in drink till I was seasick and no longer had to turn my head to look, just waited for the building to sway about me. I asked him how Caldhithe was, and he said it was hungry. Sheep didn't know they were sheep. They stayed cold in summer and could get lost in a barn. It was more quiet now, which he liked. He asked how running away was, and I said it was tiring. See more things in a day of driving than your head can hold. Forty tons of freight rearing up, ready to swallow. The land tells you how to feel and it's bloody flat out there. I asked him if he ever forgot how beautiful it was in Curdale. He said he'd never forgot a thing in his life. I asked him about a job. He laughed.

Pubs still had closing times in them days and folk needed to be told to piss off home, instead of begging them to come out. It was late and the doors were locked to newcomers. Only folk left drinking could've floated up against the ceiling like pickled eggs. Heard someone rattling to get in, pounding on the big door. Barman yelled, "We're closed." Heard another rattling, the delivery door to the side smacked open and in came Kit Jones. Now, that was a pub man. Wore a red fleece full of white dog hairs and the zip was bust so his wife had sewn the throat up. Made a hobby of carving walking sticks and he needed them because he didn't half hunch. How fell people often are. Get to walking crooked from forever going uphill. For all that he was a good bloke to have about. Grumpy, tight-fisted, and mad as rabies. "If it isn't old Billy Big Dick," he said, ignoring the barman and sitting next to us. "And Steve, you're looking well, lad."

He leaned over the counter with his boots coming off the ground and grabbed a bottle of wine half-empty from the night before. "So, what's the occasion?" he asked, not stopping for a glass.

"His dad's dead," William told him.

"Eric? You sure?" he said. "I thought he died ages ago."

"Only last month," I said.

"He looked dead last time I saw him anyroad."

"When was that?"

"At Simon Nelson's wake."

"You didn't get them confused?"

"Well, somebody was dead and your dad was there."

"Your memory's shot."

"Y'know what I do remember?" he said. "I beat him in a wrestling match."

"Plenty of chance. He was twice world champion at Grasmere Sports."

"Not there, he was over at my place wanting some eggs but he'd not any cash. I said he'd have them for free if he beat me in a fight."

"How'd you take him?"

"He was good. I'll give him that. He'd me on my arse in about ten seconds."

"You lost, then."

"I carry a stick for a reason. Nearly did his ankle in with it."

"How's that winning?"

"He didn't say owt about sticks."

"You're a bloody idiot."

"Sound just like him," he said, and took another long drink. Looked over to William then. "I'm glad you're here, I wanted a word."

"About what?"

"Foxes."

"Not this again."

"Yes, this again," he said. "Biggest red bastard I've seen all my life came back last week and I can tell it's coming from Caldhithe."

"Then kill it."

"I tried."

"Stick not cutting it?"

"You'd not believe me if I told you." That's something you'd hear a lot from Kit.

I'd tell you the whole story as he did but a good half of it was about Carlisle's placing in the Third Division that year. Now, Kit was a chicken farmer. Buggered if I know why he farmed chickens in the fells but that's why he was always talking about foxes. This one bothering him was a she-fox. Big as a wolf. Talking five foot from snout to arse with a tail battered thin to a wisp, to nowt like it was a rat's. Every morning he'd two less chickens than the day before. So he put up another layer of fence. Fox chewed through that. Another layer and the fox took to leaping. He parked himself up for the night, using his rifle as a pillow, but it turned out his gun made for good bedding, and he fell asleep. The next night, he stayed awake for her, and she flew over the fence, pottered about his birds like she was at Tesco, and the chickens stretched their necks out to get it over with. Kit couldn't move for what he was seeing. Fifth night, he taped his finger to the trigger and the moment he saw her, all the bullets he owned were shoved through that barrel. And she zigzagged each shot and took her time leaving. But that scared her, and she'd not been back for three weeks. Then just that morning, she'd helped herself to a couple of birds in one go. "Not only my chickens," Kit said. "She's moved on to sheep."

"A grown sheep?"

"Saw one on my way over here, neck chewed to strips. It was either her or the offcomers are getting more fierce."

"It gobbled a sheep?" I said to him. "Show us." Barman chimed in to agree because he wanted his bed. We agreed to all piss off and find this carcass—see what we were dealing with.

As you know, you sober up from your head down, so it was as much a shock to me when I went to stand and found myself on my arse, soaking up spilled beer. I started crawling to the door, kept moving my hands in the air when William picked me up under his arm and dragged me outside. Dropped my head in the dog bowl to wake me and turned to Kit. "Where's this dead sheep at?"

"Saw it on the way here." He spun about and stopped, pointing at a muddy field. "This way."

He led us, crossed a lane and climbed its knotted banking, scrambled up stuck-out rocks in a wall, and then I heard him squelching in the muck. We walked in a line, Kit first, then William, then me, each fella more drunk than the one in front. I thought I was drying out till I got two boots atop a wall and the ground moved in waves below. Couldn't think how to get down. Felt a hand grab my wrist and it pulled me to the other side. The pub aback us shut its lights off, and it still meant something to have a night sky then. Not a streetlamp for miles. A gate was held open for me, and I felt the ground get rocky, and my footsteps hardened, then I was being hit in the face with beams of light. A motor roared and I wondered who was yelling. That same hand grabbed me and pulled me to the side of the road. I stumbled on and went headfirst over a bridle gate, found the grass was fresh cut. I heard Kit's voice: "We're here."

"You sure?" William asked him.

"Well, I've something's guts on my boots."

The two of them were stood looking at a mound on the floor. In the moonlight all I could see was a smile of bones—ribs and hips and back of a sheep in one long piece, its head in another, hide on and eyes still in, and every leg was taken off, skinned and trimmed to the joints. Wool plucked for ten yards in all directions and skin laid neat as hotel laundry. "No fox has done that," I said, the rot clearing my thoughts.

"Well, what has, then?" Kit said, tapping the bones with his foot. "No rats or birds stripped off so much."

"It's been butchered, you daft bugger," I said. "I've seen this before. While I was on the road. Met a fella that did it, killing and cutting sheep in fields at night—would have their chops sold by morning. Good money in it from what I could tell."

"What fella?" William asked me.

"Fella named Colin Tinley," I told him. "Wandered the country doing it."

"How'd you meet a bloke like that?"

"Drunk with worse."

"And he just knackered them, sold them in a single night?"

"Said he got through half a flock one time."

"Bloody hell." Could see he'd a hundred questions more. "It's impressive when you think about it."

"This going to save my chickens?" Kit started wittering.

"It's you that needs saving," William said. "I'll tell you what. To shut you up. I'll meet you with Steve up Reinstone Pass. Shred every fox in the valley like we used to. Bring the dogs."

"When?"

"Thursday," he told him. "That's when."

"About time." He stuck his walking stick in the ground. "I'm off." And that was him, walked into the dark singing some marching song only he knew the words to.

William told me to walk with him and we headed off, slow stepping to Caldhithe for two miles. Something was up. He was grinning. First time I'd seen he'd any teeth in his head, and he talked fast. Keen to be going on this hunt. When we got to the house, he found some bedsheets and put them on the sofa for me. "You can rest up here," he said. "Spend tomorrow freshening up, then we'll see that Kit's done right by."

I slept on that sofa same as I'd done three years earlier. William left a bucket for me to bowk up in, and I thanked him by not spilling any over the sides. With the doors shut, the walls were sweating, and you could've wrung a pint of ale out the cushions. Time passed to the throbbing of my head, and I showered with my mouth open and went back to sleep in William's chair as the sun warmed it. Our Helen turned up and those blue eyes looking down at me let me know how thirsty I was. "The windows in here open," she said.

"Don't think my stomach's ready for fresh air."

"I've something better. Settle you right down."

"What's that, then?"

"Work."

"I'd take a lemonade."

"Well, I've a gutter that needs cleaning. So, that'll have to do." I put my head into my palms. She came over and took my hands in her own, squeezed them tight, then pulled me from the seat, brought me down on my knees. "I'll show you the one I'm talking about," she said.

I followed her out the house, into the drylot, and she'd no need to point out the problem. One long black gutter aside the roof, swinging on three brackets, steady dripping to a puddle thirty foot below and two days gone since it'd last rained. "William said he'd take a look when he'd a day off," she told me.

"Could get out of owt with that line."

"He doesn't need any lines."

"With arms like yours, Helen. You don't need me doing this."

"You owe me." I looked into her eyes again. "And I don't like heights."

"Will this make us even?"

"I'm not sure."

"Would you let me know if it did?"

"Not likely."

We got their ladder from out the barn, slid on its two wooden racks, and raised it up, reaching to the tiles. I stomped down on the bottom to see that it would hold. "It's missing half its rungs," I told her.

"You'll get up it twice as quick, then."

She gave me her old kitchen gloves and they wouldn't roll down to my wrists. I started climbing and the breeze got stronger. Woke me inside out. The ladder sat on cobblestones, but Helen, waiting with her hip wedged in, she could've kept the night from falling. So I reached the roof and saw the guttering from its top, bunged with leaves and twigs and blackbird feathers, wet and bubbling like porridge. I got to scooping, clump after clump. Dropping handfuls to my feet. Cleared as far as each arm would reach and climbed back down to move on up the line. We each took an end of the ladder, and she asked me, "You know why this mess with the foxes is happening, don't you?"

"They like eating chickens," I told her. "I do and all."

"He's not been up to it, has William."

"Farm looks fine to me."

"It looks a mess. He goes into a field now and the crows start following. Lost two ewes in the lambing and he left them there a week."

"He'll bounce back."

"He best do something soon, or I will."

Fixed the ladder against the wall and I waited on the lower rungs as she steadied the poles. "I should say thanks," I said. "For looking in on my dad."

"I was joking before. You don't owe me."

"I should've been there. I didn't know how sick he'd got."

"Lonely more than anything."

"Not sure how much I could've helped with that."

We did the gutters all the way round till the hairs on my arms were stuck down with gunk. Helen sniffed the air about me as I stood in the drylot after. "You'll need another shower," she said.

"I don't care about that."

"Well, I do."

It was Thursday morning on the sofa, and I was woken for the hunt by Danny's dog yapping in my ear. Each bark shook me as I lay there, and they got louder if I turned or shut my eyes, so I stared back at the animal. Face pushed up to mine, its eyes the only bright thing in the room, turned from yellow to orange the more I stared, and I'd not seen a dog like it before. Heard Danny found it as a puppy, lost, howling in a storm drain—named it Snitter. It was a mongrel with a thousand breeds in it like it was collecting them, not a hair in its coat was the same type of black, and it was a different dog depending on the room it was in. In the high fells it was a deerhound, taller than any man, and sat in its crate it was a bulldog, calm, drooling, and in scrubland it was a setter, pointing out fat wood pigeons with its nose, and stood at the gates of the farm it was a Doberman with cropped ears, and in the fields it was a kelpie running across the backs of sheep, and it only had to smell blood, and it was a hound, eyes drooped and crying so deep and so loud it got dizzy. I pushed its snout away and sat up. William was in the doorway, a rifle on his shoulder. "Put the light on," I asked him.

"No point," he said. "Best get used to the dark where we're going."

"This dog's giving me the bloody creeps."

"Best get used to that and all."

The front door was left open, and the air was cold. Tucked my jumper into my britches and put my coat on quick to trap any heatglow from sleeping. They were waiting for me. Danny resting against the car door—shotgun cradled, holding the grip backwards like he'd not mind dropping it. William peeling a boiled egg one-handed. He offered me it. I don't get hungry till daylight, never have. I looked over at Danny and spoke to his dad. "He know how to use that thing?"

The lad flipped it open over his arm and looked down the opened breach. "He knows," William said. Then he told me he'd a present, opened up the boot and pulled out a .22 peashooter, placed it in my hands. Was Helen's gun I was borrowing.

We set off, me in the back of the Rover with the dog, headed to Reinstone Pass—a mountain road that cuts through the fells and marks the end of Caldhithe and the start of Kit Jones's land. Rode up the valley's saddle through lanes of wild ferns and back steep down to the bound road of the pass. One long swerve. Skirting aside boulders that marked off the crumbling ground and reached a bend where the shrubs grew in, and a wide strip of woodland took over. The trees grow short there, stripped of bark by a wind that never stops. Kit was already waiting. He waved us down to a dirt landing, one wheel on the lane and one resting on a ridge. He'd three fell hounds circling his feet. "You ready, lads?" he said as we got out, talking loud over the coughing dogs. "I've given it a good scout. Looks promising."

"Sack of spuds with a wig on would look promising to you," I said.

"A fella's got to eat." He pointed to his hounds. "And these poor bastards haven't eaten since yesterday, so they'll not wait long."

"They'll not have to," William told him.

Kit was patting a dog as it reared up, placed its paws against his chest, when he looked at Danny. "This your first time?" The lad nodded. "That's good," Kit told him. "That's good." He went off, digging in the backseat of his car—brought out this fox tail. Clean and fluffy. He started wafting it about, bringing it to life. Started barking. Handed it over and told Danny to tuck it in his belt. Held it in his hand and looked at the rest of us. "It's tradition," Kit said, and he cheered when Danny tied it to the back of his britches. Had it waggling there the whole hunt. Seems to me, tradition's just the name for things there's no good reason to be doing.

We rubbed the dog's noses in rags of fox stink and set them off. Whining, babbling, doing circles in the dark. Always combing forwards. The four of us walked in a line among rows of silver skinny birches. Chased the wind to hide our smell and moved through blind country. Couldn't see if the leaves laid over ditches or where the roots curled into hooks. Kit found two tunnels a mile in, holes the size of dinner plates dug in swoops of earth. The front and back of a burrow. We checked them both. The dogs sniffed about and the air seemed old, widened the entrances with their claws, and we thumped on the dirt above. William gripped a whistle with his teeth and blew out a fox call, put some pain into it, squeezed his mouth to tighten up the pitch to a lass's screaming. Nowt came out for us to kill so we carried on. Kept our eyes to the ground by raised tree trunks and the dark hollows under boulders. Looked for the bones of mice or frogs or chickens. Looked for fluff or feathers.

Those woods weren't big, three miles in a patch, but I was still shaky. Felt I was forever walking on a sheer drop. And those dogs were light and springy. Had to keep up as they followed Snitter.

Turned the forest and got more frantic. Went in howling on the same spot and Kit cleared the ground, found a perfect line of tracks, these hairy, diamond pawprints. Ran them for half a mile and we still found nowt—so I took to looking at my boots. A cold morning of the hunt before I could stop. Danny was bored and all. They had to keep telling him to lift his gun or he risked pole vaulting on it. He'd lift it to his shoulder instead, hold it proper, but ten steps, twenty, he'd get lazy, and it'd come back down to his hands, then the dragging ground. His dad was about to tell him off when we heard a snap, a thudding gunshot, and William yelled, "What the eff was that?"

I looked about and there was Kit, still waiting on the trail we'd come from, crouched aback a brow of rock, his rifle raised. "I saw a bunny," he yelled back.

"Could've given us a warning."

"You'd have me give it one as well?" He went crawling through the forest and came back holding a dead rabbit by its ears. Looked at us through the hole in its white belly.

"I'm getting bloody sick of this," I told them.

"By the look of you," Kit said, "you're just bloody sick. You always this pale?"

"It's called being sober." I leaned on a stiff-built birch. "How long we going to march on?"

"Long as it takes."

William hissed and held his hand up. "Where are the dogs?" No sign of them. No tails wagging in the trees. Only their howling nearby. Don't need to be an outdoorsman to know what they'd found. "This is it."

"I'm done," I said. "Enough running for me."

"Don't have time for this." William unslung his rifle. "Danny looks to be done as well. Both of you stay here."

Kit chucked that rabbit and ran like he forgot he used a walking stick, his gun swinging full circle over his shoulder by its strap. Dodging tree trunks to reach the howls. William followed. Taking his time and watching his steps. As skinny as them trees were, each one blocked your view of another. Couldn't see through to the other side. Danny stood looking as they both walked away and their rustling died down. He was getting tall, taller than I was at least, and I can never remember how old he was in any of this. "You can still go after them if you want," I said.

"They'll be right without me."

"Let's have a rest."

We started walking without a route to guide us. The sky was getting brighter and shadows formed on the ground. Doubled the number of trees. Saw a break of morning light across a slope. Not far off. Led to a clearing, so I headed there, grabbing on the boughs of bended trees, and shoving past the twiggy saplings. The moss we walked on turned to grass and the light grew whiter. Bluecap daises started popping up, still in flower, and they made a path to a rough field. I stepped out the woods. Saw a mountain ash growing from a hunk of rock. Four trunks braided into one, and the back end of the year had picked its leaves and swapped them for red berries. Wind was drier, stronger, so I used the ash for shelter. Danny followed, and we pulled our hoods up and sat down to shield our backs. I flushed my rifle, cleared the chamber, and left it empty by my side. "You're not much of a hunter, are you, Steve?"

"I don't take pride in work. It's called work for a reason."

"Way they talk about it all. The hunt. You'd think it'd be more than walking."

" Nowt good lasts more than a few minutes."

"This meant to be good?"

"Kit looked to be enjoying himself."

The sun bobbed up from a crisscross of hills far away like it'd been trapped at the bottom of the valley. I tried not to blink as it lit the broadside of the fells. Tallest among them was Shinmara, a mountain with a head of white that would stay well into spring. The east face of it raked with quarries and slate mines that'd been gutted and sold off as slab for roofs and snooker tables. The north and south face ribbed into Brimlaw Haws and Niskr Crag, curving into smaller and smaller knuckles of hill that fell to bedrock in the Irish Sea. There'd been times when I wanted it all to piss off—the mountains, the trails, the sheep, the offcomers, the hermits, the rain—but right then, I would've stayed sitting there and made a cairn of my bones.

Danny flicked my ear, so I turned my head, and he was pointing to the treeline. A fox had stepped into the clearing. Kit's dead rabbit in its gob. A young animal by the look of it, not much older than a cub, black feet, black ears, its white mouth and neck turned grey. I whispered, "It's yours, lad." Danny rose to his feet and checked his gun as if he forgot which way it pointed. Took the end against his shoulder and placed his fingers odd about the barrel. If that fox wasn't blind, then its nose was bunged up. All it did was eat. Peeled the bunny's head like pie crust and gnawed and gnawed, eating everything but the skin. The lad didn't shoot. I tugged on Danny's coattail, but he'd gone funny, both eyes open, hands whiter than the cold gave reason for, finger stuck on the trigger guard. The fox stopped to clean his teeth and caught sight of us. I got up and ripped the shotgun from his hands. Animal went to run, and I emptied the top barrel. One thunk. It rolled over, still half caught in a step. Another thunk and it tumbled into its balled brains. They write entire books on the calls of birds and deer and foxes, but it doesn't matter the animal—when they're dying, they all sound the same. It stopped twitching but there was more life in the eyes of the fox than Danny's. He took his gun, popped the shells out and reloaded. "Let's head back," I said. "Pick it up."

"I didn't shoot it."

"It's your land."

I left him and went into the forest to find the road. Every birch tree looks the bloody same, so they were no help. Would've been a path there once but all I saw was autumn. A carpet of dead bracken and sour-smelling logs. I got lost about the scattered rocks, tried getting higher up, to find my way, and on every raise the trees got thicker. Danny caught up and followed with the carcass underarm. I cut sideways uphill—would cross the pass soon enough. Smacked branches out my face and pulled up brambles and pushed against the thorns tugging on my fleece. Reached a banking where the briar was less tangled and there, I heard the baying dogs, their singing howls, and William, Kit, yelling just as awful, whipping in aside them. The rolling ground above us was covered in the hounds and at our boots the bracken moved, something running, snaking through, and out popped another fox. Had to be the one Kit told us about. Bigger even than he'd said. Could've taken any of them dogs on its own and more than a few of the shot I carried. She bolted down the slope we stood on and those hounds closed in quick. They looked different now. The dogs. Mouths scooped back dragging blackness down and their tongues flapping like they were in the way. Snitter was on her first, and he didn't stop skidding before he was biting at her leg. The fox twisted and nipped his ears, but Snitter doubled in, biting her face, her neck, till he'd something in his teeth, shook his jaw. Shook and shook as one mad blur. Other dogs caught up, jumped in, and had a go at what was left. It was in pieces by the time William could pull the body away. He squatted down by Snitter, clamped the dog's jaw and used his other hand to rub fox blood on its muzzle and along its head. "You see how big she is?" Kit said, holding the dead vixen. "Need to get Guinness in to measure her." He'd brought his daughter's camera so we could take a picture. Held the fox to show it hanging to his boots, then wrapped both kills in binbags and took them home with him. I was in the backseat again on the way down with the dog panting sweetly in his prizeblood.

When we stopped at Caldhithe, Danny pulled Snitter out the car by a roll of his neck and got the hose off the wall to scrub him clean. Rinsing the mess off with just the water and his hands. "He did good today, your mongrel," William said, and washed his own hands. Stood back up and turned to me. "Let's have a sit down, Steve."

We went to this old horse shed he called his conservatory. Had dirty white plastic chairs laid out. "Still after that job?" William asked me.

"You laughed at me."

"There's always work," he said. "Pays as much as you'd expect but I've got a house you can stay in and Helen's not so bad a cook."

"What sort of work?"

"Thinking of expanding, and I could use a good driver."

"Expanding what?"

"Sheep. What else?"

"Must be pretty big sheep you've got in mind."

"Make an elephant look skinny."

I looked at what was left of his farm. It'd never been clean, but it used to be in order. Not then. He'd a car jammed in his barn with the parts stripped out, the sides of his buildings were held up by ivy, by moss, and all the pastures I could see had grass grown higher than the walls, lazy crops of pigweed, pansies, cleavers, with dock leaves so big they billowed in the wind. "Seems like you could use the help," I told him.

Helen stopped by on her way to work. She'd some of them oat biscuits she was always making and got busy talking about the shop and the places I'd driven past at sixty miles an hour. William listened and ate, and when he'd had his fill, he stood. "I've got some work to do, even if you don't, Steve," he said. "Let me know what you plan on doing." He left the two of us there.

Helen picked up the gun she'd lent me and looked it over in her hands. "How'd you find it?" she asked.

"Didn't have any reason to use it."

"Hang on to it for long enough and you'll find one."

"I'd better watch out."

"You?" She took it against her shoulder and pointed it up at the fells. "Couldn't do it, be like shooting a puppy."

"Been called worse."

"I like puppies." She put the gun down and looked at me. "You think you'll stay?"

"I don't know. It feels good being back here, y'know, sat here and having somewhere to be. But one of the drivers I worked with, he was a smackhead. Could drive a week on the stuff with his eyes closed. I think that's where doing stuff because it feels good gets you."

"That's why you should stay."

"Because it feels good?"

"No, because you think. Don't get enough of that around here."

"Why are you here, then? You whinge about the place enough."

"When I left here after school, I went down to Manchester to be a nurse. Stuck it out for nearly two years before I came back."

"You couldn't hack it?"

"It wasn't easy. The shifts that only got longer, and I was in GI, so I had my fingers in places that don't wash off, but I could manage it. I had everything I needed. They're quite good with it really. The girls I worked with, y'know, they looked after me. I liked them. It was the city I couldn't stand. Being in the city. I'd step out the house I was sharing, and I couldn't ever stop. Walk down one street and it would turn into another one with more of the same, the same shops, same people, and it felt like they were always pushing me just to have a little bit of space for themselves. And there's nowhere to sit. For miles. I don't know when they stop. Here, well, there's always the ground for you to sit on. There, that makes you one of those tramps. You're not supposed to call them that anymore. And the buildings, they're big, like our hills are big, only they squeeze about your head like a horse's blinkers so all you can see is the one slit of cloud above you."

"How'd you get out?"

"I met William. Met him properly. Knew him like you did since

I was a kid but I'd not spoken more than two words to him. He was in the city to meet some dog breeder, and all he had to do was say hello and I remembered what it felt like for someone to be friendly again. He gave me a lift back here the next day."

"William being friendly?"

"In his own way. He cared and that's not something I forget."

"Far as I can tell all he cares about is sheep."

"Maybe. He seems better with you here," she said. "You should think about staying."

"Well, that's what I'm good at," I told her. "Thinking."

That's how it was with Helen. We joked and joked till we weren't sure what we were laughing at. Don't know if I ever loved her or if she ever meant for me to. And I don't care. Spend as much time alone as I have, and you'll have every thought you ever could and unthought them just the same. I've stared at a mountain so long I thought I was one. Called up to do my taxes and when they asked my name, I needed to go find the answer written down. But she's never left my head. Call her home or call her hope or any other words I don't know the meaning of. She'd look at me like I'm an idiot since I am one, but she still looked at me. That's how Helen was, and that's how I've always been. That's why I like dogs more than people. Why I am a bloody dog. They see you drowning, and they'll throw themselves in and drown next to you. Always hungry without knowing why. Without knowing if they need feeding. Chase after you till they die like their breath was something you once dropped.

Haata

I stayed on at Caldhithe. Kept churning the idea in my head till I heard it in my dad's voice, and it's a part of him that's never pissed off. *Should be earning money at your age.* You died with only debts. *Enough so the bank isn't sorry to know you.* When've you ever been to a bank? You can't miss what you've never had. Even when I've found a bit of cash it was never mine, just sat in my hand till someone came to take it. Money's only good as what it buys you and I could get all that for free on William's farm.

I was working again. I'd not been sick but stuck behind the wheel—I'd forgot my body, forgot how to sweat without itching, forgot that dirt washes off, forgot your back hurts worst when you don't use it. Each day I'd wake in the dark, leave the house in the dark, and go join William by his flock in the dark. Only thing I could see was my breath, and the air was sweet enough and thick enough that it was breakfast all on its own. Always started with counting the sheep, the final number getting smaller month on month till spring, and each of us had a long whistle on cords about our necks and we'd blow them to get the herd running laps, spotting lame gummers, rams with bended legs, bean ticks on the heads of lambs, new knots in their backs, wool shit-sewed in clutches above their arseholes, legs stained white or black from scours, swollen throats or crisped-up lips or teeth crossed crooked or jaw skin that sagged then stretched like croaking frogs. And for them found poorly, we'd ask if the time had come for drenching, clipping, or the fat. When the cold settled in, we'd feed them out our hands, stuff mangers with first-cut silage, and stomp the frost off drinking water. In fair weather, we'd give them turns on good feeding grounds, finishing lambs on field beans and radish, finishing mutton on cocksfoot and mustard, and we'd drive them with dogs and sticks, a scabby parade of ewes over the grasslands and up the fells to rough graze. Flock would run through Bewrith as we yelled at offcomers sat outside the pubs to pick their feet up, and we'd chase enough sheep through to put the whole village to sleep. Most days Danny would pitch in, and we'd go at it like the land itself was telling us what it needed.

The slack never loosened, and with my help, William took things further. Worked with his shirt off in the fields, and the whiter the sun got, the redder his shoulders got, and he was digging, hauling, tilling, going flat out so he'd to cool down from his mouth like a dog. He'd work and work till he'd welts on his mouth from shouting, and as much as he worked, he was also gone a lot, went missing from the earth, few days a month where it was just me in the fields. No word before he'd go. He disappeared a whole week one time. I asked where he'd been and he acted like I was mad. Seeing as that was a job requirement, he followed up by telling me I was getting paid to mind my own business. That was a joke of his. Me getting paid.

He gave me day rates in pound coins and the price per head for shearing and he let me have the run of a whole house in return for the work I did. That was another joke, the place he gave me to live in. He called it Yow House. All the time I'd been about Caldhithe and I'd never seen that building before. Like it knew to be ashamed of itself. It was far enough out from everything that you didn't think of it being in Bewrith. A two-bed place though one of the rooms had so much clutter I never saw inside, and the room I stayed in was made up for guests but the bedding shed dust when you sat on it. In the early days, I could only get it hot enough with the oven door open, and the kitchen was full of slugs till I plugged the holes. Strangest thing was the cupboards with deep scratches in them like someone had taken to using the walls for chopping boards. Spent as little time in that house as I could, and that wasn't difficult. Always work to be done.

More than helping with the flock, William wanted me for fences and drystone walls. Miles and miles of them. Took him two days to walk me the length of Caldhithe and show me where it all needed going. He'd rip what was there out the ground to prove how flimsy it'd got. I was working in places for days on end where I'd not see another man or sheep or even the road from where I stood. Just the string of fence I'd already built. William would come over to a new one I'd put up and start booting it. Didn't care about how neat they were so long as they'd take a battering.

He'd bred his flock out from my lamb Rusty and there were a few hundred sheep by then. Doing all right they were. Good eaters and yolky fleeces. Calm when they needed to be and took to herding easy. But William wouldn't have been the man he was if that was enough. All right sheep. We're not talking pets. Barely making it through a winter in the mountains was nowt and worth less than that at market. With all of them wiped out save for Rusty, they'd to learn how to find their way in the fells again, but you can't kill off every part of animals like that. It's in their blood, and we'd filled the ground with more than enough of it.

A few months in and I rose one morning to find William at my door, at the steps of Yow House. Hadn't knocked. Just stood waiting, stood in front of a car I'd not seen before—a hot hatch that lay low to the ground with a front window that wouldn't roll up. "You're driving," he said.

"Where we headed?"

"South."

"Where south?"

"Don't worry about that yet."

So we rode south. Could feel the excitement off him. His leg jittered when he sat in the passenger seat, and he pushed his chair all the way back. Couldn't see over the drystone walls in that tiny car so we were stuck looking up at the mountains like babies. Kept going out the valley and then out the mountains till each hill got flatter and softer and became slopes and turned to fields, then all the world was paved, and we were out of Cumbria. Blue sign after blue sign on the M6 warning, *THE SOUTH*. "You going to say where we're driving?"

"We'll know when we get nearer Blackburn."

"You don't know?"

"We're meeting someone."

"Who?"

"Doesn't matter."

"What are you getting me into?"

"I've never got you into a bloody thing. No more than a river gets itself into a flood when it bursts a bank," he said. Could tell I needed more. "Three years ago, I saw you burn through four generations of sheep. What for?"

"You needed my help."

"State of me that day, most folk would've helped me into a padded cell."

"What you getting at?"

"I want to know what sort of man you are. I needed help. Bollocks. You've never helped a soul in your life. You left your dad turning to tissue paper while you were off driving lorries. So, I'm asking you, what was it for?"

"They took everything from us. You know that's why I helped."

"To get back at them."

"Get back at someone."

"Well, there's still a chance for that. We can get it back and then some. Make the sort of money that lets you look down on people like us."

"Being rich wouldn't suit you, William."

He looked at nowt but his phone and we went like that for two hours till he banged on the floor with his foot, shook the car. "Turn." Slip road in the corner of my eye. "Turn, you bastard." He rocked the wheel, spun us left off the motorway. "If this is going to work," he told me. "You need to do as I tell you."

"You didn't tell me soon enough to make it."

"Then how come we made it?"

He'd got us onto the old main road—to a Lancashire no bugger had seen since the Sixties. Grass grew out the tarmac like soil, and you couldn't tell if you were driving on the verge, it was so overgrown. The houses and petrol stations and cafes had their windows boarded like they'd forgot how curtains work.

Another half an hour and he yelled again, "Turn." I swerved. "More like it."

Split off that road and onto lanes that got smaller every turn we took. Got thinner and forgot themselves to dirt and we were driving through strangers' fields, scabby fields, and they were so flat you could see to the cliffs of Flamborough. We found a white van, alone against the sky, with its slam door open and a camping chair by its side. "This is it. Park up."

We got out. William started banging on the back of the van, shouting, "Teatime, Colin."

Colin. I knew a Colin. I saw a pair of boots hanging out the driver's window, fifteen-eye black boots they were, looked to be stolen off a dead squaddie, and he kept his britches tucked into his socks. He stepped out to meet us. Not a face you forget. Lumps about his eyes like it was always the day after a fight, and he kept his hair shaved but it made him look more wild. Took a second to place him. That smelly bastard. Colin Tinley.

I'd met him two years back. In the car park of a service station—how all the best stories start. I was resting with a coffee on a bench outside and he came up to me. "How are you, sir?" He started with a business pitch. "I'm wondering if you can help me. I'm supposed to be making a delivery to Aldershot but there's been a mess at the warehouse. I called for directions, and they'd no idea about the order."

"Sounds like you'll be wanting your manager."

"That's the thing. I've got the package, but nobody knows about it. If I take it back, it'll come out my pay packet."

"So keep it."

"Doesn't work like that. Be questions if I turn up with a new telly."

"A telly is it? Big one?"

"Can hardly fit in the van."

"So you'll be wanting to get it off your hands?"

"How's a hundred quid sound? Tenth of what was paid for it."

"Let's say this telly of yours did work. Which it doesn't. I live in a lorry most of the time, what am I going to do with it?"

"Give it to your mum. Double your money if you sell it."

"This ever work?"

"You'd be surprised," he said. "So what you after? You're alone in that lorry. I can get you anything. Stuff that works, even."

"Got everything I need where I'm sitting."

"Get you a girl if you're lonely."

"Tried that once. Don't think I've ever been so lonely."

"What, then? I know some guys that can see to you."

"Christ, sheep is about the only company I've ever kept."

"Sheep I can do."

"You what?"

"Not like that, you dirty bastard. Come take a look. You'll like it."

I followed him to the far side of the car park, far from the building as possible. He opened the back doors of his van. Same one we'd find him in near Lancashire. Stuffed tighter than a whale's skin, smelled like a sneeze, boxes and boxes stacked to the roof, watches, speakers, computers, televisions, Samsung, Panasonic, Sony, all tied back with bungee cords, and there were posh wool coats and fancy trainers and in the middle were these legs and shoulders of meat, cuts of lamb, dressed and hung on butcher's hooks. Fresh enough to put blood on your hands. "What you make of that?" he said.

"You're a hungry lad."

"Dorset Horn sheep, that is, even the best chefs can't get their hands on it."

"Where'd you get a van full of Dorset Horn? Endangered, aren't they?"

"Don't ask daft questions."

"I'm not buying your roadkill here, but I'll buy you a drink. You worked hard enough for it."

He was happy with that. Went to the bar at the Travelodge, and he started telling me his life story, not that I asked him to—lorry drivers are given confession more than priests. I asked him about the meat in his van and he said his dad had been a butcher. Could dress a sheep with just a penknife. Said it was fair game. No signs telling him the lambs weren't wild. Held a fork out his window as he drove and would stab the fattest bastards when he felt like having his tea. Said he could get his hands on owt, even things you didn't know existed—didn't want to know existed. I asked him what he did for a living. He told me he was laying low. Some fellas on the east coast had fired him for being too good at his job. He'd done it all. Salesman, best in the market, a line manager for seven counties, a debt advisor, a security officer, a knee specialist, some dentistry, a little recruiting, even did international work. Said his mates called him Mincemeat. I didn't ask why or how he'd any mates. A bloke tells you his name's Mincemeat and you know everything worth knowing.

Not thought about him again till I saw that carved-up sheep with Kit Jones. To this day, I don't know how William found him. But there I was in that field looking at him again.

———

"This your driver?" Colin said, rolling his baccy midair, pouch of Old Holborn under his chin, not dropping a leaf.

"Aye, he is. Could drive a plough through a letterbox," William said. "You not met him before?"

"If I remembered everyone I'd ever met, I'd never sleep."

He looked me in the eyes, and it was like he'd hijacked them. "We need to get going," I said. "Wherever that is."

All three of us packed into the hot hatch, Colin lying on the backseat with his eyes closed. Me driving again. South again. "What you getting shacked up with this fella for?" I said to William.

"I've told you. I'm looking to expand."

"Expand what?"

"His farm, of course," Colin called out, eyes still closed. "It's something I've been looking to get into myself. As a consultant."

"Sheep farming?"

"It's honest work."

"What brings you to that?"

"There's not a hundred people in that valley of yours. Lot of prospects in a place like that."

"So not the scenery?"

"Not to look at."

I stopped talking to him.

"You going to tell me what we're bloody doing yet, William?"

"We've to check on some new stock," William told me. "With our consultant here."

Back on the motorway. We were in a new England, one that's low and grey, and between the sky and the concrete you can't tell what's reflecting what. Land doesn't roll there—it sleeps, it's exhausted. Looked at my hands on the wheel for all else there was worth seeing. I kept driving slow in the left lane, like the slower I went, the less it all had to do with me, but truth is I liked it. Not knowing where I was going. Not knowing what was waiting for me. A lot's made of being your own man, making sure everyone knows your bloody name, but I don't need that. I liked driving. I liked the shite coffee and the roads coming together as if they made sense.

A hundred miles and we were off the motorway—in Hereford-shire, driving through towns the size of bus stops and rows of houses with lawns cut short back and sides. William seemed to know the streets without a map and he got me to park outside one of the bigger villages there, called Elderbridge, on a bypass looking down from the only hill for forty miles. "It's a lovely view," I said. "Worth the ride."

"You tell him the plan, Colin."

"You're the driver, right?" Colin said to me. "We're going to a farm and your job is to see how we'd get a four-deck lorry up close. Two of them. The easiest road for loading quick with as few eyes on us as possible."

"Load up what?"

"What've we been telling you? Sheep."

"How many sheep?"

"We're thinking seven hundred."

"Seven hundred? Without anyone seeing you?"

"Don't think it can be done?"

"The farmer blind?"

"And effing deaf," he said. "You just worry about how to get the lorries in."

We rode to the other side of Elderbridge. Not countryside like I know it. The lanes there, they don't have walls, just piddly fences and hedges, and we came to these sunken roads, ancient things trod down by horses, steep banking on both sides, held back from the road by thick roots. Saw a sign for Mary Brook Farm. Headed into the main compound, and it was like nowt I've seen before. A farmhouse with glass walls that shone the sun back, could see all these bastards inside, sat up at bars swilling wine, and it had a gift shop with a hatch for selling ice cream, and the flagstones were white and surrounded by tufts of Spanish grass and potted olive trees. There were only young lasses working there, wearing spotless pinnies walking about in heels, and they all had their hair done neat and blonde. What you'd not see in the place was dirt. We're in the business of mud and here's this farm with the ground fit for eating off. Got out the car and felt like I should take my boots off. It's what they call an organic farm. Let their animals go sick for fear of medicine you or me would gulp down with tea. That's why people came. They'd get tours of the place and pick their own watercress, then pat themselves on the back with plans of saving the world.

William signed us up for the full package and we got marched about the place by this older lass, and she told us it was all super and wonderful. It had a creamery and a bakery and a room where they made gin, and we went further out to some fields, grass scrubbed clean, and they grew greens in high tunnels and the fellas working the land kept their hair longer than the lasses and wore dirt under their nails like polish. They got us to climb in a trailer with the tour group and the chatty lass kept talking. We were driven through their pastures, saw orange pigs with leopard spots, chomping dandelions and getting fat off them. In the taller grasses were half-albino cows, British Whites, with black ears and black noses like they'd been guzzling troughs of treacle. And then we saw the sheep, and I knew why we were there. I didn't know the names of most of the breeds they had. Fields of them, Lonk and Balwen and Gritstones and White Faces and Badger Faces, and some for shearing and some for eating, and Wensleydales blinded by their dreadlocks and some fluffy like cats with horns curled in five times over like they'd corkscrews stuck in their heads. And a whole flock of Jacob sheep, y'know, devil's sheep, God's sheep, patches of brown and black and white with four horns in each head, two spikes out the top and another two twisted near their mouths. Each animal worth as much as the tractor we were hitched to.

A farmer turned up, rode over on his bike, first proper farmer we'd seen all day. Came to show off his sheepdog and it hopped the fence nearest, started rounding buggers up as he whistled softly and the folk watching clapped. Colin talked in our ears. "Let's get a closer look."

No one was watching. We ducked by some hedgerow and kept low across the fields, walked over to their main flock. Stood at the gates. Saw how the lanes cut the farm into tidy squares and how they fed their animals roadside to save time. And them roads, they were paved smooth, barely driven, and wide. Fit three cars side by side. One lorry. No problem. "So this it ?" I said. "Your big plan?"

"They're asking to lose them." William moved to keep the sun off his face. "Should be someone who knows what they're doing that gets them."

Colin wandered over to the sheep, held his hand out for them to sniff and patted their backs. Walked up to the Jacob sheep and he seemed to like them. Don't know what he was playing at. Found the tallest ewe and started pulling apart her wool to look at her skin, and then he seemed to be sniffing her. Stroked her head and held her chin in his hands and he grabbed one of her horns. She jerked away. He went back for it. Grabbed the other horn and all. Started wrestling then, they hopped in a circle about each other, stepping forward and back, him twisting her head by the horns like a steering wheel. Well, sheep are dumb, but Colin was dumber. Ewe stomped stiff and shoved, shook him loose, butted his hip, and whipped a horn between his legs. He looked down, thought he'd pissed himself, shoved a hand in his britches and his fingers came back bloodied. He didn't yell. Reached to his belt and found a slipjoint knife. Sprung it free and stuck her quick, in and out her shoulder. If he didn't yell, she did. One bleat with no stopping and the herd whipped aback them, running to all corners of the field. William shunted through to keep that pillock from stabbing more.

"What you lot doing?" Farmer had come looking. Heard the noise.

Colin palmed the knife. "This not part of the tour?"

"Is what?"

"One of them got their horns stuck in a feed trough," he said, trying to keep the pain out his voice. "I was giving it a hand."

"Right," the farmer said. "Best you get back with the others."

We got in that tour trailer and then in our car, took off soon as we could. Colin sat with his britches off, legs spread over a towel so I'd to look at his swelling bollocks in the rearview the whole way. Dropped him where we'd found him, and I made him take the towel. Then I drove on to Caldhithe in half the time—roads are shorter when you know where you're going. Didn't talk about the robbery. Didn't talk till I dropped William off at his house, and all he had for me was "See you tomorrow." That's it. See you tomorrow. Left him his car and had to walk the two-odd miles to my bed.

I could see the lights were on at Yow House before the building came in view. Door left open. Curtains closed downstairs. I stepped in the hall and shouted, "Hello."

"It's only me, Steve." I heard it from the telly room. Helen was on the sofa. She looked different. Didn't know she owned a dress or how long her hair was when it wasn't tied up. "I brought you some tea," she told me.

"You didn't have to."

"I wanted to," she said. Pulled the coffee table close so I didn't have to lean. She'd a plate of cold roast chicken ready for me. "Nice day out with William?"

"I've had weeks go quicker."

"He not buy you an ice cream?"

"Didn't think to ask."

"Before you moved in, I used to come here when I couldn't sleep," she said. "Lots of people can't sleep outside their own bed. When they go on holidays or stay in a hotel. I'm the other way, all it takes is stepping into a different room and I forget what was keeping me awake."

"I don't need much sleep these days."

"You just don't know how tired you are." She poured me a cup of wine. "So, you met Colin?"

"You know Colin?"

"He's been up at the house once or twice. Strange man."

"You know what William's planning, then?"

"He tells me everything."

"You happy about it?"

"The farm needs money and William needs the farm."

"You think this is the way to get it?"

"I can't stop him," she said. "All I can do is get someone I trust close by when he does it."

"What makes you think you can get me to go with him?"

"Can't I?"

"I'm not here to be a thief."

"You wouldn't be anything like that. You're there to drive. None of your business what anyone else gets up to."

"I think you're the sort of lass who'd wear a short skirt around a fella and tell herself it's because it's hot out."

"I'm the sort of lass who doesn't let good weather go to waste."

"Do I have a choice?"

"You're still here, Steve."

Slaata

I couldn't sleep the night before. Had a week of not sleeping. But I didn't grow tired, the parts of my head that can talk sense or talk fancy just never woke.

I was sat outside Yow House, waiting where the ground was dry, and it was cold for June, when the sun takes an hour to set. A Ford drove up, a boxy one, long family car with backwards seats in the boot, it stopped in front of me as the engine kept boiling. The back hissed open, and two dogs bounded from it, Snitter and this new collie, called Jaffa, something like that, thin stripe of white hair splitting its face in two black halves. They ran at me, and each shoved its head under an armpit. William stepped out and the mongrels calmed, walked to stand aback him as he came to my stoop. "You still up for doing this?" he said.

"What if I wasn't?"

"I'd say, *Tough shit, Steve.*"

"Tough shit it is, then."

"You're driving," he told me. "That's all."

He got the dogs to shite on command and once they were done cacking they climbed in the car. Seats pressed down but no cage to keep them from our shoulders. Had their slobber on my neck for hours, chicken jelly, slippery bastards panting hot or sleeping, chewing belt buckles. One thing I will give them—they didn't bark without William's say-so.

We got out the fells, and I kept to the speed limit with empty lanes in front of me. The day's heat left the roads as it got darker, and you could see it sticking to the streetlamps, making the lights fat and the motorway green. William didn't say much other than to point the way, but I was yammering, giving him my pitch to be prime minister and filling in all the bits of my life story he'd never asked for. Them two weeks in Majorca I can't remember, a sweaty lass named Lynda, boxing matches in nightclub car parks down Barrow way. He stopped me wittering near Bolton. "What you talking so quick for?"

"Didn't know I was," I told him.

"How would you? You've not given me space to tell you otherwise."

"I can shut up."

"Don't do that. I fixed this car to run on horseshit. Knew you'd be driving."

"By feel of these pedals, this car hasn't been fixed to do owt."

"I saved it from the banger races. Still got a thousand miles in it, I'd say."

"Maybe if they're all downhill."

"I'd trust you to handle it."

"What about these fellas we're meeting, you trust them?"

"I'd not be doing this with anyone trustworthy, would I?"

"Good to see you've only half lost it."

I slipped off the big road near Stoke, rode through corridors of trees and on through hamlets we kept awake with both car beams. William would get me to stop at forking paths and lean over the dashboard to check the fingerposts, then point me left or right. Lane to lane, we got deeper into cropland, through fields of yellow rapeseed that stayed bright like goblin moss in the dark, and neat rows of whistling barley, following the height and fall of hills three ridges deep, and then I was told to slow as we came to a ditch, a lay-by with no view. A black saloon car was waiting in it. A hand waved out the window at us and we followed. Tailed for half an hour before we came to a long sweeping road and crossed a sudden treeline into acres of concrete instead of grass, huge sheds rose up about us, and beyond them were endless red-brick buildings with chimneys big as railway tunnels. The place was empty of cars and of people. Factories that'd once made ship hulls, tower cranes, race car engines. Every window we passed was rotted out its frame, every frame rotted out its wall, and we rode aside a drained canal that kept a stream of wastewater down its middle. Only industry deader than ours, but out there, the stars still hadn't come back in the sky.

The car led to this old trading estate where we squeezed down a side road between high-staired offices, and then rolled into a car park, a loading bay squared off by shuttered doors. There were two great big lorries waiting in the middle of it and two fellas I'd never met before sat on the tarmac with their backs to the rigs. Seen nowt like them lorries. One of them, this ancient road barge, must've seen out both the wars, and had a clubhead engine like a tractor and wheel arches that hung six foot off the floor, wide enough to bridge the River Eden, and it had this flatbed trailer with what looked a three-story sardine tin stuck on it. Other lorry, Christ, I could only think it was two rigs welded together. Could've moved whole villages on its back. Rose four or five decks high, and it was newer, might've been driven in the last twenty years, still had paint stuck to its sides where the rain couldn't reach, and wherever it'd come from, the insides of the cabin and the trailer were stained with something horrible and so lumpy dynamite wouldn't strip it off.

The black saloon came to a stop in front of the two men and the window wound down so we could see Colin was at the wheel. He stayed sitting as we got out to chat. "These on loan from a bloody museum, Colin?" I said. "How'd you get them?"

"Piss off. These were built to last. Would still sing if you wheeled them out in a hundred years."

"I've seen lawn mowers more roadworthy."

"Well, you're driving one of them."

"It doesn't matter what they look like," William said. "We're dumping them soon as we're done."

"That's the attitude we're looking for. Take note of it, Steve," Colin said and pointed his thumb at the fellas on the ground. "That's George and Bog. Best stockmen going. I'll let you say hello later. Bog's going to be driving this one," he said, meaning the antique. "And George will be riding in the other with you, Steve."

"I don't need anyone in with me," I said.

"You'll want George. I think it's for the best."

"Do you now?"

"You can take it up with him if you don't agree."

There was no arguing, so I looked over at George. "Welcome aboard."

I'll tell you about them two grunters. George was the biggest fella I've ever met. If you found his skeleton in the woods, you'd think it the leftovers of a dead shire horse, need the skin of one to cobble him some shoes. Could be mistaken for a mountain when he stood against the skyline thanks to his hump, his crooked back, stuck out under his shirt like someone had harpooned him and broke the shaft off. The other fella they called Bog and I've no idea what it was short for. For a bloke with fewer teeth than things to say, he could scarce get his words out. His tongue could've been swollen from the way he mumbled and his voice—maybe thick or foreign or from a part of England where they made a dog mayor and not for a laugh. Not so big as George but you could tell him to fight a brick wall and he'd do it thinking it a fair match.

"Any chance of a coffee?" I asked Colin. "If there's no time for a rest."

"I look like a bloody tea lady to you?" he said, and reached into his glove box, held his hand out the window for me. Two brown pills in it. "Get them down you."

"What are these?"

"It's your coffee break. Breakfast, lunch, and dinner as well. They don't give them guns in Iraq anymore. Just a knife and a bag of these."

"You got friends in the Mujahideen now?"

"With the right gear, anyone can be your friend."

I took them dry and all I could think about was that they'd been in his sweaty palms.

"Good lad," he said to me. "You follow us, Steve. Treat it like any other haul."

William set off in the Ford, and I climbed into that lorry and had to pull myself up each step. George was already waiting, feet on the dashboard, half lying out his seat. Stuck my head in and pulled it out, goose-honking on the smell of the rig. "I got some bad news," he said. "You won't get used to it."

I filled up on fresher air and sat down. "You can get used to owt."

"Well, that's true enough. Doesn't mean it stops stinking of shit."

The lorry choked three times before the chamber farted clear and the belts were squealing to get it moving. Even going slow its body rolled fierce. I was tempted to hold my shirt out the window for sharp bends. Get carsick even now thinking about how that thing lolled and swayed, fifty tonne in my hands, teeth chattering with the wobble of the cabin. It was more sailing than steering. All through Staffordshire and Shropshire the other fellas were red dots on the road ahead. Couldn't keep up with them, but George knew the way and called turns out early. Soon we were back on the big road. Another lorry at night. George slid down further in his seat so most of him was curled over the dashboard. "You can follow signs for Hereford now," he said. "I'm having a nap. Wake me up if there's any problems."

"That why you're here with me? Take over if I can't do it?"

"If you don't do it, I don't get paid."

"So, you're my carer?"

"Think of me how you like." He pulled his jumper over his head and used the window as a pillow. That was him out, kipping with the seat belt tugging his neck. I'd always felt strange sleeping near another fella while they were driving—trusting they'd not sleep themselves and lay into oncoming cars. Sleep's catching. Listen to a snore for long enough and it'll start rocking you gentle till you forget who's supposed to be awake. But I could scarce blink that drive.

I kept thinking of them pills Colin had given me. Didn't know if my eyes were blurry or there were dots of rain on the windscreen and I felt sick, but it was faraway somehow, and all the million thoughts I had came as shivers and I got a headache trying to hear each one. Then I saw it, a sign on the motorway, *Hereford*. Heart beat so bloody loud I thought the radio had come on. I slapped George awake, harder than I meant to—he gasped for air and kicked the window. "Some wakeup call you've got there," he said.

"Didn't have time to put a chocolate on your pillow."

"So, we're nearly there? You know when to turn for Elderbridge?"

I did. No matter how dark it was.

The two cars and the other lorry turned off and I followed. Near jack-knifed a roundabout and there was only us four on the road, and soon the hedgerow grew taller and the lanes grew tighter. Down south they're always a month ahead—have their fill of the seasons before they give us what's left, and they'd campion already blooming purple out the gutters.

I started to love the flat country. Straight roads and good eye-lines. Each house hid from us among the trees and each clearing held a pub and I saw that farmhouse. Mary Brook. With the lights off, its glass walls made mirrors darker than the sky, and the car park was empty and not a person was inside, not a person living there. It was a farm with no farmers.

George yelled and we pulled the mirrors in for a bridge. Started rattling across cattle grids, smacked my head on the roof as we dipped, and the four of us slowed and went single file about the fields, turned each corner as one long wagon train, squeezed further and further till we slowed, and every vehicle came to a stop in the middle of a lane. I half climbed out the window and looked ahead. The saloon was corking us all at the front. Couldn't see why. I started banging on the lorry roof and Colin stuck two fingers up at me from his car, telling me to shut up. Woke all the cows resting nearby and they stood, sniffing at us through the fence. "Move, for eff's sake. Move." I sat back down. "What's he doing?"

"The flock should be here," George told me. "I don't know why there's cows in these fields."

The saloon took off and we lost sight of him as he twizzled on the lanes. Tried to follow as he popped in and out aback bushes and I went for fifteen minutes, trailing, till I started thinking all the fields looked the same. Cows looked the same. The roads and their bends. We'd done a loop. Still, I kept following and we'd done another half loop when he found a new turn, down smaller lanes than we'd planned on, couldn't see out the sides for all the branches pressing in, and then we were out of the barrelled roads and driving straight on dirt and grass. Flattening crops of kale till the tyres were soaked green and we spun a bump across a raise of earth, four wheels in the air, then six, bouncing double into the next field. The convoy stopped and my trailer slid against my shoulders as I pulled the brake. With the bonnet resting on a slope, my headlights showed grass, a pasture with nowt but great dark beyond. The ground began to squirm, back and forth like seafoam. I inched forward, levelled flat, and the lights skimmed off the backs of a thousand sheep, maybe more, more than I remembered, and their bald heads would turn to look, mouthing, waiting for a morning feed four hours early. "Bugger me."

George didn't wait. Squeezed out a gap in his stiff door, flattening his head and ribs like a mouse, then ran with the lorries and cars as they drove on, slapping their sides so they'd not stump him. "Keep going, keep going." Unlatched the main gate and held it open against his chest. The whole flock was on its feet, each animal hunching back from the towering rigs, lambs under their bellies, and their tinfoil eyes reflecting our lights twice as bright. They started running sideways, backward, falling till they moved as one ripple to the pasture's end. We circled with the lorries, parked to make a tunnel, and the dogs came out to bark the sheep back from the motors, slinking between the flock's stick-legs. I saw Snitter's head pushing past their bodies, drilling to find air, climbing atop their backs and running across their hips and shoulders like a moving carpet. "Away. Away." I stood on the steps of the rig and was facing down herds of Texels, Leicesters, Southdowns clumped together by family, and across the other two connecting pastures were the Jacobs, biggest flock of them in the country. Bog's ramp slammed down, and every fella was on his feet. "Get on them, lads. You can bark good as any dog." I hopped to the ground and pulled the side lever on my lorry, brought the tail lift out, opened it to the floor through a puff of gas. "They're ours. Up the ramp. Up the ramp." William whistled for his dog Jaffa and left with Colin to muster the Jacobs. Bog and George were full of yelling, and they ran low with their arms out so the sheep were ducking out their way, and where the scrum got too thick to keep on running, they started pushing fat-arsed ewes. At night, sheep slow right down and can root themselves in mud. Have an easier time moving kidney stones. "Heave, you bastards. Heave." The two idiots' shoes sank deep and they slipped in their socks as their feet came loose. Bit their tongues when they smacked the floor. Crawled free with bruises in the shape of hoofmarks. They got just as rough as the sheep, pulling back two hands of wool, and yanking on ears like they could move them piece by piece. "You bastards, run. They have legs. Run with them. Show them." I found Snitter and got him working. "Walk up." Unclogged the flock and told George and Bog to keep at the rear, hands stretched like goalies, ready for leapers. Hammered in from three sides till the flock found the smaller rig. "That'll do." Kept them moving as the clanging started on the ramp, five sheep at a time fighting for the slope.

"That'll do." Filled each deck of the trailer even and threw pellets of grain down to stop them biting. "Move them on. Butt them back. Load them up." I felt the ground quaking with a new trampling, thumping through the soil, and a gate bucked and echoed. Colin appeared at the head of a column of Jacobs. "This is it. They're ours." Their fleeces brown and white and some blacker than sleep all over, black eyes and black horns, curled spikes that never stop growing out their skulls. Could hear William whistling a dawn chorus to get his collie racing up the flank of the new herd. "Come by. Come by." Five hundred pouring from that eastern gate, a bottleneck, toppling the fence posts and smacking into my lorry before they mixed with the bigger herd—more fearsome with their pointed heads, turning rocks from out the ground and kicking back for flight space. "Don't let them out. They're the sheep. Not you." We chased the bigger bastards down and tipped them on their side to calm them. Started loading up my lorry, steel ramp drooped with each animal two hundredweight. "Steady it, lads. Hold the ramp. Use your shoulders. Your backs are made of bone." I saw the boys getting rougher, then we all were, tossing any sheep that looked tetchy and dragging any that weren't. The dogs picked up on it. Nipping, chomping up bleats, opening skin, bleeding—on our clothes. On the trailer walls. Sheep were wobbling themselves to a fit, screaming, sounding wild for once. I knew it was wrong. "Faster, you bastards." You're trying to keep them calm. "Faster." I was lifting the rams with no mind for what it would do to my back or theirs. "It'll be right." We got them there. Could see an end to the herd in the field. Every deck in the lorry filled. "It'll be right."

I'd a straggler in my arms, a twisting gimmer, when a new light shone in the sky three fields away. Flickered on. A tall yellow square with a black cross in its middle hanging above our heads. It was a window, but I couldn't see the building it fit in. Just the light from a room. We fell to our knees and the dogs looked at us. Knew how moths felt. Knew how scuttled ships felt. "What the hell is that?" William said.

"A house by the looks of it," Colin said.

"What bloody house? You scouted these fields."

"Not this one," he stood up and started heading for his car. "Don't fret now. They're not going to see us with a shaving light. They'll be back in bed soon. So will we."

"If they can't see us, they'll hear us," I said.

"Then shut your bloody mouth."

I kept watching as Colin pulled shite out his car boot, jump leads, Jerry cans, dock line rope, digging through—found what he was looking for and rose to his feet with a long bat in his hand. A fat one made for rounders. I saw nowt move in the room and then the light shut off. Colin turned to us and smiled. Stayed smiling as a new light came on through a different window, a thinner one, then another lower down, kitchen by the look of it, and a wide bay bedroom lit up, a curtain pulled back and the shape of a lass or a child was pressed against it. "We need to piss off," I said. "Get in the two cars and go."

"We need to finish the job," Colin said.

"They've seen us."

"No stopping that now. Got to show them something else."

He walked off into the dark without a torch and I heard him start running, panting louder than the dogs, and a gate creaking soon after. I looked at William and even with his face soaked with sweat, exhausted, there was no blood left in it, so white you couldn't tell his eyes from his skin. But the other two fellas, they got back to clearing up and all William could do was join them. "He'll sort it," George said. "He's got us out of worse."

I didn't know what any of them were thinking. *Sod this.* That's all I could think. *Sod the bloody sheep.* Wide, open fields and we were trapped. Spot you as far as you could run. Lorries would get stuck in them lanes—no getting away if someone blocked us in.

I walked off. Found William's car, started feeling the seats with both hands, down to my elbow in the creases, looking for the keys. Not in the ignition, not in the ashtray, door panel, under the seat, pedal mat, glove box. Found a torch and turned it on, then *wham.* Heard a smack against my head before I felt it and my arm was pulled like a wing against my back. It was George. "You don't want to be leaving just yet, Steve." Couldn't wriggle out his grab. Lifted me to my boots and threw me, twanged against the car door. Heard my arm crack wooden. He let me fall. I blew bubbles in the muck and reached out for one of his feet as he walked off. Held my arm high to keep it numbed, and from the grass, I could see the keys hanging out the sun visor. I got myself up on my boots, and that's when the lights of that house went off again. One by one, top to bottom.

Till that day, I thought when you burn yourself, on a pan or kettle, that the scalded skin feels hot because it's burned. But it's not. Fire feels like nowt, like air. What you think is fire is just bloody pain. And I'd fire all down my arm and I looked at my fingers to check they weren't turned to candles, blew on them. Don't remember walking over to the lads but the ramps were up, and the dogs were licking the Ford's windows clean from the inside. Bog was in the cabin of his lorry, lining it up to leave.

Colin stepped into the ring of light cast down from the rigs. Didn't have that bat with him anymore and he looked drunken and his voice was gone. "What happened?" William said.

"Nothing. Nice couple. Very reasonable."

"How's that?"

"Not everyone's afraid to see sense."

"Is anyone coming?"

"Not if we leave now."

I tucked my gammy hand inside my shirt and clambered up the steps of my lorry with one arm, wriggling over the seats, propped myself against the window and didn't wait for George. Started rumbling the machine backward and leaned into a swerve toward the gate. The new haul in the trailer was throbbing and their banging wouldn't stop. I was near out that field when I looked to the others. Colin stood over the Ford and William choking it from behind the wheel, engine flat, smacking the thing when it'd not start. "It dead?" I yelled out the window.

"Looks to be."

"I'll take care of this," Colin said. "William, you go with Steve."

I slowed the rig and popped that door open, heard the dogs barking below and reached down to get them in quicker, pulled them up by their hair, their nose holes, did the same for William, flap of his coat caught in the door seal as he slammed us in. "Drive."

"What you think I'm doing?"

I let the wheel fly left, shunting to gain ground, and then spinning blind to shoot through them skinny lanes. Painted the fences silver. Shaved the lorry down. Looked at the clock—we'd done it in an hour. If Noah had us with him, he'd have got every bloody animal in the world on his ark. Could see half a laurel bush sticking out the mud flaps but we got free, to grown-up roads again with Bog tearing out not long after.

We rode on and further on away from the farm. We rode by the light of the moon and kept off the big road till day came on. Houses there were rinsed white, walls sloped under thatched roofs, sitting by hedges rounded and shaped so neat they frightened off the birds. Had these castles—ones that folk still lived in. We lost sight of the other lorry and the black saloon, but I knew where we were headed. Driving the long way, east to Rutland and the coast, meeting the Pennines and riding along them all the way to Caldhithe.

We stopped being the only folk on the road. Fifty-foot lorries, rolling steady, one ahead and one aback. Speeding Rovers that made me nervous. Lasses in minis on the way to work, singing to their music. Everything had meaning. Warnings in the guts of smeared rabbits, wrens gathering on tree stumps, cowslip wide awake at night. I'd make a fist with my hand to distract myself. Already yellow and puffing, palm purple like I'd been crushing blackberries. William had some police radio on his lap, and was listening in. "*Nowt. Nowt. Nowt. They found the car. The empty field*" Morning rose up as slowly as it'd gone but my eyes couldn't stop seeing it as too bright. The sun lay across the cliffs of Lincolnshire, across The Wash. Kept going up through Humberside, the Dales, Durham. Heard something on the radio but nowt too keen. Sheep get stolen. That's the truth.

Stopped once to fuel up and William got a bag of cheeseburgers, fed them to the dogs and me. Saw that lorry in daylight. Blood on the door. Wiped it clean with my jacket where I could, and from the sound of it, the sheep were all asleep.

I should've known something was wrong when we left the services. Them rigs are loud, but I could hear each piece of metal—each screw and washer. Couldn't get it up to speed on the motorway and we'd to crawl through moorland. William spoke up. "What's that rattling noise?"

"Which one?"

Penrith showed on the green signposts but what should've been thirty minutes took us an hour and either the lorry was getting slower or a mile had got twice as long. We'd done all right on the Cheviot Hills, but I could see the fells rising ahead and the roads with them. By the time the ground turned brown with heather, and we saw the scattered sheep of fell flocks, it was only my hands on the wheel holding the rig together. We crossed the walls of a valley and didn't make it past three big dales before the sputtering got wild. I'd only time to swerve into a patch of brambles. Had my head under my elbows when the popping from the bonnet started. William shut the windows to keep out the black smoke. The air cleared but the hissing didn't—if there was owt left to leak from the tyres or the engine it did. We got out and walked the length of the lorry. I wasn't any sort of mechanic, but I was sure your exhaust had to be attached for it to work.

I was resting my feet when Colin showed, and I stood to meet him. He idled his car on the road and looked at me. "Why you waiting here?"

"The weather looked nice," I said.

"What you done to the lorry?"

"Built to last but not for very long."

"No chance of it going again?"

"Not unless you've got a big winch in that car of yours."

"You've effed this up, Steve."

"I'll let you think that if it makes you feel better."

The other lorry caught up, chugging, didn't seem happy to be slowing. "I know another place I can go," Colin told me. "With Bog and George."

"I know a place and all, probably a bit hotter than you're picturing."

"I've had the radio on. They're looking for you."

"As long as they're not looking here."

"I'll come back if I can." He waved at the other rig, then at me, and woke his engine. I stood still in the shade of that dead lorry as they both pissed off.

Lowra

We'd broken down in Gamwater Valley thirty miles from home. A back alley of Cumbria that doesn't make it into guidebooks with nowt there save a long walk to the tourist trails. We were sat in a swale of the Limeside Fells, a waste of pathless cliffs with only a view of the motorway waiting at their top. William had found a wad of chickweed and shoved it in his gob, chewed it up like bubble gum. Stood leaning against the rig as he did. "What now?" I said.

"I'm not leaving them here."

"Take a few bloody trips in your Rover to move all five hundred-odd sheep."

"They can walk."

"Over the mountains?"

"They're hills, you soft bastard."

I looked at the nearest slopes—followed its spine of rock, over the wedge that formed the headwall of the valley and to the one corner where the cliffs dipped right down and made a roofless tunnel of stone between Han Gill and Gusty Raise, a thin mountain pass with no name. I'll call it Dead Jacob Gap. To get them sheep out of Gamwater, we'd have to go over each craggy shelf and slip across a spearhead corrie to the Mikill Barrows, to Brimlaw Haws, Shinmara, and Niskr Crag—the fells that look down to

Curdale and Caldhithe farm. It'd take fifteen hours with no time for undone bootlaces or milking blisters. "All right," I said. "We'll bloody walk."

We had sunlight, about a day's worth, and didn't need much else. I took the number plates off the lorry and rubbed the dashboard and door handles down with ice spray. Looked for rations and found a pack of Fisherman's Friend in the glove box. Had worse meals. Bags of sheep nuts—cork-shaped pellets of grain, treacle, and bone. Wish I could tell you I didn't know how they tasted. Filled up all the pockets I could find with them and got William to do the same, three pounds of the stuff in my coat and as much bulging out my britches.

We unbolted the back, and the sheep bowed their heads, made rows of horns, tangled at their base or under their chins, and packed in tight, one would move its head and make the two aside it nod. Most had no place to sit, held in place by a scaffold of ribs, shivering as if the rig were still moving. Got the ramp down and they stepped back from the fresh weather. Both of us banged on the sides and against the holding gate, chanting, *out, out*, and they banged back against the metal. Picked Snitter up by his neck and legs and swung him deep into the trailer—they found room to move then, he swam up the sides, paddling against their bodies. Sheep sprang free, one after the other, came down in pairs, belting the wooden ramp so it rattled and clapped like a train track. Our other dog was waiting for them, kept to the road, barked off their shoulder and fell on its paws from their whipping horns, herding them to the valley floor. I walked to the back of the trailer to clear the top deck and there was no end to them, more and more, falling from the railings, squeezing out the corners. Took longer to get them out than in. One last sheep leaped down and then there was only an echo left inside and two dead shearlings on the lorry's bed.

Got a count off. Twenty-five score of sheep and they were all Jacobs.

They weren't pastures or fields we were driving them into. There was no sign of rough grazing there, of other animals, other farmers. It was wild. What passes for wild up here. Great shrubs of rowan and bilberry stooped to the grass. Any sheep living there would've skinned that horizon.

We didn't let the flock rest. Kept them moving, winding along the trenches in front till we couldn't see the head of the column. Gamwater itself was no more than a puddle sat in the belly button of the valley, with shores of wet scrap soil stinking of cooked egg. It had knife-grass all about the water's edge and the sheep would get stuck in silt when they stopped to guzzle. Had to hoist them free by their overgrown fleeces. Those animals were raised by city folk, and they'd never seen a hill they couldn't leap over or found half the muscles in their backs, but they weren't pedigrees because they were sickly animals—there was strength in them when they found it. We pushed them out of that bog and led them up the saddle of the valley. The ditches got wider and lost all their green and the outcrops grew tall and stuck together to make cliffs. Swooped over our heads and covered us in shadow as we came to that mountain pass.

The flock went for it, spilling up and splashing against the skirting of the cliffs, walking ten aside in ambling chains of sheep, covering the ground, taking turns to hop from slab to slab, jumping over jutting gaps, if one slipped then twenty did and it'd not stop them for longer than it took to stand back up. We stayed at their heels, sending the dogs in where ewes would take nervy or get turned about. Slowed only where the gorge did and it was a mile in, two miles, when we couldn't see the road any longer, and we spotted five gummers straggling at the back. Old lasses, fleeces clinging to them like shedding snakes, stottering on the spot, mouths full of milky spit. I steered them on with my hands. Sheep will walk till they're dead or lame and all I could think was, *If that's what it takes.*

I felt a new wind through the pass, full of chalk so it made my skin starchy, and something was bothering me. I asked William, "Where you think he's gone to?"

"Colin?" he said. "He's more holes to drop in than a rat's nest. One pal away from any dickhead you've ever met. He'll have no problems."

"You think he can sell the sheep without you?"

"Not for what they're worth but maybe for more than what he paid."

"What's our plan?"

"It hasn't changed. Just got longer."

"Don't know what I'll do if I see the bastard again." I looked at my bruised wrist. "Any of them."

"I've some ideas." He started chewing on a sheep nut. "And there's a day of walking ahead, so I'll have more by the end."

From where we walked, all I could see was scree, upward plains of broken pebbles that rose higher and higher, across steep ledges. Rubble kept falling off one ledge and filling up another like the penny slots at Blackpool pier. We moved across layers of that loose rock and were sinking with each step. "You think we'll see Shinmara soon?" I said to William.

"Aye, another hour or two most likely." He steadied on a boulder and leaned back with his thumbs in the top of his britches. "The other thing we'll see is that Shinmara's three times the walk we've already done."

"Could be seeing worse things right now."

"Could be."

We got further up the pass, reached high enough for a view of more than our feet, and it got so we were looking down instead of up. We were at the top of a corrie. A giant hollow in the fells below, a frozen wave of rock, a punch bowl sloshing low with tarn water. Only way forward was down and through it to the Mikill Barrows. Couldn't see owt but this overhang when you stood at the edge, and we walked its rim for some time till we found a cliff wall that'd crumbled away to make zigzag ledges all the way down. Wide enough and strong enough for the flock to walk on.

We led them to the cliffs with the rams up front flattening the rushes and reeds for the ones aback. Walking single file. Pouncing sideways when they had to turn and sliding down the harsh slabs. Took most of an hour to get them on the cliffs, and seeing all five hundred crawling head to tail, binding the fellside—there were too many of the bastards. The gummers stayed with us. Watching the rest of the flock. So sore-footed, we started having to drag them to the edge, guiding their rumps between our legs till they stepped on that grassy ridge. The dogs rubbing at their sides and licking their necks to keep them going. I'd to pick one lass up and balance her across my neck with a hoof in each hand. Looked more ragged the more they walked. Squatting over every tumble, pissing down the rocks, legs bending as if they'd three sets of knees. Rest of the flock were already off the cliff—scattering about the corrie, and the gummers were crawling along that crumbling path to join them. The last leap off the cliff base was all they had. Crashed into the dirt, got up dizzy with teary eyes, looked for grass to eat and found a place to lie instead. Soon as their heads touched the ground, they were finished. Nowt but five piles of sheared wool. William crouched by each one. "That's enough now, love." Stroked the hair aback their ears.

It was the first stretch of grass we'd seen since Gamwater and the flock charged in, ripping up dock leaves and fox sedges, holding their heads back to gulp them down to their first stomachs. I wanted to do the same. The mints I had were taking as much water from me as they made, and we couldn't drink from the tarn. Water thick as half-stirred gravy and the blood guzzlers living in it had better luck supping on me. Looked about and there was one rock face slimy with liverwort had a beck trickling down it. I got on my knees and held my face to the rock, let the water fall into my mouth, waiting for it to fill my cheeks. Tasted sweeter than squash. I sat back, wet shirt sticking to me, scrubland feeling soft as owt under my hands. Shut my eyes. Not sleeping but not awake.

We got ready to leave. The sky was clear, but things can change soon as you turn your head out there. The wind was picking up, and I felt it getting between the buttons of my shirt. The ferns on the east face of Shinmara were sticking to the ground from a never-ending breeze, and that's as calm as any of the mountain would get for us. William was shielding both his eyes and looking up. He started pointing to the fells, convincing himself of something, "You seen that fella up there?"

He was looking at one of the lower folds of Shinmara, and I saw him. A figure, top half of him bright red, no more than a tin soldier to us, and not in a hurry to get anywhere. "There was bound to be some folk," I said.

"That's where we're headed."

"Best give them a wave, then."

He called out to get the dogs on their feet. Get them stalking the flock.

"We can't rest here anymore," he told me.

I looked at the collapsed Jacobs. "I'd say they're going to be resting a long while."

"Couldn't ask a better place for it."

"I'll remember that when your time comes."

"I'll crawl here myself when it does."

Made sure the fallen sheep were dead. Put my good hand deep in their fleece. Chests stopped. No blinking. No breathing. William stood watching and told me to head on with the herd. He pulled the bodies to a small dale under a cowback boulder. Resting among the heather. I saw him pull his knife from his belt and lean over each animal. Held their ears out and sawed the tags off, put them in his pocket. Wiped his hands clean on the grass and caught up to us.

Shinmara is close to nineteen hundred foot if you want to reach the top, but we were headed for a grassy shelf that eased about its southern wall. Might've worked as a drove road in an older time. The flock started lumping together, swarming over outcrops, filling gullies like a mist of brown and black with no room to get the dogs between them, and as they walked, they stripped all the grass before them. There were still no paths to be seen but we came across drystone walls for the first time, outlines of sheepfolds on the ground that'd not been used in a hundred years. We had to drive them careful through the gates left standing, use sticks to show them the way, chase the lazy bastards who'd not run.

We went on till the sun fell aside us and settled as a rind of orange on the mountain perch. The wind kept picking up, got bored of whipping us in gusts and blew without a tail. I tucked my head in and soon I couldn't lift it. All my clothes were pulled tight, flapping aback my armpits, tugging at me to stop marching. I heard shouting. William was yelling and his words were flapping about my ears. He got a hand on my shoulder and pulled me by my hair to bring me closer. "It's the Skall Wind."

"We turning back?"

He looked up to a summit he couldn't spot.

"Stick close. Best you can."

The Skall Wind. Known to the locals like a friend you'd hoped was dead. You'll only ever find it at that one edge of Shinmara, a big scoop of mountain that sucks in every bit of wind and spews it out the bottom across a ramp of earth. Can blow a mile wide and it goes like owt, never slowing, for days sometimes. Stand either side of that hurricane and you'll not know a thing but when you stand in it, Christ. If you've ever stood near the edge as a freight train rips through a station, it's like that. Except it doesn't stop. Closest you'll ever come to falling while stood up.

We'd been sheltered by a steep riser for most of the walk up, but it started splitting away, leaving us on open hillside. We took a track about this anchored slab and saw the full swell of the wind. It came down a lopsided gully with two harsh dips and soon reached a sheer drop that made its own horizon. Everything on the ramp was moving. Any grass that stayed was stubborn as back hair and any rocks buried were too deep to dig out. The only other way off that mountain was the drop.

I tucked in every bit of clothing I had on, put my britches in my socks and my coat in my britches and had my shirt pulled up over my lips and nose. The flock went on ahead for near a thousand foot and I could see the sheep already stepping out into the Skall. The biggest ram went first, its legs shaking, bare skin showing where its wool parted. No breath steady enough to carry a bleat. The next sheep stepped out, head closer to the floor, began to till the earth as it took cover aback the bellwether. More kept stepping forward and pressing up till their bodies stood the gale. Wormed further and further on, veering closer to the edge, one got brave and climbed a boulder before it got sent cartwheeling to a death we never saw. It was my turn to face the wind and I've never felt so light. The breeze burrowed up my nose and spread its fingers beneath my skin. Each second was a thousand shoves and I moved hunchbacked, stomped like a rooster with steps made of iron and tried to keep both feet on the ground. Lowered myself to the flock and grabbed on the back of the ewe nearest me, stuck my face in her fleece and put my fingers about the saddle of her muscles. William grabbed another and did the same. The dogs squeezed in and all. We were being carried by the plodding of the sheep and drifted where they led. Any strength I had blown away with my sweat. Fell down and grabbed wild for a hold of wool to pull me up. Walked as a sheep. Their heads pointed inward, rubbing shoulders and hips together to inch forward, one animal and then the other, a machine run on lanolin. I knew we'd reached the end when I felt a stronger stamping on the ground and was kicked away by the sheep I was holding. I lay facedown. William not far away doing the same. Not enough wetness to swivel my eyes, so I turned my head and saw the wind still belting a few foot away. But we'd made it through. "This why they say to always wait by the car when you get stuck?" I said, able to hold words in my mouth again.

"What you twining for? It's refreshing. You'll not need to shower for a week."

"If there was any hair on your head left to clean, it'll be long gone after that." We both stayed on the ground for longer than was wise. Not believing we could trust our boots. The dogs sniffed to check we weren't dead, and William had to hoist my shoulder so I could stagger up. The sheep weren't far off—they'd got spooked and waited when we'd not followed. Tested their jaws on moss and watched us. For them, eating and standing are the same thing.

There was a man stood by the rock face. Back against the mountain, leaning on a crook and holding a brown bottle. I'll not make like it was a mystery who it was. Only one bastard who wears a red fleece like that—Kit Jones. We'd been on his land for three hours or more. "Didn't think you lads would make it."

"Pub closed today, Kit?" William said.

"You think I'd miss this?"

"At least you can't call us liars when we tell the story," I said. Fella was swaying even with his back held by a cliff. "You not offer guests a drink when they stop by?"

He gave us the bottle he was holding, and we took turns finishing his ale. He got out some baccy to share and William had to roll it for him. I didn't smoke but there was bugger all else to fill my stomach. "Good-looking sheep," he said.

"What's a chicken farmer know about sheep?" William asked him.

"They can't lay eggs for shit." He got up, near falling himself. "What I do know is not to walk through the Skall Wind."

"Aye, we know that now too."

"You're a long way from home today."

"Got lost."

"Lost? I'll remember that next time the wife asks why I was out all night."

"Could ask you the same thing. You've gone for a hell of a stroll to drink in peace."

"Not far enough." He checked if there was owt left to sup in the bottle.

"We need to get this lot moved on, Kit," I said. "It's nearly dark. You okay to be getting back?"

"One way to find out."

He was too drunk to walk but we left him to stumble in circles, and he found his quad bike by an outcrop. Fell over the handles when he tried to kick off and took another two tries to get it started. Pootled cockeyed through a slant-sided track over a hill, swerving against the earth till he was out of sight. We took watching him as a rest before we woke the herd for the last miles home. "What if he says something?" I asked William. "About the Jacobs."

"He'll not talk."

"How you know that?"

"I don't think you're hearing me right. It's not his choice."

We looked down at Caldhithe from a balcony of bomb rock, Shinmara cut away beneath in curving terraces to the deep, and the hanging valley of Curdale was already full of night. The only light was from the cars on the Towthwaite road, and there were never any trees about but there were always singing birds. Nightjars calling out alarms for the tired dogs. And I'd no walking left in me. Just heaving as we went down and down. Came to steps of grey rock. Wide slabs like the floor of a church, forever washed on wind and rain. Had to scramble with my hands, hanging off each lip and dropping to the next. Waiting on my back till I could move again with gimmers stepping over my body. Then, with one last tall step, I fell three foot onto the soil of Caldhithe.

I couldn't see an end to it. We'd reached the pastures and the weedy cover crops and I saw a light from the main house and that brought some hope. But then the house never got closer, and it was like I was looking up at it from the ground. A small set of headlights started swinging about in the dark. Bobbed up and down through the fields as it got nearer, and when it was on us, I spotted it was Danny riding. He pulled up by the sheep. Had one piddly bottle of water with him —told us his mam had spotted us and sent him out. William got him to ride back. "Get the farm ready." I remember holding the last gates open for the flock. Like trying to get beans out of a tin after you'd bust the ring off. Felt the cobbled courtyard under my boots before I realised where we were and the whole flock ran to the barn—fell on the hay mix that'd been laid out. Some not moving owt but their mouths to chew and the ones outside having to climb the sheep in front to get in.

The door to the house swung open and Helen was stood waiting. For a second, it made me feel like it was worth it. William pushed past and went straight to the toilet, clutched the sink, slapping his head under it and letting the tap fill his cheeks before he gulped. Slammed the door shut and we heard the shower come on. I stood by Helen and the look on her face was worse than any mirror. She held me. She didn't know she was the only thing keeping me up. Wrapped tight about me in the hallway and I could feel her crying on my neck, started to squeeze me as she shook with tears, and I winced. She looked down at my arm and pulled me to the kitchen—took a tin down off the shelf. Cleaned my hand of grime, rubbing between the fingers and down my wrists. Wrapped everything but my nails three times over with loose bandage, for any good that would do. "Thank you for bringing him back, Steve." She kissed me on the forehead and left me to fall asleep hugging the tabletop.

PART III

Jack's Land

Dowra

William sorted the stolen flock and sold two hundred the next week to a fella he knew down Bowland. A hundred sheep got sent to the fat—no money in their secondhand bodies other than what could be eaten or boiled off. That left twenty good tups, breeding rams that is, and as many bollocked wethers to keep them company. About a hundred and twenty Jacob ewes. Fifty-odd gimmers ready for the next season and sixty springers with seventy lambs in them. Ten of the sheep dropped dead in the weeks after we'd brought them in, and the rest were old-season hoggs or fallow ewes to keep an eye on. We kept what was left of that flock on Caldhithe. Never found out what happened to the other sheep we took—ones Colin ran off with. William had a gun that let him rip the ID tags out their ears and he plugged the holes with new ones. He sawed off any horns that were scorch-branded, pinned them to the floor between his knees and cut them clean to their brows, sliced them off in chunks and blew away the dust.

I was left to break in the Jacobs. They're not a soft sheep like some of the doll breeds. More like goats. Getting themselves into bother testing holes in the walls and fences or getting their horns stuck in feeding hoops, stuck for hours, waiting silent for you to free them. Redecorated the farm for us, they did. Stripped the hawthorns and alders of their bark so the trees died skinny or stopped growing. And they'd eat owt, them sheep. Gobble up a leather boot or a dead bird—drinking its blood for a taste of salt. Were as likely to eat the bag their feed mix came in as the mix itself, but they were picky about grass. Turned their muzzles up at stalks that still had inches of eating in them, and I was having to bring in more pellets and grain and hay. You don't ever stop paying for the fancy breeds. They grew on me though. Would come sit by me even when I'd no food for them. I'd go out and share my sandwiches at dinner. Says more about me than the sheep, I suppose. William never much bothered with the Jacobs. He'd not check on them unless I couldn't.

It was Helen that started coming out to shepherd them. Each day before her shop opened. She could yell louder than me, so it didn't matter when the difficult bastards made four or five small herds to round up. It was more peaceful with her there, and I didn't find myself chatting as much. Listened for a change. About the village we forgot we were part of and how the Pearsons fought the Gibsons over a tree that was too big and the wheelie bin left out on the pavement too long. Doesn't matter if you own a mountain or a piddly two-up two-down, there's always gates and fences you don't want folk looking over. In the main street, there was this old building. A blacksmith's that'd not shod a horse since the days of the empire. Left empty near as long and they'd listed it, so only rot and time had the right to change owt. Helen said she went in after work most days, its doors never locked, and she put the radio on and sat there listening to it. She liked the smell of the roof beams when it rained.

Helen had this eye for them sheep like nowt else. Could spot a crooked hindquarter or undershot gums where I'd only see a pair of legs or lips. When it came to picking tups, she got down in with them and held her hand like a spirit level on their backs and crowns.

All morning she weighed and shook and combed through fleeces, till she walked out with one tup following her. Felt like I'd never seen him before. Perfect circles of black on his cheeks and a double set of horns that would make the devil blush. "This is our lad," she said. "Tried to nibble my hand off. Can tell the ones that'll make fat lambs by how hungry they get."

"My dad used to say that."

"In a few seasons, we'll have tups with horns reaching to the sky. Eagles making their nests up top."

There'd been times I didn't know what Helen was doing in the fells. This was a lass who made her own clothes, frocks fit for a lady's magazine. Wore velvet scarves in summer and flowery shirts in winter. Kept wine in the fridge and used a knife and fork even when her hands were clean. But then I saw her work them animals. All the ground she walked on seemed firm. Hidden muscles in her arms. Freckles woke up on her face. You'd point to any fell and she knew its name. Told the clouds when to burst and saw gales on the backs of sparrows and read every shade of the sun. Taught me better how to spot scours and worms and stiff lambs. Where to find mallow, asters, deadnettle, sweet pea, or wormwood and when to give them to the ewes to stop them getting poorly.

Wasn't just the flock she was good at taking care of. She'd bring me things from the shop that didn't sell. Socks thick enough to make you spring like a lamb and watertight overbritches. Lemon curd and mint cake. After a few weeks, she made a hobby of bringing along a lunchbox for me, Battenberg and buns and a lot of salad. She'd not been able to make the stuff before because William and Danny wouldn't touch it. Course, I thought it was rabbit food too, but she'd shelves and shelves of cooking books and a rabbit's never eaten so well. I didn't know what was in them most of the time, wads of cheese that stunk like damp and grains like the ones we'd give to the flock, only they were oily and tasted how I thought Greek food would. Every time I said how much I liked her food, more came the next day. The salad and the biscuits to start with, then some hunks of bread and sausage roll. Steak pies bigger than dinner plates all to myself or a stack of roast beef with cauliflower cheese. Half a trifle once. "You want to be careful, Helen," I told her. "I could get used to this."

"Take it from me," she said. "Never get used to anything if you can help it."

"You mean that?"

"It's a bad habit. One I can't shake myself."

"It's not always bad to know where you're at with things," I said, and asked her what I couldn't stop thinking. "Why'd you ever stop shepherding?"

"It was William. Couldn't stand working with him. Don't know how you do it. Whining and whining. Got so I could hear him complaining on my own in an empty room. And they were always his sheep, no matter how much I worked them."

"This lot aren't his?"

"He doesn't like them. Think he'd let them starve if you weren't here."

"I'll be starving if you're not about."

"There you go again, Steve. Getting used to things."

Took weeks to get the flock in shape but we got them there. Followed us without the dogs and we found pastures they were happy to graze on. Got them through their first shearing with us, and working like that, I forgot we'd nicked all them sheep.

————

I'd been out on Slee Rake with William—mustering the Herdwicks to a new feeding ground. Pushed through tumbles of drizzle with the ground so soggy we'd half the fellside in our bike treads. Hocked dirt from our noses as the weather kept on whipping us. "I've something for you," William told me. "Back at the house."

I followed him down the slopes on my quad bike, sliding on fresh muck, ignoring warnings from the overheat light. Got to his homestead and gave my bike a drink of two-stroke, let it cool off. He'd a new car sitting in his yard, shiny enough to see your face in the sides—an off-roader, another Land Rover from what I remember, but all sleek and vented with heavy alloy wheels. Sort of thing we'd laugh at posh bastards for driving. Led on to his kitchen, where he found me a tin of ale. "I could've gone home for a drink," I said to him.

"Give over." He got this envelope out one of the drawers. Stuffed with cash, poking at the edges, and handed me it. "You might need to put your glass down."

Handed me another envelope and another. Till my arms were full of them, weighing as much as a bag of flour. "How much is this?"

"Twenty grand. Your cut."

Some of the packets were full of flat wads straight from the mint and others were like kebabs of crumpled and muddy notes. He gave me a plastic bag to put them all in. "Now you can see what we're drinking for." He got a drink himself and we sat finishing our ale. "One rule. You can't have it in the bank and you need to spend it sensible."

"Flashy sports cars? That sort of thing."

"As long as you don't pay for it in fistfuls of cash, buy what you want."

"Seeing as your cut won't fit in an envelope, you can pass us another ale. And the nice Dutch stuff you keep for when I'm not about."

We drank more and ate all of what Helen left in the fridge. I came up with ideas of what the cash would go to. Visiting Portugal or Vegas. A caravan. French boots made of full-grain leather or robot waterproofs you could wear scuba diving. Could go private and get my knee fixed before it was buggered like my dad's and granddad's were. First thing I'd buy was a new rod. A carbon one that could curl like a whip and reel in a submarine without snapping. That's what I came up with—a lot of stupid shite. I'd been skint my whole life. Never carried a wallet, and if there was money in my pocket it was because I was buying something. And it sounds daft, I know, but I felt nowt when he handed me that cash. There's tall fellas and there's short fellas, that's how I see it. You're born to be one or the other, and just the same, you're born to be a rich fella or a skint one. That twenty grand—it was like giving a bald man a wig. Doesn't mean he's got hair back on his head, does it?

I got up to leave and William came to see me out. Half through the door when he said, casual like, "I need you to clean up that spare room in your house. I've got someone coming to stay a while."

"Who would that be?"

"It's Colin. Needs a place for a few days."

I'll not tell you what I said to that but he stopped grinning. "It's my house, Steve," he said. "Let who I want stay there."

"I thought you were going to kill him if you saw him?"

"That'd not get that stranded lorry moved or that cash in your hand, would it?"

"You're right," I said to him. "It's your house."

For the next week, I didn't see William. Didn't pass any word on to him or drive near the farmhouse. Kept working like I was meant to and near forgot what he'd said till I came back to the house and found a white van resting in my spot. Rust holes on its sides and laundry bags of tools and clothes sat about it on the ground. House was sore with music. With a hundred beating drums. Went in the telly room where the stereo was and the room stood empty, so I switched it off. Turned about and was face-to-face with Colin. "Not your sort of tune?" he said.

"I like songs with words in them."

"Got some Celine Dion."

"So you've made yourself at home, then?"

"You know how it is, Steve. Spend too long on the road and you forget what standing still's like."

"Just keep this rubbish down when I'm in."

"I'll do my best."

Took a while for me to piece together why Colin was at Caldhithe. He wasn't an outdoorsman as you'd know one and I'd my doubts he planned on working. At first, I didn't notice him. I got up early and came in late, and he was always out. If it wasn't for the hairs in the sink or piss drying on the wrong side of the toilet bowl, I'd have thought his room was empty. Then one day, I came home and had to check my eyes. There was no front door. Walked to the other side of the building and there he was, shirt off, leaning over a pot of wood stain with a fag in his gob. Finishing a door twice as thick as the walls. "You've not been locking the door," he said to me. "Need you to start." Jammed that hunk of wood into the frame downstairs.

Two dead bolts, a slide lock, a chain, and it needed a good shoulder to get it open. He'd boxes of window bars in the hallway that he put up the next day, filling the rooms with prison light. From that point on, a lot of folk started coming to the house—they'd stop for ten minutes and were gone again. Colin had an even bigger lock on the door to his room and there was a shotgun he kept in a golf bag by the hallway and a bumbag full of shells he wore wherever he went. William didn't want to hear about it.

I kept working. Harder even, so I was out the house where I could fix to be. I thought of leaving but that took planning, and it wasn't all bad. Colin might've been a gun-shagging, bone-breaking drug dealer, paranoid about everything save getting the clap. But he was a laugh. Not always a good one, mind you. When he wasn't dressing a deer for the freezer on the kitchen floor, there were card games and dirt bikes and lots of lasses visiting. If most of the folk that came by only stayed for ten minutes, well, the women he got visiting, ones with fishnets that couldn't catch owt, they stayed ten minutes longer. One time, I found Colin sat on the sofa with a fox next to him. A live one. Wore a dog's collar. He told me he'd found it in a snare he'd put out. Had it on a chain and kept talking about how he'd train it, put it in a sheepdog trial. Gave it strips of bacon if it sat on command and took it for walks. Let it sleep in his room. Would hear it barking like a child at night. Thought he might pull it off and have a little pet for himself, till one day, he got steaming drunk and shot it.

About that time, Danny started coming by a lot. To Yow House. At first, he'd sit quiet in the armchair and watch Colin. Be offered puffs of foul baccy or powders from out a padlocked suitcase and the lad would say no. "Have an ale, then." And he'd have an ale. Colin let him clean his guns. Soaking the barrels with solvent and buffing out the stocks with rags. He showed him this lever-action rifle he'd got, one that could pump out bullets quicker than a grease gun, and they'd go using it on squirrels and spotted fawns. Danny would bring his dog Snitter, and Colin took to the mongrel keener than the fox. Brought him along on his strange day trips, on deals, on hunts. Trained him on gunfire till you could shoot apples off his head. Trained him on rabbits let loose in a pen. Left the dog to go hungry, so being riled up felt normal, then fed him up on fresh-killed meat. Soon enough, he'd got the lad trained and all. Paid him to sit at the big door while Colin had birds in his room and them lasses would stroke Danny's hair as they walked by and tell him he'd be handsome in a few years. William didn't want to hear about any of that either.

I'd come back from work and gone to watch some telly. There was newspaper lining the coffee table and a salmon hanging off, head yelling at the floor, gills pulled red inside out like a bow tie and a tail so long it folded twice against the rug. Colin was hunched over it with silver fingers and his arms covered in blood. He was filling a bin with guts, using a serving spoon to get its liver and its heart, then he started using a gully knife to chop the rest up. No idea where he'd caught that fish. None that size in the becks running through Curdale. "I didn't think it could stink worse in here," I said to him, and sat down.

"What you talking about? That's the real smell of a lake. Make a candle of it if we had any sense."

"The fells growing on you?"

"I'll be joining you soon. Cleaning out ewes' arseholes to stop the flies settling."

"Why did you come out here, then? It's not for the sheep."

"Because I can be."

"So can a lot of people. Usually they're running a guesthouse."

"Not that like. I can do anything I want here. Say the word *copper* and people will hand you their loose change. Don't even know what the police look like."

"There's coppers about. William won't shut up about Simply Red. Fella that did the farm in."

"There's ticket wardens. Stake out a toilet to make sure no tourists are pissing for free. Lollipop ladies. Got them to watch out for. Anyone who knows his way around a baton is sent to the cities."

"We've always looked out for ourselves here."

"You're lucky to be rid of them. It's the coppers that cause half the problems."

"No doubting that," I said. Looked closer at what Colin was up to, tried guessing how big that fish was. Four foot if the table was two. "So, what's that sea monster getting carved up for?"

"Got a woman coming by. Special one, needs wining and dining."

"Which one is it this time?"

"Alexa."

"Them heels she wears put holes through the floorboards last time."

"You can have a go when I'm done."

"Christ, you'd be scooping out your own giblets if you were any more of a pig."

"Me, the bloody pig? I've seen you with William's wife."

"What?" I got up and tipped the side table without meaning to.

"Calm yourself," he said. "I don't blame you. Little old for me but there's no shame in that."

"Might not be the coppers you need to worry about."

"That's the thing. I did worry about you. When I first got here. Till I saw you skipping out to meet her every day."

"What's that mean?"

He answered by taking up his knife and cutting the fish from the neck back. First the goodish bits, cut thin to the smell of the knife. Then whacking it through to make steaks, one loud chop at a time, splintering the table to grooves that let blood spill on the carpet. "It means I've got less to lose than you."

Staying out Colin's way got trickier when it wasn't only the two of us living there. I heard voices downstairs when I was in bed, getting louder and heavier. So loud, they could've been in the room with me. No idea what they were chatting about since all I heard was swearing. They kept the music down, but made up for it by stumbling, banging, shooting guns. Left the house deaf. At least we didn't have mice anymore. I went down for a glass of water, and I saw them, those two grunters, George and Bog, sat at the kitchen table with Colin. Four crushed tins of ale for every one of them and they couldn't see me in the hall for all the fag smoke. I left the house without even a *how do*. Headed straight to William. "Now it's the three of them, between the two rooms?"

"That's for them to work out."

"You remember what that bastard George did to me." I held up my hand to him.

"Why you'd let him?"

"He jumped on me in the dark."

"What I remember is you trying to leave us there."

157

"I'm not getting into that."

"You should be happy they're here. Going to help you with the sheep."

"I don't need them."

"You might, Helen's not to keep doing it."

"Why not?"

"She'll not say it to you but she's exhausted. Got enough on with the shop." His voice got stronger as he said that. "Bog knows his way about an animal, you can take him."

"I'll work quicker alone."

I was tending the Jacobs on Helen's last day and she was there like normal, giving them a drench of worming medicine. Worked through to dinnertime and said she was having a day off from the shop. She kept stopping, looking over, looking till I caught her eye. "You hungry?" she said.

"I am now. What've you got?"

She'd brought a rucksack with her, and she led me a few fields over, to a beck crowded by oak trees, where we sat on the gritrock beach by its banking. The bag seemed endless once she opened it. Laid out a blanket for us and placed china plates on it and tub after tub of food. Curled her legs up under her and passed me a bowl, filled it up with yellow soup out of a thermos. We had lime cordial in champagne glasses and a roast chicken with little herbs on it, posh ham with crumbs and thick veins of fat, cheese that made you cross-eyed, and as many of her oat biscuits as I could fit in my cake-hole. Spuds and soda bread and butter with hunks of salt you could see. Strawberries fat as goose eggs. More salad than could fit on a side plate. We'd talked so much while working, I didn't have much left to say. We ate till we couldn't eat any more, and she lay back and looked at the sky through the tree branches. I sat watching her. "I want you to take something," I said.

She looked at me and I passed her that twenty grand, folded up in a plastic bag. She flicked through the wads of cash. "This your cut?"

"It is. I need you to look after it."

"Not safe in Toad Hall over there?"

"Not much is."

"I'll look after it, Steve." She put it in her rucksack, then turned on her side away from me. Went to sleep. I sat there ten minutes before I headed back to work.

Dick

Colin was an animal but he was house-trained. Bog and George, well, they were trained for something. There was always one of them up to man the door and they'd sleep anywhere. On the sofa or under it, toilet floor, outside in the sun, in the mud, in my bed when I was out working. Any lock I put on my door would've been used to keep me out like as not.

I said to myself, *If it gets worse, I'm gone*. Said it again and again, near every day till I forgot what owt else looked like. Our shower head was broken in the first week, and I saw them washing their privates in the sink. The fellas were blind to dirty plates and ate out of pans or on the bottoms of them. If it couldn't be cut from ear to ear or out of a tin, they weren't interested. Ate grouse and partridge and venison when they went out with their guns, and rainbow trout or char when they took their poles. What was left of hares or rabbits from their dogs. But most of their diet wasn't food. They were their own biggest customers, and you don't need plates for snorting or smoking. They'd be punching tables one minute and falling muzzy, lost in the curtains the next. Speaking of dogs, they'd a pack of the bastards living there, slit-eared things they were, with all their weight in their jaws, trod shit upon shit into the carpet and taught each other how to fight when they were let in. Had them collared to the side of the house with spools of rope otherwise. Not just the dogs that fought. Fellas came to drink and then they came to box.

Dancing pop-eyed, punch-cut faces with loose teeth as prize money, and they were all loose soon enough.

You'd think with me being a stiff old bastard they'd want me out. But they liked me. Couldn't push each other when they were already half off the edge and seeing themselves in my eyes made them tougher. Always calling me in to show off the telly that got bigger every week or offering wet meat with shot in it or a spoonful of hash. I knew how much they were selling some of that shite for, so it wasn't nowt offering it up for free. I guess when you steal everything, money looks funny in your hand. I say they liked me. George bloody didn't. Acted like I was a fella who never paid his round, took owt I said as wrong as he could, and wound up the dogs if I ever went in the room. I took to sleeping in my car or the odd night on William's sofa. Some days bedded down by the flock like a shepherd from the Holy Land.

It was Danny that worried me most. If he went to school, it must've been in secret, and I'd see him walk out of Yow House at all hours. One of the last nights I slept there, I was woken at three with a pounding at the door that threatened the hinges. It was Colin. "You need to go get Danny."

I sniffed the air to sharpen up. "Get Danny from what?"

"Bog's come back from a do they were having. He's a mess and there's something about a girl. I'm not getting involved."

"William not going?"

"Not answering his phone."

"Where's the lad at?"

"Said it was in a farmhouse. Twenty minutes down the road."

"There's only Montgarth that way."

I pulled on the clothes I'd been wearing the day before and

stepped over the pillock sleeping in the hall. George was sat by the door, rifle on his knee and a tin of cash next to him. He let me out and locked up again. I was sloshing in my wellies to get to my car. Headed to William's house and lay on the horn for him. He stuck his head out the bedroom window, and I waved him down. "Bit early, even for you, Steve," he said.

"Danny's in trouble."

We took the quick road to my dad's old house, and William was sat there next to me, coat over his stripy pyjamas. Soon as I saw Montgarth peeking over a hill, I'd to swerve to avoid a girl on the tarmac. There was a whole gang of young folk walking on the lane, staggering, holding on to the walls, pulling the stones out of them. One lass squatting by a gate to take a piss, frock so short she didn't need to lift it. I asked if they knew where Danny was and got told to eff off. I kept going to Montgarth. The gate to the road was wedged open with a white boulder and we parked up by the house. Stepped out, and I could feel the music with my feet. Folk streaming out the house, some of them older fellas and they weren't so plastered as the teens they drank with.

The house looked how I remembered—only newer. Jarring. Like I'd squirted soap on my toothbrush and stuck it in my gob. The slate walls were washed black and even with the chaos, it looked neat. Tidy flower boxes and a welcome mat. The door had been bashed open, the lock shattered, and I could see there was hotel art on the walls and this iron casting of a sheep by a shoe rack. It was all glowing yellow, the hall and the rooms, from plastic bags the kids had put over the lightbulbs. We went in, and there were two people left in the front room. Danny and this lass named Alice. She was sat against the wall, eyes closed, hair wet with spew. Two slices of bread and a spilled glass of water by her feet. Danny was sat holding her hand, half the buttons on his shirt pulled off. Club music was hurting my ears and I'd spent thirty bloody years working machines with blasting cylinders. William pulled the radio out its socket and whipped it to pieces against the wall. I shook Danny. "What's she taken?" I said.

"Nowt."

"She's not just having a kip."

"Bog was handing them out. Some sort of pills." Only useful thing we got out of him. Tried giving her water but it fell clean out her mouth—bowked more on herself instead.

"Okay, Danny." His eyes were so big I could see myself in them, holes to China. "You're going to have to carry her." The lad stood and gave his cheeks a slap. Got ready. Scooped her up and staggered back. I reached out to steady him. Crab-walked through the hall, the door, and placed her in the Rover. I spoke to William as he sat aback the wheel. "We need to take her to the hospital. The big one."

"She doesn't need any hospital."

"She's only a slight thing. Must've thrown up more than she weighs."

"Take her to our place. She'll be right."

"Are you that far gone?"

"Give over. She's had a little too much," he said. "And, anyroad, I don't have answers for any of the questions they'll have. Do you?"

William drove my car, and I asked Danny where the lass lived and what her parents were called. Got nowt. We took them both to Caldhithe. Pulled the car in and Helen was waiting. She looked in the back and opened the door gentle, got the girl on her feet, got her talking, moved the hair from off her face. Told us she'd be fine. Left me to walk Danny in and plonk him on the stairs.

———

A week later and I was on the slopes of Brimlaw Haws with William, marching the Herdwicks to a vale of grazing heather. Ground full of wild thyme that made the air smell of roast dinner. Best view in Caldhithe up there. Can see the whole of Bewrith village with every ridge in the valley crisscrossed in front of you, and the clouds low enough to cast shadows a mile long. All you've got in life is what you can look at. Best make sure it's not a pavement full of dog shit or the wrong side of a supermarket checkout.

William went to tend one of the gimmers that was limping on the way up. "Get this ewe held down," he yelled. I went over and pressed her shoulders flat while he grabbed her flanks. Got hold of a hoof, overgrown it was, twice the width of her leg, like a melted candle in his hands. He used his knife to scrape the muck out, then carved down the edges and swore loud after he cut the quick of her foot. It was left to me to plug the bleeding. I pulled up some yarrow to hold against it. "Losing your touch, William," I said to him.

"Like you've never nicked a sheep."

"Nicked it? You about chopped her leg in half."

"She's fine."

"It's not you that's got to deal with her if she's left lame."

I pulled the yarrow leaves back and the blood had slowed. Left her to get up and walk the rest out. "I wanted to talk to you about something," I said to William.

"What?" He cleaned his knife and stuck it in his belt. "If you needed my permission to talk, I'd spend all my days giving you it."

"It's Danny. I think you need to stop him spending time with Colin."

"You not confusing him with you? Who is it that wants to stop spending time with Colin?"

"I'd be glad to see him gone. Not going to lie about that. But the other night was only the start of it."

"He's a young lad. Lads drink."

"He'll get hurt. Get someone else hurt."

"Who's he going to hurt. That daft girl Alice? You?"

"Could be anyone."

"If you're scared of a bloody kid, I can't help you with that."

"What's Helen think about what he's getting up to?"

"I thought you wanted to talk to me. You want to know what Helen thinks, talk to Helen. Not me."

"What does she think?"

"She thinks you should mind your own effing business."

"Sounds like her."

"Is this what you really wanted to talk about?"

"You asked me to help you out."

"I asked you to help," he said. "Not to help yourself."

"Done more for you than anyone I've ever known."

"You have. I'll not say it was for me, but you did it all the same. And that's enough now. You don't need to worry about our Helen anymore. Or my lad. You only know what things look like from the outside because that's where you are. You're getting good with the sheep. Stick to that," he told me. "Now, Colin. He'll not be here long. Got a big job coming up and then I can't see him wanting to sit in that house forever."

"What bloody job?"

"Make the last one look like the school run."

"I'm not driving any lorries again."

"We'll talk about that later."

"Nowt to talk about."

"A first for you, then." William was done speaking before the chat was over, but it was a few days later that he finished making his point.

It was the day of a big England match. I can't remember which, but we lost if that narrows it down. Forecast strong wind on the low grounds and gales on the high fells, wind fierce enough to pick up boulders and squash you under them. Rain to match. Pull your body to the deep of the nearest tarn if you got caught up in it all. There's this old saying, *if you're comfortable, they're not*, but I'll always choose comfortable over dead.

We'd gathered at Yow House to watch the game and wait for the storm to calm itself. Had the camping chairs out and a tarp stretched from the building to make a plastic shanty for sitting under. They were all there. William, Danny, Colin, Bog, George. Bunch of their mates. Whole crowd of them, never seen so many shaved heads, lads with flat caps and earrings, lasses with heels and leather straps that coiled about their legs. That lass Alexa was there, sat on Colin's knee, had this bright blond clump of hair, like someone had shot a spaniel and stuck it on her head. By the time I stepped out to join them, most of them couldn't walk. Been supping from bottles of vodka with crooked labels—would vanish to fumes soon as you poured a glass. The game was at halftime but none of them were watching. Their eyes were on a mud pit drawn out in the ground. They'd been boxing again. A fella was propped up against the wall of the house—eyes swollen shut and heavy breathing. Big bloke, he was. Name was Ricky Windmill. If you know owt about fistfighting, then you know who he was. Swung his fists so fierce one time he knocked out half the crowd. George was propped up in a plastic chair and there was a lass pouring a bottle of ale down his gullet. From what I could tell, he'd flattened the other fella, this Ricky Windmill, and they were right proud of him for it.

I helped myself to some vodka and held my mouth open in the rain to clear it out. Heard them talk about the fight. How George had taken six windmills and then smacked back so hard the other fella was doing roly-polies in the dirt. They kept talking and soon it was about who could beat George. Ricky had been a champion at one point, made a living with his balled hands, so there weren't a lot of names to put forward. William had one. "Steve could take him."

"Steve?" Colin said looking me over. "Couldn't take a kiss from my nan."

"He was a world-champion boxer."

"It was wrestling," I said. "Only ever done a little boxing." William wasn't lying either. I'd been a world-champion wrestler when I was twenty-three. Only thing is that in Cumberland Wrestling, the world starts in Kendal and ends in Carlisle.

"So you know how to box?" Colin said.

"I'm not fighting that big bastard."

George leaned over the table. "Good choice. I already snapped your one hand. Don't want to break the other."

"You snuck on me in the dark."

"See, he wants to bloody do it," William said. Pulled out a fold of cash from his pocket, licked his thumb, and counted it. "Two grand to whoever wins."

"I don't need the money," I said.

"Well, I do," said George. "So you're effing doing it."

I'm a fella who likes to sit and watch, get my hands dirty if it's needed, but I own a nailbrush for a reason. Everyone was shouting at me, cheering, and George stood up, blocking out my view of the fells. Drained his ale and waited in the mud. Started howling at me. Scooped up a handful of the muck and rubbed it across his head. I got out my seat to leave, to go lie in bed, and William and Bog grabbed my elbows, held them tight. Dragged me. I pushed back, and all William said was, "Save it for George." If I'd not had a few drinks myself, I might've walked away. But seeing that lardy beggar stood there, I'd not mind a battering if I could get a smack or two in.

Colin stood in the middle of us and held our arms high by the wrists. "Keep going till one of you stops. Twenty seconds to get up if you fall down. Ring ends where the mud does." He nodded and that was it. Colin was still standing there when George slammed a full-hand fist at my head. I heard a static no one else could, and I saw that swaying hulk like I'd not done before. He might've had five inches on me and been fifty pounds more dense, but he carried one gutful of black Polish beer and a heart in need of metal stents. There was no stepping out his reach—both arms the ropes that held the ring. He hooked my head and deepened the dent he'd made. I threw my body at his armpit and teased a swing that missed. Then smacked him back, smacking mad, popped and thumped, whacking ripples in his belly, cracking quick his outgrown hip, one, two, one, two, the oysters in his back, right and left and soft and bone. Couldn't touch his jaw. Ducked by his other armpit and punched each ladder of his ribs. I wasn't thinking. Stuck my bare foot forward and curled it about his ankle—each chair rattled as he fell into the pit. "You twat. You cheating bastard. You bleeding dickhead."

Colin ran in calling foul, grabbed my arms so George had time to flop, to roll, to get back standing, then he knocked me dizzy, spun the earth, and began his clobbering. My cheek, my neck, the plate of bone above my heart. I made to squirm like someone throwing up. Curling closed as to collapse, sick of beatings, sick of slaps, and I stomped instead, crushed his toes and clicked his heel. Let him fall and gave an elbow. He rose through and grinned while swaying, bleeding from his brow and nose, dripped and dried across his chest. I caught sight of William and he looked more pissed off than George. He'd paid for beatings that weren't mine to hand out. We didn't stop. Saved our spit and were all done talking. Wheezed as if our breath's allergic and raised our necks, circling like cornered dogs. He was looking for my feet now and backhanded any dive I threw out. He hunched and met me eye to eye, him near blind with black blood, no blinking in his right. I jabbed the left and went for it, *thlick*, *thlick*, *thlick*, till the orbit of his eyeball was dark as the skull beneath. Heard a voice in the crowd. "He'll kill you, George." I stottered back and threw one last punch that brought us both tumbling.

Ricky Windmill rolled me off him when I couldn't lift myself. He stopped to check George was breathing. It was Danny that pulled me to a chair and gave me water. "Remind me to never piss you off," he said.

Two grazing teeth dropped out my gob and sat there on my lap.

"And you were asking me to sort these fellas out for you," William said, pulling a chair up. "I'll have to split the money between the two of you. Might've said you were the winner if what you did could be called boxing."

He put the notes in what was left of my hand. Couldn't hold

them. "Don't worry," he said. "I'll hang on to George's share. If he doesn't make it, you'll get his takings."

"Not enough to kill that bastard," I said.

"Not for lack of trying."

He held back my head and looked at my eyes and ears and would've had a look at my hand if I'd not moaned. "I don't know how good of an idea that was, Steve. You gave him a beating he'll not forget."

"Neither will I."

Colin's pals gathered about George, standing in a circle, each one pressing a towel to a different cut or bruise. And soon all their mugs and glasses were messy with his blood. They opened fresh bottles of brainwash spirits and were no longer wincing as they gulped it down. They could only talk by shouting. Booze had taken all their strength and given it back in double helpings. Their cheeks were red and swollen and their eyes began to float and land on me. I toppled my chair as I rose from it, couldn't steady myself, knocking tables, plates, and tin cans, bumping against the outside walls to keep me walking straight. I couldn't drive and could scarce walk, so I headed to my room.

The latch on my window wasn't strong enough to keep out the storm and I woke in darkness to the clacking of its frame. It seemed the pain through my body hadn't gone to sleep and it was waiting for me, worse than when I'd got it. I wasn't alone. Colin was resting against the metal footboard of my bed, squeezing my big toe. Held his shotgun softly in his arms and used its muzzle to scratch his chin. He was sweating standing still and I could smell it harsh as vinegar. "That was a hell of a fight," he said.

"What you want?"

"Wanted to check you hadn't got itchy feet. Wouldn't want you to miss out on the rematch."

"I'll leave Caldhithe if I like."

"Don't plan on stopping any time soon if you do."

"We can talk about this tomorrow."

"Y'know, it would've been better if you'd killed him. I owe that man things you wouldn't believe. Could've cleared my debts today."

"Fights go wrong. Nowt to get mad over."

"Funny though, isn't it? If I emptied this gun at your bollocks, well, that wouldn't be meaning to kill you. Don't need both balls to stay alive. But you do everything you can to end George and since he's half bull, it doesn't take. Yet, I'd still be the bigger crook?"

"We can talk tomorrow."

"Tomorrow it is." He got up and headed out. "You get some rest now."

Yan-a-dick

The front door was wide open and the house was empty. Hosing it down outside and more light from the drenched fields than the sky. I couldn't tell how long they'd been gone, Colin and his pals—they'd left a pencil case stuffed with cash, taken the guns down off the walls, left wads of soggy toilet paper about the place, parcels of blood.

I didn't wait. Left with all I had. Put on my two wax coats, my waders, and a pair of boots slung over each shoulder. Left the thousand pounds William had given me on the coffee table. Walked peglegged to my car and drove to see Helen to get hold of my cash. Looked at her through two scabbed eyelids. "The money, Helen," I said to her. "You still got it?"

"You've only given me three weeks to spend it." She got the money out of a biscuit tin she kept next to the bleach and stain remover. Handed me it.

"Have you seen Colin about? Them bloody numpties that follow him and all?"

"Not since yesterday. Not seen Danny or William either."

"They'll show up."

"Will they be looking like you when they do?"

"At least I won the fight."

She told me to get washed and have a cat lick shower. Came in while I was soaping up and left me a towel. One of the bad ones from the back of the closet that stank of drip oil and she put it in the bin after I was dry. Didn't want her washer getting infected. Would've done more for me but she didn't own a plaster big enough.

I went to see my dad's old friend. The fella we all called Uncle Lanty. An hour north of Barrow, to a stretch of coast with grease beaches and pulped fish and bunker fuel in the air. He lived on a square plot of land by the dunes at Solhead. Never built a house on it but there were sheds and cargo containers and run-aground boats tipped on their sides, all resting about this ancient shothole used by Georgian lime miners. Piles of treasure anywhere you trod, scooters with twenty mirrors, wardrobes filled with dead folks' clothes, salvaged chairs from sunk airliners, a cigar case of coins from Burma, unexploded bombs clad with trawl netting, trunks and trunks of well-worn porn that dated back to the Silent Generation. Everything washed up there—old Lanty himself. Couldn't tell where he slept or where he ate. Most of his money came from breeding ferrets and he'd a wall of a hundred hutches built of scaffolding slats.

I clambered over dunes and marram grass to reach his gate, and he was stood there, fiddling with a ship's tiller. He put down his tools and came up to me. "Do I know you?" he said.

"Been a few years. I'm Steve Elliman."

I put my hand out to shake his, and he looked at my raw knuckles.

"You could open both your eyes back then."

"Could keep them both shut too. Didn't work out so well."

"How's he doing , your dad, Eric?"

"He's dead."

"So bad?"

"I'll let you know when they've a cure."

"I only get farmers out here when you're bored of farming."

"Something like that. I need a van I can sleep in."

There was one reason to go see Lanty. He could get you owt. I don't know what it is, but if you know a fella who breeds ferrets there's nowt he can't get his hands on. Everything he owned was for sale and there was always at least two people interested in whatever caught your eye. I gave him six grand and he gave me a camper van from the Eighties. Threw in a two-stroke generator, electric hob, copper soup pot, bag of teaspoons, and some rolls of wound dressing. That's how it worked. He never haggled on price—you just got more and more stuff or less and less. At least half of it worked when you got it home. "I've another grand here," I said and showed him it. "I'm looking for a rifle."

"A what now?"

"The pointy things. Use them to put speed holes in cars and get money at the bank if you forgot your PIN."

"And what'd you be wanting one of them for?"

"Deer."

"Deer?"

"Big ones."

"Big enough to do that to your face, I take it?"

"New breed."

"I've heard of them."

He went off to one of the containers and came back with a canvas bag, told me not to look at it till I was well out of Solhead. Had a stiff-trigger Remington inside with handfuls of flat shot cartridges rattling about the bottom. Paid out another hundred quid and Lanty fixed it for two local lads to help me get the camper van back.

I parked it on Low Crag, the van, on the border of Caldhithe, veering down into Montgarth. Headwall at my back and a hillside knotted with crowberry for a garden. My dad's house was always there, always in view of the window, and I could see offcomers coming and going, bringing their kids and wives or some lads for a piss-up.

I healed up there for a week. Had to use this orange hot lamp heater to stop from freezing and the dry air made my bruises itch. Wrapped my head and hands with bandages and stuffed my bed-sheets with all my clothes to stay warm. The water tasted of the plastic tank it was kept in, so I only drank it with orange squash or boiled it for tea. Lived off food that could be cooked one-handed. Listened to the radio to pass the time and never sat anywhere with-out that rifle in reaching distance. I tried to sleep in the day and sat looking out the window at night. Wind would rock the body of the van and smack the walls, and I'd go check it was the wind. *Door's locked. Window's locked.* Got sick of getting out of bed so I sat by the door. *Gun's loaded.* Cooked holding it, shat holding it, did sit-ups holding it. Started thinking about shooting myself with it just to see if it bloody worked.

By the eighth night, I was strong enough to walk without hurt-ing, so I went to The Crown and sat wet-through at the bar getting half pints of lemonade. I looked about, and nobody kept my eye. Had a mask of yellow bruises wrapped about my head and, in them days, the stories told by the fire were all about Caldhithe and the dancing mad bastards living there. They'd not forgot I was one of them. At the start of drinking time, the locals came in. Cowslip Pete from the Horsetooth Brewery who bought three pints of his own ale each night so they'd keep stocking it, a ruler out to check the foam head was shorter than his thumbnail. The middle of The Crown had a Viking bench that could fit ten people, but only Ian Little Arms and his sheepwife Susan sat at it. Their old black lab would wander about, feeding on bits and brats from off the floor tiles. If you could hear someone talking loud, there was a good chance it was Mikey Powers. He drove fifty miles once a week to sign on then whined more than working fellas and made bastard king of Curdale his job, talked about how Towthwaite up the road had a post office, and it was time we got one. Tried to get the Spanish barmaid to remember his name and complained about foreigners when she'd not. Foglight Mathers—killing himself on drink in front of all of us and us keeping pace so we'd not have to watch—would stand on his own head for a shot of rum and you'd make sure he'd not waste what was left of his days wearing out his boots on the slate. I said *how do* to each of them and got less back. Ian gave me a game of darts because I was the only one he could beat. No other bastard wanted a chat till Simply Red stepped in.

He was on his own. Dragged out a stool and got in a cider. Was still in his uniform—black shirt with three diamonds on the shoulder and handcuffs dangling off his belt. He was a thirsty lad, ordered his second pint before his first was done and Cowslip Pete stepped forward to pay for it. As many thought Red a hero as a monster for what he'd done with foot and mouth. Called him Inspector Tapemeasure—if you were two inches into the three-mile zone from an outbreak, your animals were getting thrown in the trench. By the end, he was one of the few left calling for the culls to continue and they sent him in to wipe smallholders on his own.

Red moved two stools over till he was next to me, unfolded a piece of paper, and placed it on the bar. *Crimestoppers*, it read. Photo of Colin on it, looking grimmer than usual.

Location. Yorkshire, Northumberland, Durham County, Lancashire, Manchester, Staffordshire.

Suspect name. James McKenzie.

Nicknames. James Brennan, Colin Tinley, Mincemeat.

"You know him?" Red asked me.

"You'd not be asking if I didn't."

"How much you know about him, then?"

"More than I'd like."

"He's been living at your house."

"Never been mine."

"I'll tell you what I know about him, then. Sound good?"

Told him to do what he liked.

"This isn't the first place he's taken over. Nowt special what these bastards do. They find some poor sod no one cares about. Fellas just off the streets or finished doing time. An old bird who doesn't know how many pills a day she's on. Kids in council flats whose parents aren't coming home. Get friendly with them, y'know, bring them round a PlayStation or make them cups of tea or find a lass for them. Giving grannies surgery painkillers. Start off stashing gear at their houses, selling it from out the sofa cushions, getting them to sell it, and then they start with the financing. Sign them up for dodgy credit and short-stop loans. You know how it ends, don't you?" He took a long drink of his cider. "Here's the thing about Colin. Thing I can't figure. He doesn't look for weak folk—the old blokes, the spanners, the ex-squaddies. He finds people to make them weak. Last time it was a fella in Stanley and he's doing twenty years in Wakefield now. Before that, in Blackburn, we don't know what happened. But they had to cut the rope out a man's neck once he'd hanged himself."

"What's it you want from me?" I said. "Go cuff the wanker."

"For what? A half-flushed toilet full of cannabis?"

"That's not my job."

"Don't worry about that. It's what you've got planned I'm concerned with."

"Only concern I've got is whether Carlisle can beat Scunthorpe next week."

"We know what you did in the summer. Whole valley figured there's something odd about the flock of Jacobs. But these fellas, the ones in Yorkshire that William's spying on. They won't play about."

Rest of the pub was carrying on normal. "I don't know what you're talking about," I said, not lying for a change.

"I'd arrest the lot of you if I could, but I can't," Simply Red told me. "I don't want you dead or anyone else getting hurt."

"Arrest me for what?"

"The case is finished, Steve. The one fella we had talking is in hospital now."

"Who'd that be?"

"Kit Jones. Looks worse than you, and even if his jaw still worked, I doubt he'd talk now."

"Kit's in hospital?"

"You not heard?"

I got up to leave, and Simply Red went back to his drink. "Call us when you get a chance, Steve."

The wind was full of Irish rain as I made for the van, and I was frog-fingered and frog-toed with the windows steaming. Rain seeped in as I sat there feeling sick. Kept thinking over all the things Red had told me and I felt sicker. I slept wet and cold hoping it would heal the rest of me quicker. I lay for hours like that till the sun woke me.

I heard smacking on the side of the van again, but the curtains were still as the breeze. The door shook. I saw the rifle leaning on the wrong wall. Lock on the van was weak as a matchstick—snapped with a pop. William came in, wax coat dragging muck inside and the stink of dog and fleece oil. He was never tall, but he was never bigger than when he stood there looking at me. Short slope of the roof making him seem endless. "I'd say death's found you, but I think you were looking for it," he said, and threw one of my shirts at me to clear a seat. "Time to get up, you daft bastard."

I sat on the edge of my bed and saw I was skinny for the first time in my life. Only thing dry was my waders so I put them on and pulled a coat about me. "Why you not been at work?" he asked me.

"I'm on holiday."

"Well, the flock's not. You could've taken them with you. They'd like the Costa del Sol this time of year."

"How's George?"

"He's better than you."

"I talked to Simply Red last night. Had a lot to say for himself."

"Why you think I'm here?"

"Going to make sure I don't talk either?"

"Are you going to talk?"

"I've nowt to tell him."

"Then I've to make sure you work. And you can sleep with both eyes closed. I've told them not to kill you, Steve."

"So, what's this other job?" I said. "This robbery?"

"Don't you worry about that. The sheep need tending. That's what you need to worry about."

He stood up to leave and shunted a path through the messy floor. "Why you've not killed him yet, William?" I said. "When we were lost in the fells with five hundred sheep, you'd not talk about much else."

"If I killed him, he'd be dead."

"What you get by him being here?"

He leaned on the back wall.

"I was born into all of this. Same as you. What was the one thing we were always told? You need to work hard. Even if you're milking a dry cow. You don't ask where the milk's gone—you milk it harder. As long as you've worked till you can't anymore, you've done all you can. Believing if you did that long enough, it'd make you rich. At some point, Steve, you need to get that the hard work isn't what comes natural. It's easy to get the shit kicked out of you. If I pass up a chance to make more of this farm, more of myself, because I'm scared, then there's only one person to blame when nowt changes."

"That what you really think?"

William stepped out my van, and I was left to get back out into the fells.

Been days since I'd seen the sky without a pane of glass to hold it back, and it fell on me as a fog that hung low and stuck to my clothes and weighed heavier than fag smoke on my chest. Both flocks were in the lowland fields, waiting in their hundreds, foddered to keep them full and resting lazy on the folds of outcrops ready for the autumn tup. The summer had made their fleeces sprout and ripen so they scarce clung to their bodies. The ewes had taken to rooing themselves against the whirlstone cliffs, getting rid of their stinking wool.

We wanted beauty queens for our best rams—so we started with a dipping. A Lancashire lad named Paul Spittle turned up, brought his long box trailer filled with chutes and ramps and paddling pools. Clattered as he drove. The dipping machine was hammered to the floor and the fella tubed in a bath of bug wash for the lice and ticks and blowflies. Took three days to get them all through. We'd a platform resting at its top where we sat a friendly ewe to calm the flock. Led them up the metal slope and had them resting each at the slam gate before they took the plunge. A two-foot fall into brown frothing water that stunk of toilet cleaner. Horns scraping on the panelled sides as they tried to edge the tank. We looped steel crooks about their necks to dunk each head and left no dry patches for the lice to hide on.

Then came the shagging. Turned the sheep out in two big fields, one holding all the goodish gimmers and proven breeding ewes, the other holding the chosen tups. We'd to spray them with squirt guns to tame their wicked thoughts. We raddled each fella. Fed them with one hand and used a rod globbed with oil and powder to paint their bellies to the far side. Green or yellow or orange, bright as watercolours down their legs. You can see on the backs of the ewes who's been tupped by who, and by the end, the dirty beggars can have more colours on them than an oil spill. The teasers went in first. Rams fixed the same way as a fella with too many kids. Got the ewes warmed up so the lambs would all get born at once. Every teaser has his own chest of paint and they'll rut till they can't stand anymore and even then, they'll still have a go. I used to feel sorry for them, the teasers. Shagging half-finished for a living. But now I think they might have the best deal of the lot. Next, in go the tups, and once the tupping's done, the sheep walk dazed. You've to stop them heading for busy roads and light them cigarettes while they get soppy and want to cuddle.

182

For the longest time, our best ram had been Rusty and there were twelve dozen rust-red fleeces in the flock that took after him. Went to get him for that tup, in one of the outer pastures called Siberia, where we'd left them to see the end of summer. No spotting the bastard. I lined every ram against the wall and climbed the tallest stile to look out, and all I found was reddish wool on the barbs of some stretched wire. His tracks went for five miles into the fells and stopped near Midscar Swale by the roots of this alder tree. No other sheep had taken off, and I wandered into the night to find him, poking sticks through lumpy marshes and scouting every gully. Spent the whole next day looking and couldn't even find a body.

It was an early winter that year. Snow packed about the van so high some days I couldn't leave. Went to bed and rose in my fleece. Door would freeze at the bolt till I poured the kettle over. There was a week of whiteout with only the black rock shelves of the Mikill Barrows to be seen through the covering of snow. Even the roads were lost to us.

Got wrapped up in my dad's hair coat and tried on these new cowhide boot covers to keep my socks from wetting. My quad bike's battery was hibernating in the cold snap and that meant I'd to walk the buried trails to our sheltered pastures. Carried two bags of sheep mix atop my shoulders to hand-feed the Herdwicks. Waiting for the ground to thaw. Squinted through the blind white fells, and a bag slipped out my hand. Knelt in the snow to pick it up and heard the sky breaking. A gunshot rang across the farm from the same direction I was headed. I dropped both bags and started walking quicker. To this day, I've no idea why I ran toward the sound.

The sky was clear but there was no warmth in the land. Tried covering itself with fog to heat up. Had to wade through the stuff and I started seeing new footprints in the snow, four aside and sometimes six. They led to a gate and the snow was slurried on the other side, a mess of hoofmarks, and I walked the pasture's borders and found our ewes pressed against the dry rocks. There was blood on the ground, thick, thick blood. Bright and fresh and melting all it touched, a long smear of it, drag marks. I followed it till I heard voices. Saw three hooded men in the field. A tall bastard with a long gun in his hands—had to be George, no other bastard big enough. And then there was a skinny fella with his hands in his pockets and I knew that must be Danny. And the last fella, one squatting on the ground, was Colin. There was a dead ewe on its back, fleeced hide spread out beneath and its white head the only thing with skin still on. Colin was using the gut hook on his knife to rip its stomach out, and he looked up at me. "Steve, I wasn't expecting you." He kept cutting. "You can have some when I'm done." Flayed the meat from the joint in its back legs, a hundred flicks of his knife, jammed his thumb in to pull the tissue apart. I watched as he lifted its leg off and cut through a string of muscle before passing the meat off to Danny. "What the eff are you doing?" I said.

"Getting dinner." He dug his knife under a flap by the ewe's spine.

"You can't kill these sheep."

"Can't go on the road. What are we supposed to eat?"

"You eat your own bootlaces before you touch my sheep."

Colin put down his knife. Ran his filthy hands over his head. "Your sheep?"

"They're as good as."

"I've no time left for you, Steve. You eat at my table and still whine the legs are wobbly. Now, we gave our word to your pal, William, that we wouldn't kill you. Though you deserve no less. But sheep are made for being killed. If these were William's sheep, I supposed we'd have to think twice. But they're your sheep, aren't they?"

He nodded at George, who went off to the wall. I heard bleating, heard him dragging a gimmer by her fleece, dragged her along the ground aback him, then threw her down in front of me. Shot her through the neck. "You can dress that one, Steve." Colin threw his knife at my feet. "Don't want to?"

I went for the blade and George swooped in, hooked my foot with his so I fell on my face. Started scrambling to get up and felt his boot pressed on my back—couldn't move without him letting me. "You look a bit like a sheep now," Colin said. "Go on, walk around like one of your flock."

I didn't move.

"You make them walk. It's your turn." Felt the tip of the blade on my hip, so I put my palms in the snow and shuffled up to them with my knees. "Don't stop," Colin said. Kept going with them all watching. "What is it I hear you boys shouting every day? Come by. Walk up." George pulled back my coat and was threatening a scar if I slowed. "Sheep *baa*, don't they, Steve?" I spat and got a kick to the mouth. I spat blood. I got on my knees again and made a rumble in my throat for him. "Sounds like you're taking a shit. Do we need to get another sheep in so you can remember how it's supposed to go?" Roared out a *baa* then. Sound I've heard all my life. Bleating and crawling for long as they were yelling. Crawled over to Danny's feet and he stepped back, ruffled my hair. I'll not tell you how long that went on for. My hands were white as the ground when they let me go.

I was back in my van. Only thing that kept my hands still was the rifle in them and it was too dark to see by the time I remembered to switch the heater on. I could hear music, thudding through walls, but nowhere for it to come from. The cupboards were punched out and I couldn't picture who'd punched them. And there was the gun. All the things I could do with it. Every part of me, my hands and my stomach and my eyes, had its own way of feeling hate. If it could tighten or cramp, it did, and if it couldn't, it shook. My dreams were subtle as a pair of tits and in all of them I was still lying in the van. They say you have six dreams a night and I saw three times as many uses for a bullet. Waking up didn't feel right and daylight didn't feel right, and I'd say I felt numb if they weren't opposites. It was a night that lasted two days.

I was starting to nod off on the third day when there was a knocking on the door. I'd been shutting sounds like that out for so long it wasn't till it got louder and didn't stop that I looked over. "Come in."

Helen stepped inside. Hair tied up and eyes drawn so black and deep I wasn't sure they were open. She turned the lights on and cleaned up without saying a word, put the cupboards straight on their hinges and scraped the food off my plates. She'd brought a blanket with her, thick one full of duck feathers, and it smelled like her. She gave me it and sat down on the bed. "William said you were sleeping under a pile of rags."

"I don't keep them in a pile."

"It's not so cold in here. Bit hot to tell the truth."

"As long as there's fuel left in the genny—should stay like this," I told her. "What you doing here, then?"

"William's out for the night. Thought I'd check on you."

"What's one got to do with the other?"

"You might find out if you stop asking daft questions."

I stood up and made us some tea. She made my bed.

"I wanted to ask you something," she said. "About Danny."

"What about him?"

"They want him to do something, Steve. Something bad."

"I've nowt to do with the robbery they're planning."

"But you could. You could go in place of Danny. They don't need him."

"You could go in his place and all."

"William wouldn't allow it."

"You've picked a weird time to care about what William will allow."

"He doesn't listen to me anymore."

"Why don't you take Danny and get out of here?"

"He doesn't want out. All I can do is try to keep him safe." She sat down and took her snow boots off. "So, will you do it?"

"I'll have a word. See what can be done," I told her. Knew I was lying as soon I said it. I mixed up my tea and looked over at her. "Now what?"

"Shut up for once," she said and put her head on the pillow. Waited for me to lie down aside her. I went to kiss her mouth and she turned her head. Went to kiss her shoulder and she turned her body. She sat up, got off the bed, and found her boots. She'd not look at me. Walked to the camper door and I didn't hear it open. The lights went off. She was moving in the dark, sound of her britches slipping. She walked past the hot lamp heater, and I saw her skin all orange. Felt her hands reach out for mine, and she blew both palms warm—placed them where she wanted, then settled in my lap. Took my belt off and pressed my legs together with her own. She kissed my chin, my nose. Searching for me. She wore a thin chain necklace, and I held it in my mouth, then she pulled her head back. Made me bite it off. And if I didn't hold her up, we'd have fallen off the bed, rougher than I thought I'd be, and she pinned my wrists back long after she was done. Some bloody teaser I was.

Taen-a-dick

There was no running from Colin. Only keeping my distance and I'd plenty of that. By then, I knew Caldhithe like the Lord's Prayer. You might think there's not much to know of a hill farm—you can see near all of it from anywhere you stand, then turn about and see the rest. There's the top of a hill and its bottom and no chance to get lost, only stuck. But there's a million ways to measure a trail. I knew which gates were stiff and the walls with three-foot drops hid on one side, the clay ground you can run on and the bogs and silty ditches that can suck your boots right off. The crushing boulders that were loose and the ones you could unload a tommy gun on without a dent. I even knew the crackslips of quarries you couldn't get a body out of.

Wherever I worked, I kept two fields between me and any off-comers. Moved my van every day. If I was going somewhere, I drove. Worked with my back to the Rover and kept the rifle loaded under the seat and a billhook knife on my hip.

The snow went away but the air got colder and the world got smaller with my hood pulled tight about my face. I took the winter to fix up walls that I'd seen tumbled. Back end of the year is as close as it gets to quiet on the farm and some days it's so quiet you'll talk to yourself to prove you can still hear. It's what you've worked for all along—winter. The ewes in lamb are sent off to find grub on the coast, keeping the fat on them for when they need it. There's a patch of salt marsh in Winnadale for them, that William called The Nunnery. Rest of the flock was left to curl against snowdrifts and fed on sugar beets. The Jacobs had to bunk indoors. Kept warmer than me.

It'd been a month since that night with Helen, and I was stumbling back from a heavy session at The Crown. Rolled into waves of drunken sleep and was woken from the sweat of my sheets by my phone ringing. Screen read, *Danny*. I answered it. There was breathing and clacking on the other end, banging, loud banging. "Hello?"

"Steve," Danny said. "We've effed it up."

"Why you calling me?"

"It's just me and Bog here."

"Where?"

"They'll not stop following us." His voice caught on his teeth. "I think they're dead. All of them."

"Tell me where you are, Danny."

"We slid off to a bung road near Culbeck. Where they do the chariots."

"Hold tight."

"I can see them looking for us."

"Then don't let them find you."

I was in the Rover before I'd hung up, on the road to Culbeck. A village an hour from our valley, not even big enough to be a hamlet, spun off from the main road in a quick of the country with mountains either side and the Dales to the south. I crossed the River Eden at four places and took the back way, hopping town to village. Riding aside great bare fields with birches praying to winter and the lanes stripped to mud by tractors. There wasn't a car in sight till I got to Nelby-on-Toldale. A place with a name that takes longer to read than drive through—a mile or two from Culbeck. There were two jeeps out there. Big bastards. Ploughing concrete with their bull bars and fat racing tyres squeezed into their wheel wells. They rode slow on high beam, lighting up the lanes they went down and the wooded tracts and verges. There were fellas hanging out each window, waving hunting lamps from rifle ends, yelling into roadside ditches, and blowing out the skyline with tinted spotlights. They swung their heads and dog stared as I went past.

I took a blind left into dirt. Driving on roads I didn't know, I looped back on Nelby so they'd not follow. I'd got myself lost. Reversing out of dead ends and gated driveways and trying every fork both ways, cut through a deer park and out to Culbeck Bridge. Came across two lightless houses and a church and found my way onto a private road, a double-wide one with deep grooves where they raced the horse and trap. Set next to a wild paddock and a row of hand-built sheds with tables full of harness frames and two stacks of bended wheels. There was a pony still awake, looked a skeleton half lit, and it was grinning before it drew its teeth back across a fence post, chewing on the wood. The road opened out to a paved cliffside—rose over a tall banking with skinny woodland sloping all about. Tread marks streaked across the road, stunk of rubber melt, and the fencing from the clifftop was torn away. It had to be the place.

I picked up my phone and rang the lad. Yelled out the window for him, and I heard a smothered ringing among the trees. Saw the shape of Danny moving, climbing up that cliff, and he stopped to peek out before bringing himself in front of the headlights. His face was stained from head to chin, looked like muck at first. He stumbled closer. Dried blood. Dark under his nose. I left the car, went to him and he lay against my chest. "You're all right now, lad." Sat him down in the passenger seat and gave him pain pills from out the glove box. He told me what'd happened. "We got there, to this farm in Thirsk. Dad and Colin and George, they left me with Bog to round up the sheep. Left us half an hour before they all came running back. I heard shooting. They told us to do the same. *Run. Run, you bastards.* They pissed off in their cars and I got in the lorry. Bog drove and drove and, at some point in the Pennines, two cars came on us. Bumped into the trailer and ran against the rig. We got out the hills with them still tailing and Bog lost them on a short junction. I got him to spin off here. He'd not seen this turn on the cliff road. I've not got him out yet."

"Out of what?"

"The lorry."

"Where is it?"

He pointed to the cliff.

"Is William dead?"

"I don't know where he is."

"You said they were all dead."

He was closing his eyes, falling back in his seat—awake but choosing not to be there. I took a torch from the boot and walked to the road edge. Shouted down the cliff. "Hello." Only heard my voice back. What was left of the lorry lay across the slope. Took chunks of the banking with it as it rolled and twisted, swung about on its neck. Its head fell one way, stripped back to engine, cabin crushed, rearing out the dirt, and its artic trailer fell another, sides peeled in layers, skidded to a stop. Forty foot of steel. Bigger than most houses. Down one side spilled the bodies of the sheep, some already buried from the crash, tucked up against the trees, wool plucked and hanging from splintered steel. I began lowering myself, steadying on tree trunks and slow footed where the soil was sparkling with glass. Got level with the rig. Some sheep had lived, stottering about the banking, skin rolled like socks, trying to walk on bloodsticks. I followed the animals to their source. A hole blown out the trailer, a bite mark big enough to drive the Rover through. I looked in that torn chamber and couldn't understand what I was seeing. There was tread-plate floor where the roof should be and vented walls and livestock gates pressed together, spun almost, and there was a paste of hooves and hides and balled-up innards, spit strands of flesh, and nowt moved unless it could drip, and anywhere I stuck my light there was hammered meat and ewes cut into pieces no butcher could carve. I turned the torch off and heard Danny coming down the cliff. "How many were in there?" I asked.

He stayed quiet.

"How many sheep, Danny?"

"Two hundred."

"But look at them." I nodded at the sheep still crawling. "They're scrawny buggers. I'd not take half of them for free."

"They didn't want the sheep." He was rubbing his eyes. "It wasn't a farm."

"You'll need to talk sense, lad."

"They were growing grass out there. Y'know, like dope. Barns and barns of it. It was a gang that runs it all. Colin's old mates. Called them the Brown Hill Boys."

"And that's who's looking for you?"

"They're looking for the cash we took. Never seen so much. Two kit bags full of money—had to drag them."

"We've not long," I told him. "They'll find this road soon enough."

The lad's nostrils were billowing wide enough to see his skull. Kept putting his hands in his pockets, then taking them out as if it felt wrong. He tried lifting one of the dead sheep before he gave up. Tried carrying one of the living animals. "We don't need them, Danny," I said. "Where's Bog?"

"Course we need them."

He wasn't listening.

"Get back to the car," I told him.

I shone the torch over the ground looking for that idiot Bog. "You dead or not?" I called out. Moving sheets of panelling and te-pees made of snapped axles. "Speak up." Went the length of the rig and got to the cabin. So crumpled you'd need a knife to pry it open and scrape out anyone stuck inside. I stepped back to look higher up and trod on something soft. Bog's thigh. Used both hands to dig him out. He wasn't awake but he'd not a scratch, save one long cut along the seam of his left shoulder. I could still hear a rattle in his chest. Felt a pulse and picked him up, shifted him to my back and held his fingers together across my neck. Found Danny where I left him. "Drop that ewe and get to the car." Shouted when he didn't move. "Now." He ran to the road and left me shouldering Bog. The fella bleeding through his shirt, then mine, and I felt him on every nub of my spine. Sinking with the weight of both of us. I clambered till I could finally roll him over, faceup on the tarmac.

Loaded Bog in the car and laid him down—stretched and stiff along the backseat. Rolled up a tarp to make a pillow and hooked bungee cords about his body to stop him shifting on the drive. Wasn't going to wait for those Brown Hill Boys to find us. Doesn't take long to search the woods and roads when you're looking for a lorry. The big road. That's where I needed to get to. The Appleby

Bypass. I found a new lane, one come unsealed, and I needed light to drive it, switched low beam, high beam, rode leaning forward, with my eyes against the glass, owt to keep us hidden. Pitching up and down the potholes like an oarless rowboat. Riding near blind in a tunnel of stinging nettles. Would face a bend, light up a birch tree, and think two naked legs stood in the shrubs aside me.

When it looked as though the lane would end, when we found a fence, a wall, a house, a field—the way would turn, and the roadside would grow more wild. Had to be heading somewhere. With the windows down it smelled of sleeping garlic, and I saw some other light. A way off. Floating above the ground. Flickered aback the trees. I slowed the car and shut my beams off, and when I blinked, it was gone. Kept on riding and it soon came back, a bright light across the woods, if I sped, it rushed to match me, and if I stalled, it waited long as I did. I'd had enough. I was done with lanes. No time for signposts or quiet for the neighbours. Bollocks to the winding trail. Mounted a verge and found another fence and when I reached a gate, a closed-off stretch of pasture, I smashed on through, ripped up the grass, turn after turn, field after field, Danny in and out to hold the gates, and when that other light had long since dropped away, I stopped cross tracks on a railway dyke. Saw it led to a bridge and a black stretch of road. To a way home. We got on a carriageway and went far as Carlisle to water down our scent. "Next time, Danny," I said. "Call the AA."

"Don't have their number."

"Well, you can forget mine and all."

I rode down through the northern fells, on the safe roads by Derwent, Thirlmere, the sheltered string-thin lakes. Took my time on Lower Drot Lane into the valley, rode long round Bewrith before reaching Yow House where William's car was parked. George stood waiting in the frame of the main door staring down the sights of a boxlock shotgun. "Stop playing," I told him as I got out. "You need to get Bog inside. If he's not broken his skull, he's a hell of a heavy sleeper."

"Where's the bloody lorry?"

"The lorry? Where were you lot?"

George stayed at his post as William and Colin both stepped out. I helped them carry Bog into the telly room and laid his boots on one end of the sofa. We all stood about looking at his body, scared to touch him. "Is he dying or not?" Colin felt Bog's forehead and then listened to his wrist. Moved his lifebare body, placed his head atop one hand and turned his knees both sideways. Bog let us know he wasn't gone yet by bowking orange gut foam that frothed as it came out. William took his knife and cut the arm from the fella's shirt to work on bunging up that wound. Handed me a dabbing rag and some rubbing alcohol. "Now, that's not for drinking, Steve."

"You must've had plenty of time for that while you were sat here."

"We were about to come looking for the lad."

"You shouldn't have needed to."

"Who's that talk helping?"

"I've done enough of that," I told him. "No help left to give."

I walked away, went outside and got in my car. Out of petrol. Tried starting it and it didn't even choke. Slid the seat back and shut my eyes. Still felt I was staring into that crushed lorry. I picked up my phone to have something to do with my hands, playing with the buttons—I wanted to call somebody. Put in Simply Red's number.

It's said that men don't show feelings. You cry at the football or your dad's funeral if he's earned it. Tell a woman you love her only when God's watching. Scared of nowt but getting scared. That's bollocks. I've met every breed of bastard they've made. Smelly bastards and bastards with broken brakes, bastards with no money and bastards with too much, and bastards that can only say the right thing. They're all bastards. Some are just let to forget it till they get hungry. Never met one who wasn't filled with anger, and the angrier you get the less they say you feel. I've felt it. Anger. Still got the scars—some I cut and some that were cut into me. It's not just a feeling, it's all of them. Never been sadder or happier or hornier than when I was fuming. And I'll tell you something else. I'm not sorry for it. It gets things done. Crying's for when you want someone else doing it for you. Now I'm telling you, sat in that car, that day, I was Jesus. I was no longer a man. There was not a bit of anger in me. I wanted it all gone and didn't care who did it. I picked up my phone, one bar of charge, and pushed dial. Two clips before an answer. "Hello?"

"Red," I spoke slowly. "It's me."

"Steve? It's bloody late."

"Is that a problem?"

"Give me a second." Heard him sigh. "What've you got to tell me?"

"It's the robbery."

"What about it?"

"Worse than we thought it could be. You need to get to Caldhithe."

"Now?"

I was about to tell him to get there while they still had the money when there was a slap against the car window. I dropped the phone. William was there, towering in the dark—yanked the door open with me against it so I near fell out. "Who you on the phone to?"

197

"Piss off." I tried pulling at the handle, but his hand kept the door wedged open.

"I want you to come back in the house."

"I want to get off to bed."

"You can sleep in the house."

He picked up my phone and started saying hello into it. No one there. Simply Red was gone. He lobbed it over the wall into a patch of briar. He went for me then, grabbed my shoulder, got his nails in the joint, and dropped me to the grass. "Get in the house." Had his knife unclipped and held it like a dagger. I walked in front of him and was marched into the telly room. "Danny," he said as he walked in, "get Bog upstairs. George can help you. Let us know if he wakes."

I sat down in Bog's wet patch and William found a space next to me. "Steve, you know I don't like to pry. You live in your shitbox, playing hide-and-seek with the sun. That's how you want it. But I've to ask, once more, who were you on the phone to?"

Colin was watching me.

"And I'll tell you once more," I said. "Piss off. None of your business."

"You work for me. It's all my business."

"Don't remember that being in my contract."

"Look, Steve, I'm not going to do owt to you if you don't tell me. But I will leave this room and not come back till Colin says to."

"No need for all that, it was Helen. I was calling her."

"Why would you be hiding that?"

"I know you don't like it if we talk too much."

"What makes you think that?

"At one point it seemed like you had some funny thoughts. About her and me."

"I'll tell you what is funny. I saw your phone. Wasn't her name on the screen. You don't have her saved on there?"

"I don't know anything about how phones work."

"So, you know her number by heart? That it? Very sweet of you. I'll let her know." He got out his own phone and wouldn't let me see it. Tapped at the number pad. "There it is," he said. "I've got Helen's number up. Tell me what it is, and I'll let you off to bed."

"I already said, I don't know owt about phones."

"It doesn't matter," Colin butted in. "You said you saw his phone. Just call back the last number."

"You what?" William said.

"Christ, give me his phone."

"Bollocks," he said, and thought for a while. "This is what we'll do. George will come with me, and we'll find this phone. Colin, you see if you can get him to talk before that."

"About bloody time. I've told you this is how it needs to be."

The door closed after William and Colin pressed his ear to the wall, listening for when we were alone. His face was twisting. I couldn't recognise anger in it or sadness or fear. He was guarded with everything he did, but right then, there was something coming off him, a violence so single-minded the rest of him went slack and blank. "I need to head outside a minute," he told me. "You have a rest."

Soon came a scratching at the door, a clawing, something pressing to get in. "Easy now," I heard Colin warning. "Easy." It opened and there stood two dogs, taking turns to enter so they'd space to fit. Snitter walked in first, sniffed my privates, took a lap to check the room, and then sat darkening the corner. See his eyes but not much else. The other dog only had a length of rope to move, and he pulled it tight at that. A huge white dog. Heard them call him Jack. And from his skinny back legs his body grew and grew, a wide rack of ribs, blobs of muscle up his arms, his neck, needed them to hold that head—jaw so big his eyes had only room to squint. Stretched white skin that made his pink mouth look forever bleeding. Colin led him near and went to drag the coffee table over to my knees. Dropped the leash and poor Jack was caught leaping midair when Colin picked the rope up and reeled him in. "You like dogs, don't you, Steve?" He sat close, facing me.

"Might've liked a few of the ones this grunter's eaten."

"I don't think you would've."

"You might be right."

"So, about this phone. You want to tell me?"

"What is it you and William think I've got to tell?"

"That's fine," he said and looked down. Jack was heaving so hard he'd given Colin rope burn. "I'll need your help with him." He slackened the rope and gave the mongrel room to sit between my knees. Told me to put my hands together, then wrapped my wrists with the barely holding leash. Stroked the dog's head and started talking. "Y'know much about them Brown Hill bastards? I effing do. Was with them for nearly ten years. Now, they're a smart lot. Got rich without lifting a finger. Had some poor sod growing their gear for them and they'd have kiddies selling it all through country, from St. Brides to Beadnell Bay, and they'd sit happy in their pub getting sloshed." Jack was bored of waiting, lunged at my face, and only Colin's hand hooked in his collar kept him an inch away. Barking. Barking. I pressed against the cushion and tried to tuck my lips in. Colin jerked the dog back to his feet and kept on with his story. "They had another poor sod, the Brown Hill Boys did, whose job was to make sure them kids didn't forget which pocket they put their cash in. Ten years I did that. And I got good at picking sellers. You'd think it'd be the daft bairns you were after. Do as they're told. But that's all they'll do and there's only so much you can tell a person. I wasn't there to babysit." Jack looked at Snitter for a while and that only seemed to stir him. This time his cold nose and his teeth caught on my cheek before he was brought to heel. "It's you that's supposed to be doing the talking, Steve. For a man who never shuts up, I'm not sure about you. Be doing you a favour by killing you. So that's no threat. And I'll have you know I don't believe in torture. You seen on the bloody telly what the Americans are doing? Dressing them up like witches, the Iraqis—stacking them naked, three fellas high for a game of hide the sausage. Laughing as they do." Both front paws rested on my legs, and to help slow the growling, Colin tugged on my jumper, let the dog have a play with that. "I've tried it before, y'know. Not letting them sit for a week. Blasting Spice Girls to break glass. So starved they forget their names. It doesn't work. Gets you a confession, if that's what you're after, but if it comes from pain—may as well be talking to yourself." He stood up—having to yell over the throaty howls. "So, I want you to understand, when I'm braying the shit out of you. It won't stop. No matter what you say."

The door opened then, William letting yellow light in from the kitchen. "What you doing to him?"

"You said it was a race to break him."

"You're the expert," he said. "We didn't find his phone, but I found out who he called."

"Who?"

"Simply Red. Just seen him heading up to the house."

"How many are with him?"

"Looks to be on his own."

Colin turned back to me. "What did you say to him?" Had to remember how to speak, and my words got stuck together. "If your windpipe's not working, find a new hole to speak out of."

"Nowt," I told him. "I said nowt to Red."

"He didn't come to make a house call on his own."

"I didn't have time to speak."

"So, he doesn't know what's happened?"

I nodded. Colin threw me back to the sofa. "Where's George?" he asked William.

"Bolted the second he heard a copper was coming."

"We'll take care of this. Get the light off in here so he can't see this idiot. Get it locked." He wound Jack's rope in. "I'll put the dogs in the cellar."

I watched as they left. My hands still tied. Saw them walk out the door and stand under the bulkhead lamps on the outside wall. Ground beneath them was brown—dead as the soil. Their shoulders were nearly touching as they waited, hid their necks with their collars and stuck both hands in their pockets, only pulling them out to slap at the winter gnats that circled in the light. Didn't wave or nod as Simply Red walked up. He'd made an effort. Wore a black tie and a long black coat that covered up his flak jacket. He was a foot taller than either of them and his bobby helmet put ten inches on top of that, its seven-pointed star and crown looked polished, had cuffs and zip ties hanging from his belt. He rested his hand on the grip of his baton as he began to talk. I wriggled over to the windowsill and placed my head on it, neck not fit for the job. Couldn't hear all of what they said. Red asked question after question and he sounded sort of jolly and sort of scared. Could see that red hair of his under his hat, thick enough to scrub the burn off pans. "Would you lads mind taking your hands out your pockets?"

"It's bloody cold."

"It won't take long." Colin took his hands out and lit up a fag. Stepped forward and offered Red one. "Gave that up when I got married."

"It's late," Colin said. "Come back tomorrow."

"A quick look."

"Take a while with nowt to find." Red went to unsling his radio and Colin took another step.

"Have a look round now. Come in. There's lots of gear for us to share. And lots of cash and guns."

Red pulled out his metal club and swung to clear some space. "On the ground, lads. On the ground." Didn't wait, he smacked down and belted Colin's knee. Hooked him to the floor and weighed him down with all his body, snapped one wrist in handcuffs and whacked his stick to stop the other fist. I saw William step away and then come back holding a roofing slate. I slammed against the window and tried to give a warning. Screamed easier in bad dreams. Red looked up and caught my eyes. The first smack dented that helmet and it fell back, hanging from his neck strap-wise. Next smack of the slate had him on the ground next to Colin. Blood came gentle out his ear, dignified somehow. Soon as he hit the floor there were hands all over the copper keeping him pinned. William reached for his knife and locked it. Stabbing and stabbing at the vest, only bruising, ripping the fabric, fella wriggling in the dirt, fish-kissing the air. Three hands tugging at the straps on his vest, tore open and the knife went in. Never seen William move so fast, twenty times, poking holes in him till he slipped into holes he'd already made. Till there was no getting back up. Left the dead bastard on the ground where they stuck him.

PART IV

Blessing the Throats

Tedder-a-dick

In all of this, I've talked a lot of death. Animals sent to the fat. Culled and slurried. Blood enough to float a gunboat. But before Simply Red, I'd never seen a dead body before, y'know, a dead fella. Come close. Warehouse in Shropshire, a bloke's knees rolled flatter than oats under fifty tonnes of rig.

I thought it'd be different. Dead stock and lamped rabbits and sick sleeping dogs. They all end up as bodies. Whole thing went slow, one of his hands fell open at the side of him and the other curled up like a trotter, lying on his chest, and he stopped moving. Remember feeling relaxed when it was done. That's wrong that, isn't it? It's like, there's a part of you that's always waiting for death to happen, seeing it a thousand times over when you lean too far off a bridge or cross a road carblind. So, when it did happen, that bit of me took over, like I'd been expecting it, like I was trained for it. Another thing to deal with.

William and Colin picked him up, soft as hunting dogs, pulled his belt past his belly, one grabbed his armpits and the other his ankles. Spilled sideways through the main door and placed him on the coffee table in the telly room. Colin sat back in an armchair watching Red's hands dangle and his blood filling up his hood. With the yelling finished, Danny came down the stairs and saw what was waiting. The mess they'd made, on the door jamb, the walls, the carpet. Like toddlers in the kitchen. So much blood the house stunk of iron. The lad closed his eyes, placed his hands over them to make sure, and he left the way he'd come. William stood by my patch on the sofa, wouldn't look at the table, and he asked me, "You call anyone else?"

"Don't think I'll call anyone ever again."

He asked one more time. "Did you call anyone?"

"No," I told him. "Just Red."

We watched and we watched, me and Colin did, like there was more to come, like we'd never seen owt so interesting, like we'd no idea how long folk stayed gone. "We need to get rid of him," William told us.

"No matter what we try," Colin said, "they'll come looking for him."

"You want them to find him when they do?"

"Find an eyelash and they'll have found enough."

"Don't leave any eyelashes, then."

"You can't get rid of all of a man in half an hour."

"We'll get rid of all of him at once. In the ground. Won't take any time."

Colin stood and went to the table. "Time to show me your bloody fells then, William." Got to work on Red. Smoothed out his shirt and did up his buttons, where the buttons still clung on, and he zipped his jacket and stroked back his hair. Wiped his hands on the policeman's black britches, then he felt in his pockets, deep as they went, pulled out a stiff hanky. A set of car keys. Took them outside, and I heard him calling George. *Feeding time, you big bastard. Come feed.* That monster stepped out the dark as if he'd been waiting to hear his name. Got told to take the copper's car far as he could. Take Bog with him. If he'd not found he was lost, then he'd still further to go. Colin came back in with a bag and sheet. Stretched the bag till it turned white over Red's nose, and he tied a knot with its handles down by his chin. Unfurled the sheet and let it fall across the body. Their foreheads pressed as he tucked it in aback his legs and shoulders. He left the room one last time and returned with a rifle, swinging off him by its strap, this massive gun, built like it could chop down a tree, an old man's Enfield, old enough to have seen the sands of Normandy. Seen out Waterloo. "What's that for?" I asked as he filled his pockets with junk shot—wildcat rounds he'd stuffed with double powder.

All he said to me was "Can you still walk?"

"Last time I checked."

"We'll all take the one car. William's car."

"What's the gun for, Colin?"

"What for? Well, there's the blokes we robbed and the police inspector we stabbed." He looked out the window. "And you never know what else you'll run into up there." Soon as he'd loaded it, Colin used that rifle for pointing and if he was talking to you, you were talking back to its muzzle.

He said William was driving us, but the boss man's eyes were swelling out their sockets—full red rims. Colin shook him. "Get your tools, man. We'll need them." He called through the floorboards and told Danny to get the dogs ready. Yow House would be empty. We'd take their yapping with us. He told me I was carrying Red, to look after him, and I said nowt at first, didn't stir, and he pulled me by the give in my jumper. Pulled me to the floor. Then pulled me so I was on my feet, and I grabbed out for an armrest, then a doorknob, swung with the hinges, tried making it outside. "Where you think you're going, Steve?"

"I'll stay quiet," I said.

"You'll stay where I can see you."

"I'll only slow you down."

"I won't let that happen." He gave me another push, put the gun into my back, twisting—made me stand before the altar. "I'll see you in the car."

He was under a sheet, Simply Red, but I could see the shape of his face and feel him watching me, and there was nowt keeping it tied about him. So I hugged him close. Took the warmth he'd left inside my arms. And all wrapped up, he looked small, y'know, small for such a big fella, and I was holding him up by his back while he was pulling me down by mine.

They were all looking at me from that fancy off-roader. Scarce left its barn and still smelled of sweet plastic. William at the wheel, the crazy-brained dogs in the boot with Danny, and Colin balancing his rifle across his legs. I placed Red on his arse against the open side door and got in the back. Dragged him by his armpits, and hand on hand I hauled him up and rested him on my lap. Those dogs had calmed, and the turnspit Jack was breathing on my neck—he reached down and started licking at the sheet.

The car set off, rattling on the cattle grids, slippy on the wet grass, William clinging to the helm against the thawing dirt, and we rode to Brimlaw Haws. We rode in coils about the land, skirting higher, ridge to ridge about craters of gravel, we cut across it all and bridged the folds of sandstone with four fat muddy tyres. I'd no thought to where we were headed and all we went was up, to places no cars should drive, made new roads through waves of rocky hills that surged and crashed on either side. Saw north by the few lost trees that bent in search of sun, but we'd none of that. Didn't know how it could still be night—three hours out of bed. We strained the motor, driving straight up, on the brink, stopped and seized. Heard it ticking. Oil cooking in the vents. The bonnet popped, hammered mad, and raced us on another thousand feet. William's eyes got so wide they filled the rearview and he looked at me. "What happened?" he said. Really asking.

"You'll have to tell me," I said. "I don't know what I saw."

"I couldn't think."

"I'd hope not."

"He lost his bloody mind. Coming to the house alone."

"That's my fault."

"He was crooked."

"They always are."

Put his eyes back on the moors, and we reached Dando Cove. The biggest outcrop on Caldhithe. Bulges out of a wide plain of grass on its own, like a brain being pushed up from the earth, stripped back to rock on its top and sides. Rain-cut cliffs all the way about it, cliffs jutting out of them cliffs and small ones atop them. We were headed to its eastern edge, to its tallest point, and that's when William said to us, "There's not much further we can go."

"We out of petrol?" Colin asked.

"We're out of mountain. Least what this car can handle."

"You think they'd look this far?"

"Not on purpose."

"Pick a spot, then."

He rode on for some time after that, bumping on limestone pavement by the cliffs, from one mountain rooftop to another, and he came to a crag that rested on a slope of Brimlaw, curved and twisted like some sea-roar shell, made a long wall with enough shelter for trees to root and there were junipers so old they'd grown sideways, low and wide, branches hugging the ground in grass-green heaps. "This'll do," William told us. The car stopped, hissing loud as wet rocks in a fire, and on that hour's drive, we'd put five years on its clock. I was more stuck in my chair than the seat belt, but the two fellas got out the front. Dogs jumped free and joined Colin as he took a piss. And a drowsy smell fell on me—Danny puffing on a rollie. He stayed hunched where he'd been sat and smoked quick to get a headrush. "Danny can stay here," Colin said, still waggling his privates. "Keep a lookout if anyone follows us."

William looked his son over. "Why'd you bring him up here?"

"Good to know where everyone is."

William opened the door by me and pulled out his gear. A roughneck shovel, a pick, a trencher, stacked beneath my feet. Placed them on his shoulder. "We're not done yet, Steve." Watched as Colin did his britches up and whistled for the dogs to follow. "We're not done yet."

Red was mine to carry. Lifted him to rest against my belly button, only place I could keep his weight, and then I set off, him pointing feet first. Followed William as he led on through a dirt strip across the acres of scrub and stone. No torch to guide him. And not seeing what I was stepping on or where the path was taking us—it began putting me at ease. All that fear and all that danger. They were somewhere else. The turf had no give, made my bootsteps bouncy, and with the night sky bobbing way above, I felt weightless and that helped me bear the load. Walked on shale and walked in bracken and the stems we trampled had a wet and bitter scent. There came a trickling ahead. A beck washing along its rocks. Flowing down from Toom Tarn, it was thin but it was fast, and it split the fell in half so

I'd no choice but to cross it. Wanted to hop over the stream but it soon made me wade in, frothing where it met my legs, trying to turn my body with the current. I lifted Red clear of the water. Seemed important to keep him dry. And when I reached the far banking, a wind rushed in aback me—picked up the edges of the sheet to show me Red's white fingers.

It was among a spread of drum hills where we laid him down. A spread of hummocks, rolling humps, big ones, near three times my height, and there was hundreds of them, in rows, with dens of broom and heather at their base. Growing up, my dad had called them giants' graves. Red was tall, I'll give him that. He'd need a ladder each morning to shave his chin. But I don't think a giant's dead hole was big enough. We'd need a grave the size of Curdale to bury what we'd brought.

William went among the hummocks, counting loud each hill he passed, four rows deep and six rows down, *twelve, thirteen, fourteen, fifteen*, and there he rested where they dipped with Colin not far aback. "Here's where we'll put him." I turned up and settled in the pit, tried to place Red neatly but he slumped and found his own place to wait. I cleared a space. Pulled up the heather and its hairy roots, weeded patches of hungry grass, and rolled away the loose tumble-rocks. "How deep we want him?" I said, looking up at Colin.

"When do we hit the sea?"

"Fifteen hundred foot."

William stepped in and stuck a shovel in the ground. "That's a start."

We all got digging. Colin worked the surface with his axehead pick, swinging overhead and chopping up the soil, pitching squares to make a trench, deep slices that he dredged and dredged so we could rake out all his churn. Me and William, we tried stomping on the shovel blades but the earth we were digging up was peaty, tough, and close to frozen. I got right in there. Two-handed, scraping, pushing through, stabbing out the clods. Each scoop of soil I lifted was taken by the wind, and when our hearts beat so hot we near threw them up, we'd stop, and Colin would have me lie in the hole to measure when was deep enough. Took five turns to get us there but he was happy when just my nose was poking out. I went to move Red and a fresh gust of wind blew his sheet clean off. First time William had looked at him since the killing, and he knelt over the dead man. The dogs came in sniffing, and he smacked away their snouts. Dragged the body by himself and stumbled on the grave. Squashed Red's neck so his head would fit, and placed aside him all his things, his hat, his cuffs, his smacking stick. Then we sat looking over the edge. Our faces red and the mountain in our nails. William finally shut his eyes, leaned back, and turned away. "If that's not deep enough," I said, "we'll need a ten-tonne crawler to finish off the job."

"If they know where to look," Colin told me, "doesn't matter how far down we stick him."

"I don't think I could even tell you where we are."

"I'm sure you'd have a go." He spat through his teeth as if to water the ground and got up. Sat on Simply Red's chest and took out a folding knife. Grabbed one of Red's hands—the fella was getting creaky now, so he'd to lift his arm up like a lever, and he got sawing through his fingers. "He won't be needing them any time soon."

"And you do need them?" I asked him.

"Don't want them to know who it is."

"I suppose you'll have his teeth next?"

"You reckon I need his eyes?"

"He's a body full of blood. You can't cut it all out."

He laid the knife down and Snitter came over to clean the mess off the blade. He stroked the dog's head and patted him along the shoulders. "You think I've not done this before, Steve?"

"I've no stomach to imagine the things you've not done."

"I'll tell you what I haven't done. Haven't got caught."

"Then cut away."

"If no one talked, every prison would be empty."

"Who's talking? I've not talked to you once. Your name's not Colin. I like it that way. I don't want to be remembering you, and I don't want to talk. I know everything that's in my head and yours and William's and the dogs'. Even Red, I could take a guess at what's in his head right now. Don't need any talking to know what you're thinking, do I?"

"Why'd you come up here with us?"

"You'd shoot me if I didn't." He laughed at that. "You think I'm an idiot, but the only thing I can't figure out is what to do about you."

"I don't think you're an idiot. I just don't think it makes a difference."

"It doesn't."

"They'll find this grave," he said and took the gun in both hands. "They'll find whoever's nearby. Find their own answers in that."

"It's only us in these fells. You can say what you mean."

"I'm going to kill you."

Was then that William let us know he'd been listening. Hadn't time to open his eyes before he smacked Colin, once, right in the

215

head. That didn't drop him. He swung again and fell across his knees, twisting, slipping in the growing mud. Got up and slipped. Used each slip as one step closer, and there wasn't much in his smacking, but two smacks. Three smacks. They added up. Colin turned and scratched red stripes in William, and they locked their heads and locked their bodies. Two trout on the same hook stranding a riverbank. I saw Colin's hand reach out, feeling, he got his knife, gripped, thrust it, one cut ducked, and he slashed that coat. I found a coward's rock and threw it, dinged Colin's back and made him shudder, let William sweep his ankles. Sent him toppling. We had our chance, climbed out the pit and then we ran and ran. Shots fired at us in the breaking night, three bangs and one bark loud and one bark quiet. And we ran.

Medder-a-dick

There's a laziness in living that your body's keen to hide. No matter how fat you get, how forgetful, how blind, there's a skinnier fella in you and he knows what running is. Lazy since that's all he's got, that one run in him, one he holds tighter than a bee's goodbye sting.

I could never read without my glasses, but right then I saw it all, the shaggy moss, the tracks, the seed stones, the milk-white rubble. The greatsome gullies on each side that peeled away into the dark. Felt I'd brought on the gloaming an hour early or tricked the sky to fake a dawn. Let me go flat-out where the ground was stable, quicker than the scree, strides the length of two men—an odd forty years of trying and I'd finally caught my breath. We scuttered in and out of those humps, some we jumped, cleared twenty feet like stepping stiles, felt bullets coming, skeeting by our boots, and I saw the dogs closing in, high hopping along raised ground, and the one sound worse than barking was the quiet when they'd sprint.

Falling through the hurtling country, I could see the route we'd come from. The trail of bracken. The walls of Dando. It was faster down but steeper also, no stopping, even if Colin shot me dead, I'd still beat him to the bottom.

The car. Nowhere else to go but there. The fancy car with the power steering that never worked. I lowered my head, right down, slowed me but it halved what I gave for target practice. I knew the rifle Colin carried, he'd let me fire it, once, maybe twice, could drop a deer at three hundred yards and I'd a second to every step and two steps to make a yard and with a stretch of endless fellside that meant distance was the only cover and it was always ten minutes up ahead. If I could still hear the shots, at least I wasn't gone. Kept telling myself that.

I looked down, no easy path left to run, came to the head of a hill that slanted where a hunk of Brimlaw had rolled away, jutted as it went, rock over rock, call them steps if you were a mouse. But as I said, no stopping. Set off on my toes, pressed my weight into my treads, stretched my muscles going lower and got tap dancing, drop to drop till it levelled out. Started sliding on my arse and on my hands, and saw my knees come through my britches, saw them pink with scramble burn. Then I saw the car. Waiting in a shrinking mist. A lovely bloody mist. Tried to gulp it as I went and felt a deafness creeping over—we'd not heard a shot since plunging off that ridge. For all his ailing, William went faster, and I heard him shouting, "Danny. Danny." I reached the bonnet and rested on it. "Speak up. You stupid lad, where are you?" Felt myself over to see I'd no new holes. Still waiting for another thunk. "He's not here." William was pulling at the driver's door, a foot pressed on the panelling so he near tore the handle off.

"Where is he?" I said, looking about, squinting at the nearby stacks and bumps as if my eyes could bend. He kept shouting for his lad, and I told him, "Stop yowling. We only just got away."

"Why would Danny lock it?"

"Probably heard the shots. I doubt the car would start again—way you drove it."

"We can't leave him."

"Won't be much of a search party if we're both dead."

"And there won't be owt left of us to shoot if we keep running like this."

We tried each door and stuck our knives to pry the windows. Might've smashed our way in if we hadn't heard a howl from somewhere in the bracken. Looked about. The fells never seemed more naked. Nine hundred square miles of unending tracks and not one way out.

We wanted a cliff. One we could climb and find a soft-rock shelter to wait and hide in. So we headed northward, where Brimlaw reared up on its shoulders—it's not short of cliffs but we were nervish farmers with sickly joints. The sun had come out cold and it filled the crags and painted those rocks red. Showed us a stony tower that sat on friendly blocks, went up in layered faces till it took off as one slab, straight like a wishing well, with cracks and cracks. I learnt to climb that day. Could walk and heave the first few boulders but soon I'd no footing, and all the ground rose upward. Let my boots slide into holes and gaps, took it slow, crawled where the cliff stuck out and meathooked my hands in where they'd fit. Dried my fingers across my shirt and could feel my body dangle as the fog clung to our backs. *Not so far down. Not so far down.* Doesn't matter how many times I thought it, it was never true. Came to ledges stuffed with bracken, and I tore out leaves for handholds. I swayed over to where I could move on both boots and sidestepped a ramp for twenty foot, and there we found it, a buttress broad enough to stand on. William reached it first and hauled me up the final step.

I looked out to where we'd come from, the humps, the car, the block fields, and saw them blurry against the skyline. The wind had turned, and I felt it streaming in my face, and the gale brought with it the birds we'd woken in the cliffs—stock doves, jackdaws, stonechats, and a buzzing swarm of thrushes. Flew as if we might catch them and glided in a line with their wings straight as sheets of paper. And with their chirps they woke a blood hawk who soared and joined the hunt. I looked out further still and saw a figure, one in a hurry. We all look small from far away, but he looked scrawny, had a yellow coat tied about his waist. I turned to William and asked him, "Is that Danny?"

"Aye," he said, shading his eyes with his elbow. "Thank Christ, I think it is."

No sign of Colin, but nearer to us I saw Snitter and Jack on the grassy shelf we'd left. Sniffing footprints as they went. They swerved across the bumpy land and swerved back again like crooked rivers, stuffed their heads in each crumbly patch, and herded in the mountain. They'd stop, squirmy, thump their legs, and hold a bark as each step brought them closer. Soon both came to sit at our feet some two hundred foot below. "Dogs can't get up cliffs." That's what William told me. "They'll get bored soon. Wander off." We were bored ourselves not long after. Aback us was a wrinkle in the cliffside, deep enough to crawl in, two pillars of rock that made a narrow den in their middle, roofed over with a chockstone that felt always close to dropping—what outdoorsmen call a hide puller. Squeezed out all my back pain as I found a place to squat among the thick plates of rock. William joined me, and he talked for a change, chatty, trying to stay sharp. "I don't blame you," he said. "For calling Red. Just didn't think it would be tonight."

"You don't have to do this now."

"Might be the only time I have."

"I didn't know what else to do."

"Maybe it was the right thing. It's been coming to a head."

"There was nowt right about that."

"Y'know, when we were at that farm in Thirsk earlier. And they found us, two truckloads of the bastards, screaming, coming out shooting like they'd been waiting. I thought that was it. I couldn't see a way out. They were riding up on us and three of them were blasting out the car window, nearly tipped it. Two sat on the field gate. No reason for us to have made it, and when I couldn't think of owt better than closing my eyes and flooring it, I felt grateful. Happy, even. What you make of that?"

"We should all be so grateful to die," I said.

"Lots of folk are. I ever tell you what my dad died of? I didn't know you so well then, so I don't suppose I would've. It was arsenic. Must've taken half his life to finish poisoning him but it did. It's what they used to dip the sheep in, and you had to dip in them days. Not like they didn't know it was bad for them—my uncle and granddad wouldn't go near the baths, but they sent my dad in as a kid to loosen up stuck ewes. Naked he was. Sloshed about with not so much as a glove on. Thought if he was starkers it'd not be so fierce, not getting it on his clothes meant it could wash off quick, and if it was okay for sheep and we ate them, well, how bad could it really be? They'd not let you use it if it was so bad, would they? They do it again and again. Lying so much it gets to be your fault for listening. But we're not stupid as they used to be, eh? They stopped them using it, the arsenic, replaced it with something as bad from what I remember, some Vietnam mosquito killer, but it didn't matter. It was in the ground, not far from here, and we've been using the same place to rinse sheep since fellas with top hats were doing it. Nowt grew there, but nowt does out here. Does it? Y'know how we found he was dying of it? It wasn't his cough. They all smoked. They all coughed. His wet barks were seen to be a good thing. Getting the tar up. He was always shaking like this." He wobbled his hands at me, twitching his fingers. "Got so bad sometimes he ate from his plate like a cat. But he drank so much—course he shook. They all drank. They all shook. What got the doctors saying it was arsenic was his skin turning black. Started off with these freckly things under his arse and armpits, and then he'd wake up looking like he'd fags stubbed out in him. Big patches of black and grey on his arms. One on his face. Months of that. He didn't know owt by the end, who he was or how his body worked. He looked healthier dead, and I tell you what, never seen someone look so grateful."

"He might've been," I said. "But it's not our choice when's some fella's ready to be put out their misery."

"That's not a choice anyone's fit to make. After that foot and mouth business you left here—you got to leave. I was done for. I've never once used an alarm clock. No need. Used to be, every morning I was up at five. Couldn't sleep in if I wanted to. But with the flock dead, it wasn't till I was eating breakfast that I'd remember there was nowt to be up for. I sat not trying to wake anyone—watching telly on mute or going for a walk so I didn't forget how. Few weeks of that, and I saw on my arms the same rash my dad got. Arse and armpits. Hard as scales and they grew bigger every day and I'd rub bits off in the night, so the scabs were always raw. Couldn't see it as owt else but the same poisoning, and I felt weak for the first time in my life. Could scarce remember my name. It was on one of them walks that I decided to end it. Put myself out my misery, as you call it. It cured me, that did. Doesn't sound right, does it? Wasn't any bloody medicine. It was a one-shot horse killer. Kept it in the pouch of this coat wherever I went. I could do owt because it was always there. Nowt mattered—for good or bad. Lost all my money? *Bang*. Wife left me? *Bang*. Put out my back? *Bang*. I always had a plan. That rash went overnight and the weakness with it. Pain was all in my head."

"If this goes on any longer," I told him, "might have to try out your cure for myself."

He dug into the lining of his wax coat and pulled out a revolver. This small gun made for finishing livestock. Not much bigger than his palm, and only room for a single rubber bullet. A squared-off muzzle and holes drilled in the barrel to take out all its kick, and a contact safety pin so it could only fire when he pressed it to his temple. "Just ask for it. Anytime you like, pal."

"Think you might need to start carrying two bullets."

"At least four by my count." He put the gun back and shook the coat about him. "How long have we been up here now?"

"Not been keeping track." The sun had filled the air and the ringing in my ears had dimmed. "I'd say about an hour."

"You think he'll just piss off?"

"He can't live up here."

"We do. Or near enough."

"Nowt to stop him waiting for us on the farm."

"The police will come. Get a helicopter in."

"Is getting them mixed up a good idea?"

"They're already coming for me. Best make them work for it."

We sat like that as a rack of clouds chased off the bleary weather, and I'd been on the edge so long, I could've slept right there. But soon a grey wind drifted in. Full of smoke. You think something's on fire before you know it. A brashy smoke, a woodless smoke, the smell of Guy Fawkes sparklers. We moved to look. A long black plume growing where the car had sat. Colin was there. No one else for it to be. And next to him, on the ground, on his knees, was the fella with the yellow jacket. Our Danny. We heard this yelling, one that never stopped, coming from a place I don't have in me—it was Colin calling for us. With my eyes closed I made it out. Just one word he was cutting his throat with. *William.*

He was whelping next to me at the sound of his own name. Had to stop him jumping to the fell floor and he said, "Why the eff were we sat here?"

"Doesn't matter now."

He checked where we'd climbed up and looked along the rim. Called himself a stupid bugger, and I went to see what made him swear. Only feet away on the cliff's western side were gentle ledges— lift your knees and you could stroll along them with both hands in your pockets. "We need to think this through," I told him.

"If we're going to sit here thinking, it may as well be about bury- ing my lad."

"You want to die?"

"You've not been listening."

Didn't judge his leap as he climbed down the easy path, and I went not long after. Dropped each ledge, two legs over, and sprang rough off my hands. We didn't run now. Needed something in us for when we got there. Stalked our own trail to find our way and travelled low or in the shade and we talked with our hands or at a whisper. "What's your plan, William?"

"Get my son back."

"Running into a bullet won't do that."

"I expect not."

"What we going to do, then?"

"I already told you what I'm doing. As for a plan, you don't want to be filling your head with nonsense when you need it most."

We'd come to a trench filled with scruffy bed straw and we heard that forgotten barking. Came from overhead, from atop the trench's banking. It got closer till a dog leaped down, moved to head us off, moved soundless as a sun speck on my eye. Don't know where Jack had got to but now it was only Snitter. Dug in his legs, as if to spring, and showed us his black gums. Growled like swallowed glass, and any move we made, he barked to burst our ears. He backed up as if we'd put him in a corner. Think I heard William say *Eff off*, and then he bolted, left me with the mongrel. The dog that wouldn't scare. I waved my arms, straightened up my back, and made myself look bigger. Then so did he. His jaw popped as he bared his crushing teeth, and his hairs stood up from end to end. If I went to kick, he went to bite, and his snout could nip in quicker. He pounced up and there was only sixty pounds of him, but he pressed them all on my chest. His jaws snapped at my face and throat as I held his ribs away. Threw him off and he bit my swiping hand. I got my coat off, waved it at his head, he snapped over, under, slipped on through and whipped his snout—bit into my thigh. Held on. Shook and shook and tried to drag me. He'd one big mouth but I'd two arms. I grabbed his back legs and hoicked them up and we spun, rolled to the grass. I got him pinned. Had him tight about the neck and leg in a knotted cradle. We both lay panting, and as I held him, he seemed to grow and his fur got blacker and his bark got louder, till I couldn't keep my arms together. He stood and pricked his ears, he'd heard something, a sound too high for shepherds, and he looked to a sunken peak of Brimlaw. With that, he tore across the open hillside and was gone without one last thought for me. No one saw that mad dog again. I reckon whatever was calling him led him into the highmost fells. Found something there to tame him. He'd not be the first to be taken by them—heard them calling for me once or twice.

Felt blood in my socks and squeezed my ripped fingers with my good hand. The way I swayed with one leg trailing, and my clothes on ragged, and my hands pressed above my heart. A monk who'd paid his toll. I kept moving, kept to where the ground was smooth and wound my way with heavy steps, the rocks, the ridges, my hand railings. Almost peaceful as the world slowed with my thoughts.

Reached the clearing where we'd left the car and heard a sound of talking, the words roaring above the wind. Taught me twenty new words for arsehole. William waited in the open, lost inside his coat, legs forked to keep up steady, and his spud gun drawn, held aiming hipwise. Could only half see the others aback the bends of mossy turf. Danny was on his feet, I could tell that much, hands up by his ears, and he kept them still. I crouched and moved to the car. The paint scorched off and the glass missing from the windows. I wafted away the ash and fumes to get a better look. Colin was there. Mud dried on his jeans and jumper, wore them like a suit of clay, looking faded—this dusty man from out the east. He stood loose and easy with that long rifle full of .303s resting underarm. "We can all leave," William said to Colin. "Get out the valley. Out of England."

"You go first. I'll wave you off."

"I've nowt to gain by giving you up."

"You spend all your time whining. *They don't care about us. They don't care.* But you still don't believe it."

"What's that matter?"

"What've you got to gain? Everything from where I'm standing."

"The money, then, you can have it all."

"You think that's yours to offer?"

"So there's no deal to be had? You kill me and my son no matter what?"

"I'm still deciding on Danny."

William gripped the gun in both hands and took a step closer. "You don't get to end this."

"That's what the gun's for."

Danny's hands had begun to tremble wilder than he could stop. Closed his fists and squeezed them about his head. That trembling spread and his body rocked in fits. When the guns took aim, he ran and pushed off against the rock. I guess his legs were jelly. Would've smacked the ground if Colin hadn't swooped in, slowed him with a fist rammed into his chest. Made a thump so loud his body sounded hollow. No air left to scream so Colin did it for him. "What the eff you do that for?" He grabbed the lad's hair and looked him in the eyes. "I'll get to you later."

William had one bullet in that single shot horse killer, and I knew he needed to get in close. Gun couldn't fire till it was touching skin. I leaned back and kicked the Rover—clanged and clanged so Colin shit himself, and he turned with his gun and fired. Shot a hole from door to door. The bullet twanged, skidded on the ground, and wedged inside my boot heel. He went to rack the handle and have another pop. *Clink, clink, clink.* The bugger jammed. That trusty British bolt action. William rushed in and swung his revolver, tried to press it to the bastard's neck. He couldn't miss. Some safety feature. Colin shifted his leg and slapped the gun away. Let his rifle drop, strap looped, slid to his armpit, and he grabbed out, got William's ear between his fingers and pushed him off. Couldn't kill his balance. William started whipping with the handgun, chopped the air, clipped Colin's brow, made him stotter, made him duck, made him flap his shoulders. Had the muzzle one-handed in his face and Colin clapped William's wrist, trapped it against his own chest, closing, tighter, and turned the barrel skyward. Smacked William's skull with his own and they fell—slammed into the rocky ground. Both moved slow now, as if wrestling on a lakebed, and William lifted himself on his forearms, tried to stick the revolver to Colin's head. Slipped the trigger. Rolled away. Stuck again and it was fended off. Colin pressed down on the earth and sprang up with his knee, knocked William back, the handgun dropped. Kicked into the heather. Colin rose with his hand on the rifle end and whacked its wooden stock right into William's chin. Watched him slither underneath with a spreading beard of blood. Colin took his rifle, smacked the chamber, shook out the sticky round, and pressed the butt up to his collar. "This is how I always should've done it."

"Had plenty of chance," William said and closed his eye. All I could think about was whether he looked grateful.

Heard three thuds. One after the other.

A small bang, the rifle hitting the floor, and Colin falling on top of it.

He smacked into the dirt like he was made of the stuff. No blood spilling or holes blown out his skull. Just Danny standing with the revolver in his hand. A humane way to die.

Mimph

I didn't want to be the first to get up, and when I was, my brains hummed like they'd made a home on the ground. I hopped without my arms to balance, reached for the car, still burning hot, soot on my palms. The hills and sky were swirling, taking turns to sit atop me, and I kept on my feet. Seemed the earth below had turned to one big bed made of comfy, worn-in rocks.

Danny sat with his arms on his knees, nowhere safe to look but up, and I put my hand out on his head, part to comfort, part to stop me from falling. Took his fingers off the handgun and stuck it in my britches. He asked me, "Is it over?"

"Since when's that stopped us?"

"Are we safe now?"

I didn't answer. William had scarce moved from where he lay, and when I say he held his face in his hands, I don't mean from shame. I dragged him to a boulder and sat him up against it. You're not supposed to move folk with wounds like that, but I thought some brain damage might do him good. "Chin up, William."

Went to tell me *shut up* but whistled out a spurt of blood.

I sat with him. "We going to bury this fella as well?"

"Not up here."

I looked at Colin. The back of him. It's always hard to tell if someone's breathing when they're facedown. "What we going to do with him?"

"Don't touch him."

Not long after, there was a panting aside us, and out came Jack, slinking along, that hairless white coat of his. He went to Colin and sat right by him. Looked strong and sad like he was bred to. Waited on and waited on. Rested his jaw across the dead man's shoulders, and if he'd ears left to droop, they would've reached down to his whiskers. When Colin didn't wake, he curled up in the fella's crooked arm and fell asleep to pass the time.

We were all waiting. As if we might wake up somewhere else. No signal on the phone we had and the only moving we did was to hug ourselves. A droning rose in the valley, covered the fellside, louder and louder, a booming *thip, thip* noise. Spinning helicopter blades. It did a flypast. White and red it was. Flattened the grass and flattened my ears. Blew up clouds of chalk, and I waved, and they didn't wave back. First person to reach us was Helen. On her feet, alone, in her bobble hat, her baggy waterproofs, and it always seemed to end with Helen. Said she saw the smoke, and she went to her son and held him.

There weren't any sirens or lights when the coppers came from all directions of the mountain and all at once. *Help's coming. Don't move. Don't talk. Don't touch anything. Help's coming.* More and more of them, some with guns, and if I moved an inch, they'd point them. Went about the heather and turned over bullet casings, split open the car boot, and poked sticks through the reeds and tall grass. Heard swearing and it passed from man to man like blessed wine, and one of the coppers came forward, spoke to the only fella not wearing a helmet. The fella in charge. "They killed Red," he told him.

"They what?"

"Simply Red. Inspector Marsden. He's dead."

Some smart-dressed fellas turned up—fellas what
they were doing. Got cars out there and moved us in a
hospital down Lancashire four hours away. Asked m were
family. Asked me not to talk to Danny or Helen till t ken
statements. William. I don't know. Put him somewhere h n't
talk. They sewed me up from my knuckles to my nails and n h
up to my privates. Wanted me in for observation. I told the
haustion's not an illness or else I've never met a full-grown fella
wasn't sick.

I'm telling you this story, about us, about them folk who died
and I'm telling it like I lived through it. There's parts of me that did
but more that I carry about broken, waiting for the rest to be buried
with them.

The trial and the investigation never seemed to stop. When you
thought it was coming to an end that was the start of the next bit.
Questions the police asked weren't how you'd imagine. Wasting
time seemed their aim—dull question after dull question, talking
like they're your mates, nicer even, so nice you think they might
be selling you insurance. Coppers aren't supposed to lie, but asking things they know the answer to, that's allowed. They keep them
coming. Telling you they only want information, to know what happened, but it's still them choosing the questions. "Can you tell me
about the work you did for William Herne?"

"I've never worked for William."

"You've not been working at Caldhithe farm for the last three
years?"

"I've worked the farm. Wasn't working for William."

ot your boss?"

my boss. Doesn't mean I work for him."

oesn't?"

e's in charge and it's his farm but he doesn't tell me what to how it's to be done, when to start the day or finish it, how to n a sheep or brand one. When I can stop for a lemonade. I turn o I don't. He doesn't count my hours or pay me."

He doesn't pay you?"

"You look at any of this and think William had money to give her people? I get some of the cash from selling animals and day rates for shearing or dipping and a place to stay and some food to eat. Close to paying me as he's ever got."

"So you're not contracted to work for him?"

"A bloody contract? With William Herne? You're asking the wrong questions if you're asking that. Unless I wanted my organs on offer in the small print, I'd not sign owt he put in front of me."

"What does that mean?"

"Means he liked a steak and kidney pudding."

"Can I ask why you did it? If there was no money?"

"If you do this work because you want money, you're too stupid to ever make any. And if you do this work knowing it pays bugger all, well, I guess you're bloody mental. I've worked for blokes before who were always trying to get me to work for nowt. Paying me six hours to do a job that takes ten and filling my pockets with pay soon as I shook their hand so I couldn't say no. Asking for seconds like the first plate was empty. For them fellas, I'd see to it they got what they paid for and not a thing more. With William I would've given everything because that's what he asked for. Because I'm a shepherd, and if that's not an answer, well, I tell you how it is. You're born in a field with nowt but a fire for company, one that about keeps you hot, and you don't know where it came from or how you got in the field or how to start another fire, but you know how to keep it going. And the one thing you do know for sure—if you don't feed it, that fire's going out and you don't want to be the one to let it."

For all the months of talking and cold cups of tea, the case was simple. Colin was dead. No arguing that point. And he wasn't born with a bullet in his brain, so he'd been shot dead. Simply Red was twice deader, and when we told them Mincemeat had done it, hacked bone to bone all on his own, well, they were happy. Dead men can't stand trial. The corpse doctor stuck his finger in Red's side and said it must've been a thin knife. So thin they never found it. They stumbled on the stolen lorry and what was left of them sheep, and we pinned that on Bog and George. Never caught those two and the coppers were happy. Lost men can't stand trial either. Still keep my rifle nearby in case they show up. Now, William. He copped to shooting Colin and called it self-defence. First time he stood straight was when he was being crooked. Lawyers never questioned that he did it but killing folk is only a crime when they say it is. That's what went to trial. Hard to claim you didn't mean it when they found a gun in your hand. Said he carried it for work, the humane killer, a tool of his trade. They almost bought that. He was in a suit at the trial's closing. William Herne. Like a dog in a jumper. Still had the creases over the knees from when he'd bought the thing. He stood. Lone fella on his feet in a room of thirty people, and he put his notes on the table, so they'd not see them shaking in his hands. Looked at the judge, then his solicitor. "Can I speak now?" he said.

Nodded *yes* at him.

"I'm William Herne, you've heard a lot about me, not just in the last few weeks but in the papers. And if that's my head getting too big, then that's the first thing I'm sorry for. But you've not heard much from me other than to say I killed someone, that I'm a killer, whether I wanted to be or not, and that's only part of what I am. I've been a farmer for over forty years, not including time off for breast feeding and foot and mouth, so there's not much I know outside that. The man I killed, Colin Tinley, he was sick, and I asked him in, knowing what he was, and he moved in knowing how afraid I'd become. I'd be dead if I'd not shot him, and it's lucky you're not here to say what's better. So, I'm asking, that when you judge me, you're judging that I let it come to this. I was protecting my family, my wife Helen and my son Daniel, but it was me they needed protecting them from."

Judge looked at him with squiffy eyes. From what I understand, that's not how you're supposed to go about it. You say sorry or you say nowt. "Thank you for your statement, William," the judge said to him. "My uncle was a farmer, so I'm not without sympathy. I want to ask you about Caldhithe." He made some notes on the paper in front of him. "How many sheep have you got on it?"

"Nine hundred ewes, twenty rams, and two hundred-odd lambs."

"And what will happen if you're not there?"

"I see a thousand years in their blood. They see me as the fella with a bucket of molasses. They'll not miss me."

"Is there someone who can look after them?"

"There's my wife, Helen, but that'd mean giving up her job, which isn't right. And there's Steve. Do a better job than I could. Not just with the sheep."

"You trust he'll stick it out at Caldhithe, even with you not there?"

"I do."

"Thank you for your honesty, William."

They gave him five years for lesser crimes and William didn't get to see the fells again before he was locked up. Think that was a part of why it was so lenient—most of the sorry bastards he puts away, what's he really taking from them? Moving them from one shithole to another. As much a punishment as a treat for some. Every fella is due his length of rope.

PART V

The Old North

Yan-a-mimph

Coniston Old Man is a copper mine near three thousand foot tall. Call it a mountain but the insides must be hollow these days and the paths on it trod to nowt, so all of it's a path and the summit's cast in slate, shoeshined like a Roman cobblestone. It stands alone without a ridge to hold it up. A lump ripped out the fells or a wart on the back of them or a sea cliff that got left twenty miles behind and it keeps one of its sides rough to walk on and the other soft, so you get to pick what's worse. Covered with blast holes that are shortcuts to the stomach of Cumbria. I've not been to its peak but once or twice, and when you're up there, there's a reminder you're trapped in a steep-sided bucket off the west coast and on clear days you can't put a knife-edge between the salt sea and the sky and on claggy days you'll not see either. It's busier than ever with offcomers, and they come for nature but there's none to be found. Everything special about the fells is in our heads and truest on maps and the only wildlife left is what ambles up on weekends. For the longest time, I thought it was named for an old man, y'know, because it was meant to look like one. A humpbacked fella lay on his side, drunk or sleeping, working a big fart or ready to die. I looked and I looked. Fifty years I looked, squinting till I saw my eyelashes. Trying to see that old man in the rock, if only his nose or an eyebrow, and I did see him at times. I was up there not long ago and talked to this offcomer, told him I was searching for the old man, planning to sit at Goat's Water till I could see him proper. He said to me, there was only one daft old man up there and he was looking at him. Told me it was nowt to do with old fellas—longship Ostmen had named it with their Viking words, something like Ald Mane, and we'd all been too stupid to say it right.

Doesn't stop me looking for him.

I'm no rambler. Your legs and knees and hips aren't made to go forever, and you're born with only so many mountains in you. I'm saving what I've left for Caldhithe and the land of my flock. But every few months, sometimes years between, I feel a pull to go up Coniston Old Man, felt it more and more after William went away.

It's a tarn I'm looking for. A small mountain pool I swam in the first time I went up and I've not been able to find since. I get itchy when I think of it, like when you're in bed and not sure you've turned the burner off, and all I can do is go check. Prove I didn't make it up. I'll tell you how it was back when I found it.

It was a summer day fifty years ago, a hot day like they used to make them, and I was on my way to school. There was the one school, and all the hill people sent their kids there, from Black Fell to Birkby.

You'll not believe it, but families used to live here. Worked the hills like they'd not been chained to them, like it was a choice. All you see now is offcomers wrapped in blankets outside Italian restaurants. Every home empty but not for sale and the living rooms and linen closets turned to sleeping space for hotel workers. When offcomers did turn up, they treated the hamlets like base camps, friendly, going to pubs for warm ale and settling for cheese and pickle. It was nicer somehow before they made it all nice.

The bus would drop me far as White Claw Beck and I walked the rest of the way to the school, through Briggle Bottom and a paddock of Dales ponies till I reached the low grey building we were taught in, stretched out like a barn, six cow-stall classrooms set back-to-back, and you'd hear all the teachers talk at once through the thin walls. It was quiet that day. As I got closer, I saw there wasn't a person about to make noise. Place was empty and it was the first time I'd seen it without lights on, and minute on minute, I felt more I shouldn't be there. Went to the double doors and tried opening them, knocking on them and nowt. Peeked in the window, stuck my head through this opened slit and yelled. Nowt.

I was on my own, fourteen or fifteen, sat at the top of the big steps, picking at the rubber on my shoes. Thinking how long I'd to wait before that was long enough to say I'd tried. How long for the bus to go the length of the big lakes and turn back. If I say I waited on them steps for hours, you'll know I couldn't count. And if I say I didn't know what I was waiting for, it didn't matter because a lass showed up. Saw her walking through the fields and stared at her. I was told staring's rude but there was nowt polite in my head.

Her name was Helen Yalden.

She was in the year above me and seemed tall and had big eyes the way we thought models did. We'd fight over a seat when she'd finished sitting on it. Got jealous because my mate Tom lived on her street in Saddlesby. Well, she was staring right back, keeping my eyes as she got closer, and held tight to the strap of her bag at the bottom of them steps. "Where is everyone?" she said.

"Must've slept in," I said to her.

"I slept in. They're just not here."

"At least we know where they're not."

There was something about the way she stood skinny in her uniform, hiding in it. "You're Steve, aren't you? One of the farm boys."

"Farm boys? What are you, then?"

"Normal."

"What your parents do?"

"They run a guesthouse."

"What's wrong with farms?"

"People like you live on them." She climbed the steps and sat next to me. "What day is it?" she said.

"Monday."

"I know it's a bloody Monday. I mean is it a holiday or something."

"I'm a farm boy, we don't do holidays."

"Well, I live in a guesthouse. Holidays is all we do."

She got out a diary and flipped through it. Swore when she saw the date.

"So it's only us that showed up?" I said. "What do we do now?"

She answered by getting a fag out and held the tip an inch from my face. Filled her mouth with smoke and let it out her nose. "You not going home?" I said to her.

"You not?"

"If it's a day off, then I'm having a day off."

"You want to spend your day off at school?"

"Do I heck."

"What's your plan?"

"Give me the rest of that for a start," I said, taking the cigarette from her fingers.

"That as far as you've got?" Looked at me and leaned back. "I want to go up there." She pointed to the hills over our shoulders, the lumps making up High Furness.

"Which one you want to go up?"

"The tallest one."

"That's Coniston Old Man."

"I know."

"What you want up there for?"

"It's what people do when they're on holiday, isn't it?"

"It's what bloody idiots do."

"Well, that's what we're doing."

She didn't wait for me to finish puffing. Started walking to the back of the school, quick like the fells were set for demolition, and she hopped the fence though the gate wasn't more than a few yards off. I followed like she knew I would.

Tried not to look as if I was rushing to catch up. She led out the school fields and clambered through hedgerow, hopscotching over cowpats, and she didn't slow when we came to the half-hid woods and the trail of buried ale tins, then we were walking on farm roads. Flattening ourselves against walls to let tractors and trailers past and stumbling over thirty years of hand-filled potholes. We came to a gate and took off through a crop of naked oats. I was about running to keep up with her and she only slowed three miles out the school. Wafted her hands mad to keep the horseflies away, like she was too good to share her skin with them.

We kept going till the fields stopped having linseed or barley growing and till the pastures stopped having walls and then we were in the base of the fells, wading through the marshes and the meadows as if paths were a weakness. The muck soaked her white socks and our school shoes got dipped in bog, coated in silt, and they dried twice as heavy. We finally gave in and followed a trail, and we did that for a mile before she stood still at a small outcrop and turned to face me. She pointed to the ground in front of her and told me to stand there, right close. Taller than me she was, and she put a hand on my shoulder, using it for a post, and dangled on one foot, then the other, so she could take her shoes off. Shoved them both in my bag. We kept going—her barefooted. Avoiding the slopes of scree. Ended up in a gulch, looking down the edge of this overhang. She started talking to me then, y'know, really talking—about Mrs. Fletcher's moustache getting fuller and The Osmonds and owt else she could think of. "So, you work on the farm?" she asked.

"Course I do."

"Every day?"

"Every day the sheep need feeding."

"How much you get paid?"

"Why would my parents pay me to work?"

"They not believe in paying people?"

"They don't get paid."

She went to tell me what she thought of that but was stopped by a loud crooning that sprung up aback us. These horrible, curling aw-hoos coming from the throats of hounds. Dog trumpets. Sounded like a bloody lot of them echoing across the mountain. There was a wedge of rock towering above my head, and I saw a foxhound standing on it, panting, eyes hid aback its ears, looked about and then at me. Ran down the boulder with not a slip and came up to us. She went to pet it, and another appeared on the rock, jumped down, and then another and soon a whole pack of them was standing on the boulder's head, racing down to us. Thirty dogs yapping. Seemed bigger the closer they got. She stepped back and fell into me. Clinging to my shoulders and her hair blowing in my face. At the time, I thought her clumsy. I didn't get that she was thinking I might protect her—that she didn't know who I was.

The hounds rubbed their sides together, slung their snouts over each other's shoulders, and jumped in closer to us, started climbing each other to get higher, a pit of white bellies stacked three dogs high, and I could feel them tugging and growling. Had to stop from kicking out and getting my leg chewed off. I kept still as her. Would've fallen flat if they weren't propping up my knees. I put my arms about her and my fists in front of my face and heard a shouting from the rocks. "Huic to him. Huic to him. Huic. Huic." It was the huntsman. Long coat and a stick dragging across the ground like a match. Booting his way through the pack, shunting the dogs and all their red heads turning to meet his eyes. Forgot we were there. Hounds nipping at his boots like they might carry him to the bottom of the fells. Helen stayed in my arms till the pack was out of sight. I let go and she stood in the middle of the trail with her hands under her armpits.

"You still want to walk up this thing?" I said.

"Not really."

"You want to head down?"

"Not really." She faced the summit. Peak still looking as far off as it had at the foot of the Old Man.

"You can't wait here forever," I told her.

"Why was he telling the dogs to hike?"

"Got to yell something to get them moving."

"There's no reason for it?"

"The reason is that's what they bloody yell."

She started clapping at me, yelling, "Huic. Huic." She took off running, still yelling, still clapping, and I ran after. If there was a split in the path, she took the steeper one, and if that path was paved with rock, she'd run on a bank of turf. The spines of mountain above had turned to valleys beneath, and the better the view got, the harder the rambling got. I asked her if she needed her pumps back and she told me to chuck them. Didn't want to wear them again. Told me to take mine off instead. We followed a trail laid down by sheep with not another walker out there. Path got jagged and we were hopping as much as stepping. She'd wipe her feet dry with her hands and scramble at head-high cliffs till she hooked a ledge and sat on it waiting for me. But with every ledge, the summit only seemed further, and we were both hungry and our necks were pink with sunburn. Without thinking, we moved sideways where the ground looked flatter and kept going. Came to mounds of shale from a hundred years back—spoil tips from the slate quarries. "You ready to say we're lost?" I said.

"What you mean, lost? Can still see the top."

"No way to get up there unless you reckon your shoelaces will hold us for the climb."

"You didn't want up there anyway."

"We going home?"

"I want to cool off first."

"The sun's setting soon."

"Let it."

If we weren't lost, she did her best to make us. Started balancing on ridges and jumping across steps of rock. We moved along that hillside till there was no view to be had and the ground lolled from steep up to steeper down. Spotted one of the few trees and headed for it like it'd give us directions, and it was there I saw a tarn set into a nearby dale. Not a big one. Could've mistaken it for shade. Set flush against a cliff and moving at a trickle over its split lip, down a patch of bog, settling in swamp grass. She led us along its crooked shore, and it was a tarn so clear the sun couldn't stick to the water. Could see every rock and hunk of algae and it was shallow but deep enough to float in. "This'll do," she said.

"You going to drink from that?

"I'm going to swim in that."

"Swim?"

The darkening sky set everything blue—blue cliffs and blue heather and blue ragwort. Ground felt warm and the air was dry. She got ready to go in, no warning and no shoes or socks left to take off. Only three buttons on her frock. If that water was clear, all I was interested in is what the sky looked like. "You not getting in?" she said.

"Could be owt in there."

"It'll be all dark soon. You won't see anything."

"What's left to see?"

"You tell me."

I got in, whelping from the cold, and I don't know how long we stayed but I wasn't getting out first. I know that. The night's meant to be good for hiding though there's plenty it brings out. I couldn't bring myself to look at her, stone naked, but her reflection was fair game. Knew where she was by the ripples lapping at my chest, and they shivered smaller as she waded close till all the tarn stood still. No one knew where we were, including us, and there was no one to see us up there, except each other. Times like that I wished I'd paid attention at school. Must've said something about lasses.

"Is this what you want?" she said.

"Hypothermia?"

"No, to live here. In the fells. Keep living here when you're older."

"When I'm older? I'm the only farmer's lad still in school."

"Sounds lonely."

"You get used to it."

"I think you've been around them sheep too long. You always follow girls up mountains?"

"I wasn't following you. Just liked the look of where you were going."

"You ever done anything without being told to?"

I reached out for her hand, and she took mine. I thought about kissing her and started crying. Not able to stop. My cheeks were already wet. Felt her pruney hands on my face and then closed about my waist. "You're all right, Steve," she said. "You're all right."

Taen-a-mimph

When I heard William getting sentenced, I'd only one thought, *Not bloody long enough.* They'd taken five years from him and given me them. I wanted more.

I don't know how I thought it would be without him, but each morning from the foot of Caldhithe, I could see two dim lights in the valley, Kit Jones's place and Peffer Farm, each settling their own terrace in the foothills. I'd walk the land, from the birthing pastures to the Washpit and on to the rutting grounds and the crop-land slopes and into Siberia. And wherever I'd see the herd that day, I'd start the first count and drop a stone in my pocket for every score. Tried to get as much done before the sun came out. No point wasting it. I'd a list of chores that ran longer than a year and they were written on my hands as blisters. Sowing wheat and sowing rye, sowing early barley for slaughter lambs, sowing turnips, kale, rape-seed to break the soil, sowing clover and cat's tail, tilling, mowing, threshing, machines to do it for me, drying beds of wet crop and baling all that's left, black-wrapped bundles in walls a pin could burst, feeding sheep on cold plates of silage, feeding them on nettles, guzzling troughs filled up with rainwater, fixing bollocks, fixing foot rot, fixing motors, driving a thousand sheep with one dog, shout-ing, screaming, bawling, penning them in with my legs, with fences, worming, dipping, tupping, shearing, lambing, swinging babies back to life and feeding mams the newborn fat from each yellow finger,

mucking, bloody mucking, grassy, sweet and sticky, tagging, dock-
ing, fresh-cut tails wagging on the floor, swearing, bleeding, shitting,
smelling strong as petrol, drenching every mouth to dribble, and
burying all the fallen stock the knacker man wouldn't take.

And then by midday, she'd be there. Near every day Helen was
by my side, would close the shop early or open it late, and you could
say it was a family business again. I was right proud to be working
with her and to be seen with her in the village. And she'd bring dinner like she used to, and we'd stop and talk like we used to. Then we
worked. They were long days even in winter when there wasn't much
day to be had. All we did was work. I'd tell her she looked good. "I
bloody don't." I'd put my arm about her. "Am I in the way?"

Sheep got to be healthier than ever, and we bred out a champion
Herdwick with a back flat enough to hold a grain tank. There was a
closeness in that. Putting ourselves into raising out a flock and seeing the good that came from it. I thought if we had a ewe with the
squarest head or neatest teeth it would mean something.

Put my arm about her one time, a year into it, and she kissed me
plainly on the mouth and grabbed me, y'know how I mean, firm like
you'd hold a ram, like she'd a spurt cup to hand. "What you doing?"
I said.

"This is what you wanted, isn't it?"

"Not stood up. Not in the horse shed."

She let go of me. "You think there's more to it?"

After that, I guess she got lonely or whatever you'd call it, and
she'd come by the van some evenings or lead me over to her sofa
after a mug of tea, and I'd never been so sad at spending forty years
alone till I wasn't anymore. Not that she was mine. Fell in love for as
long as each day lasted, lights out early to forget ourselves at night,

and those first weeks, the creaking from our bodies was louder than the bed. Started my workdays aching for a change, and they're the only aches I never minded. It might've not all been new to her but sometimes I'd catch her smiling, and that was new, and when she'd be snoring next to me, on top of me, pins and needles in my arm, Christ, even now that reminds me how to breathe. And I'm not forgetting where it all came from, she bloody didn't, sat naked on the bed and talked about her husband, but we kept going with it as folk caught in fast tides. I've heard deep-sea divers get giggly underwater and want to take their masks off. There's some happiness in drowning, and I took all of that I could get. It went on, and each time I held her, I felt her getting thinner, getting smaller, and at times it would be like I was doing the job of her skin—holding her bones together. "You need to eat more, love."

"Just me and Danny. I don't need to cook so much."

"Let me look after you, Helen. I want to."

"You don't know what that means."

"Can we go to your bed? The lad could walk in any minute."

"He's never home."

"There's no room on this sofa."

"We can't go to my bed. I've not cleaned my sheets."

When I said it was a family business again, I wasn't including Danny. I can't tell you much about what he got up to because I never saw him. His mam told him if he wasn't in school, he'd to be in the fields, and he'd carry on like a prat when he was. Hold a pitchfork backwards and prick his own guts to make a point. He wasn't a little lad anymore, and since he was old enough to help out proper, he was old enough not to. Anytime he saw me in the farmhouse it was "What you doing here?"

"Am I not allowed to be?"

"I don't know. Are you?"

"It's your house. You tell me."

He'd tell me to eff off, so I did. I'd have crossed the street to avoid him if we had any of them on Caldhithe.

For months after the killings, I'd been stuck in my camper. Eating dinner on my bed before I'd turn over and go to sleep. I wanted to get out of the thing, and I felt Yow House aback me, following like a hungry barn cat, coming closer when I wasn't looking.

Was heading to the camper one day in spring, and I saw a car parked up by the old house. Helen's silver jeep. I followed Yow House's grassy trail and pulled in close to the big door. They'd not cleaned the house after Red died. The police. The council. I went inside where the windows had been left open so the carpets soaked and stank. Heard our Helen panting. Heard a scrubbing noise. She was in the telly room, in her bra and britches, hair tied back, on her knees and elbows, rubbing a rag into a stain across the floor. "What you up to, Helen?"

"You'd have thought all the rain getting in would've washed this out." She kept scrubbing, working out from the corner. "Only made it worse."

"There's no cleaning this up."

"There's so much of it."

"We'll get somebody in."

"You know an exorcist?"

I took a step back and heard a squishing. Whole pile of rags on the floor twisted brown and black. "How long you been cleaning?"

She wasn't listening. "You open the shop today?" She kept scrubbing. Pushing with all her shoulder. Watched her scrub to the middle of the room. "You've to stop now, Helen."

I took one of her wet hands from the floor and she slipped it free. I picked her rag up and she started clawing at me to get it back. I grabbed her about the waist. "What you playing at?" she said.

"I'll do it," I told her. "I'll fix it."

For maybe the first time I'd got a plan. Wasn't right what I was doing in the farmhouse with Helen, for everyone to see, for Danny to see, and there was a whole house sat empty. Only needed a paint job. That was where we'd live, I thought, me and Helen.

I backed a trailer to the forewall of Yow House and put owt not bolted down into it, ripped up the carpets and pulled out the cupboards, not looking at what I didn't have to, two pairs of gloves on, and I dropped everything off at the tip. Plastered the walls and painted all the insides a new colour—green like the lake of a quarry. Wanted to make it right nice for her. Each weekend, I'd go to see Uncle Lanty and bring something new home with me. These bonny pillows ripped out of a river boat with willow trees sewed into the covers. One of them fancy rugs from Persia with a thousand red diamonds on its back. Chrysanthemums and hyacinths and lilies and a crate of daffodils. I wanted a garden. Wanted something that wasn't secondhand, and even flowers from the shop aren't new. I started scratching it out at the back of the house with curved borders to make a path and fences to shade the dirt and I dug so far down the plant beds could drain straight into the Solway Firth. When I wasn't working, I was in that garden. Had been waiting close to a year to show Helen what I'd planted, and she came by on her own, stood with the hyacinths ankle-high. I was on my knees with the sun warming my back. "You got any stale bread I can have?" she asked me.

"Feeding pigeons?"

"It's for bread-and-butter pudding. William's favourite."

"Oh, aye?"

"He'll be here tonight. Want to have it ready."

"Will he now?" I stuck my trowel in the ground. "I do have some bread. It's not stale but you're welcome to it."

She said thanks and looked at what I'd done. "That's a lot of lilies, Steve," she said. "It'll look like a graveyard if you're not careful."

Five years I was supposed to get, and no one told me otherwise. Two years and William was back on Caldhithe. They'd let him go early to free space for muggers and dope dealers, but it was a while before I saw him. He stayed holed up in his house for weeks. Helen stayed close, hand-feeding the soft bastard, and making her way about in the dark to save his eyes the work of shrinking. She told me he slept on the floor by the bed with a pillow under his belly like he'd eaten bad Chinese, letting the floorboards cool him. The farmhouse had a way of telling me not to go up to it. Gates felt heavier and the windows darkened.

I'm not sure how much William knew about me and Helen. There was no secret in it. I wasn't hiding. And I didn't find owt good in knowing she wouldn't be happy with him—that's all the revenge he needed.

I kept my watch over the flock and made a sheepfold for them with my eyes. A month like that, then Helen stopped working soon as William said he wanted to start, and he came to meet me in a pasture. He shuffled through the fields, holding his wrists across his back. Sneezed when he caught sight of the sun. He'd always been a man in control of himself and prison had deepened that—didn't place an ounce more of himself on the ground than he had to and could enter a room quieter than car fumes. But that sort of control only comes when there's something in need of controlling. No man can hate himself and keep living. He either learns to love the parts he hates or cuts them out and hopes what's left is strong enough.

"This you back, then?" I said to him.

"That okay with you?"

"Long as you've not forgot how to work."

"Only thing I'm hazy on is mucking out."

"Good enough."

He went to see the flock. Pulled a ewe close and ran his hands through her fleece, rubbed strands of wool together in his palms as if starting a fire. Got stuck in down to his elbows. Stroked her ribs—hoping not to find bones too easy. Flipped her over and squeezed her udders for lumps. Held his eyes to her hooves like periscopes and rattled his thumb across her teeth. Came back when he was done and leaned on the gate. "They're looking fine, Steve."

"Good sheep always do."

"Helen says you're the boss now."

"I'd sooner give orders to the fells than you."

"And they'd sooner listen."

"You any new plans for Caldhithe?"

"Just looking after it. I suppose that'd be new for me."

The weeks locked in his house were less hiding and more getting ready. Must've thought of nowt but the farm while he was inside. Started each day before me and stayed out long after so I'd no idea if he ever stopped his toiling. He'd watch the sheep keener than a dog and triple count them each morning and each night. If a ewe stumbled, he'd polish her feet, and if she wasn't eating enough, he'd place his ear on her stomach to hear for rattling or bloat. Got so there wasn't much for me to do on quiet days. He was rabid on getting the perfect shite for spreading. Stored manure with the good sileage till it turned sweet as honey and he wanted more of the stuff. Drove the valley asking for spare cow shit and goat shit and chicken shit, and he mixed different pats together to find the best recipe. He'd get on the floor with his hands in cack, listened for grit as he rubbed it between his fingers and gave it a taste for acid like a soap maker. He dried it in a pile outside the house so he could see it from the breakfast table. Ended up with the most beautiful shite you've ever seen.

On the day of spreading the ground had to be drier than navy biscuits, and I watched him drive the spreader across six fields. Got each row tight as backstitch. In the seventh field, he'd been going so long every window of the rig was smeared with muck and at the end of the row he kept going, didn't see the stone walls, brayed through one of them and conked out the other side. I ran over, huffed engine smoke while I pulled him out the saddle, and soon as he was on his boots, he was picking up the boulders he'd knocked down to start rebuilding.

———

When it was time to do our taxes, we sat down, the three of us—Helen, William, and me. Takes days to get it done and you need to get the dogs in to round up all the paperwork. Asking which bastard can't write down ones or sevens neat and taking turns to check what emoluments and accruals and other bollocks are supposed to mean. Found a price for every fat lamb sold and for every thin lamb dead. National insurance contribution. No quicker way to bring a grown man to tears.

It was three in the morning when Helen got the final form ready to send off, and William sat looking it over. Tapped something into his calculator, then looked at it again. Brought his face down to the page. "How can that be?" he said.

Started smacking the papers on the table. Hard enough to tip over his tea.

"How can what be?" Helen said to him.

"We must've done the numbers wrong."

"You can do it again and again if you like. Not like you've bed to go to. You'll not find a different figure save maybe a few hundred quid."

"It's less than last year."

"It was a duff year. Lambing was strong all over. You know how that is."

He ripped the forms to dandelions. "Do it again, Helen," he said. "Do it right this time."

———

We had the shearing planks out and the whole flock penned ready to go with three days of clear weather to get them bald. We needed everyone working to get it done quick and that meant Danny. I'd clipped hundreds of sheep and had a stack of wool stinking by my side, trying to get each fleece off before the slam gate came down. Had one gimmer in my arms on her back, doing a tango with a set of clippers, when I heard a yelling. I went to see the fuss. There was a ewe on the floor under Danny's feet, blood running along her leg and big clumps of untouched wool down her front. "Get her fleece out the way before that gets stained." William was speaking to his lad. "You stupid bastard."

"Settle down. It happens," Danny told him back.

"It's happened one too many times."

William picked up a set of shears, and I could see they were dry as owt. The blades were stuck with wool. Hadn't seen a drop of oil. "Look at this bloody mess," he said.

"They're yours."

"What?"

Danny held up his own clippers. A clean set. "This is what they should look like."

He didn't like that. William turned to me. "Steve, I need you to piss off now."

"Not the first time you forgot to clean them," I said. He threw the dirty pair at the wall aback me.

"Piss off."

I went outside and stacked more fleeces. Thought I'd hear yelling at some point but there only came a wet smack and banging, denting, the sound of scuffling boots, and I saw that injured ewe bolt back to its pen, spreading blood through the flock. I was about to go over when I saw Danny climbing one of the fences, wobbling on his arm as he jumped over, and then he walked away. One of the last times I ever saw him. He left the shed, then the field, took one of his dad's cars, and he was gone from Caldhithe.

Not long after, I heard William's shears going again and each sheep bleating wild as he held them down.

One evening I'd gone to The Crown, and I saw Helen there. She was on her own and she was never much of a drinker. Had three empty packets of crisps in front of her. "What you doing here?" I said.

"Getting too crowded in the house."

"I thought William was never there."

"That's one way of putting it. I can't be around him when he's like this."

"What's he up to?"

"Keeps saying daft things."

"I can have a word with him if you like."

"If you're heading that way," she said. "Make plenty of noise when you get up there, let him know it's you." I kissed her then, to say goodbye, in front of everyone, and she put her hands on my chest as if to push me away but somehow held me closer.

I drove most of the way to the farmhouse and parked up by the rough trail leading into the drylot. All the lights in the house were on and the ones in the barn and kennel and in the old horse shed. Any curtains were left open, and you could see into every room and every corner of them. Pictures on the walls, of windmills and rivers, and calendars three months out. The big door was swinging wide in the breeze. Made it seem less welcoming.

I stomped every few steps to sound off like Helen told me to. "William?" I yelled his name as I got closer. "I'm heading in." I heard a clattering move from one side of the house to the other, things falling to the floor, the cracking of wood, and what must've been pots and pans chucked at the walls. Stuck my head into the hallway. Smelled like a camping stove in there, a hot smell, sweet almost— made me feel nice and sick. "William. We need to talk." There was noise in the kitchen so I followed it to find William sat down. His chair and the table were the only things not thrown to the floor. I'd say he'd lost his mind but he didn't look crazed. Well, he didn't look sane either, I suppose, but he'd no hair left to be out of place and he was dressed. Except for his feet. First time I'd seen him barefoot. He was sweating fierce. Might've mistaken him for having stepped out the shower or having flu. At first, I thought he was supping some odd purple drink then I looked at the bottle in his hands closer—it was methylated spirits. "What you got there, William?"

"Knew you'd turn up."

"Helen seemed worried about you."

"I've not seen her in days. Think she went to visit her sister."

"What you got there?" I said again.

He looked at the bottle and placed it on the side. "I couldn't get the oven going," he told me.

"When you ever cooked owt?"

"I'm not feeble, Steve. I can feed myself."

"But you've been having a bit of trouble, haven't you?" I found a tea towel, wet it, and brought it to him. He didn't know what to do with it. I took it and placed it on his forehead and on his neck. He let me. "What's all this about? Helen said you've been wanting to redecorate."

"It's been tough."

"It has."

"I'm figuring it out."

"You want some help with that?"

He stood up and offered me his chair. "Get yourself a drink. I need to get washed up. We can talk then."

I cleared things away while he was gone. Sweeping the food and rubble from the floor. Hiding away the spirit. Searching for a second chair that still had four legs. He came back down to the kitchen smelling of lavender, and asked me, "So, how we going to start making some money?"

"That's the problem, is it?"

"Can't keep going like this. I'm paying to work."

"It's the farm that's worth owt. Just need to keep it going till you can retire."

"It's Danny's farm. I can't sell from under him."

"The lad want it?"

"Course he does." He pulled a leaflet out his back pocket, unfolded it, a golden eagle on its cover. "What you heard about rewilding?"

"Sounds made up."

"A fella came to talk to me about it," he said. "From some charity, I don't bloody know—wants someone to have a go at it. Said they'll pay us for it. Safe money. Good money. Plant trees instead of crops and turn the pastures to woodland, he reckons. Not for felling or owt like that. Fill the dirt with roots so deep you can lift a field clean out like it's pot-bound. Solid trees. Alders and yews. No bloody pine needles. Enough trees they can start planting themselves and give the rocks time to grow hides of lichen and raise the earth another foot. And they'll bring cows in to wander feral. Ones with ribs big enough to build houses out of."

"No sheep?"

"They're greedy bastards. You've seen it."

"What they need us for, then?"

"You still think we're farmers? Raising bloody livestock. I've never taught a lamb to leap. We build walls about them and wonder how they'll feed. They need us for what they've always needed us for. To do what they'll not. With all the trees come all the leaves and soil as we've never known it. Grass that'll not stop growing and dinosaur ferns. Then there's the birds and the rabbits and the squirrels and they'll fatten themselves like we do, so they can't do owt but bloat. And that means they're bringing the full Ark to Caldhithe. Falcons to gobble the thrushes up and wild cats for the wild rats, and for the big bastards, the deer and that. He was saying they'll bring in wolves. Imagine. A grey wolf on the slopes of Shinmara. I'd lose a few sheep to see that."

"How many sheep need to die before it's wild enough?"

"None of them are getting out alive."

"You think there was no reasoning to getting rid of them? The wolves."

"They got rid of them because you don't need teeth if there's only porridge in your bowl. The weak control everything because they have to. I'll tell you how it is for them. I was there the day they sold Wenlock Jackson—most expensive dog in the world, they said. Everyone at the auction was clapping as the numbers got higher, but all I could see was the dog. Wenlock, a collie, had him on a leash as they walked him back and forth in the sales pit. And that pup's what they call pedigree. He'd an odd set of eyes, one blue, one brown, hips didn't fit in their sockets and the hinges of his bones pressed against his fur. Slinked along the ground like a torn squeezebox. Now, they see one of our dogs. One of my dogs. Run a fifty-score flock down a crag. Swim through floodwater to round up stranded lambs. And they say, that's a sheepdog, not a collie. It's how they do things. They get tired of walking and say the mound they're resting on was the mountain's summit all along."

"Is there owt you've not got figured out?"

"I know what I need to do."

"Making the whole place wild?"

"No, with this mess I've made. I'll sort it." He stood up and started walking me to the door. "You can tell Helen, she's fine to come back when she's ready."

The next day, I found William stood in a pasture filling a trough with water for the Jacob sheep. His eyes clear and every bit of him save his face and fingers, from his neck to his boots, wrapped up in that wax coat, back pocket bulging. Sun had turned the waxed cotton yellow and there were two years of creases in it. Shoulders filled out more than I remembered they did, and its tail flapped in the wind, billowing, like two men could've been wearing it. I went up to him. "This you back?"

"It is," he told me. "So, get to work."

Tedder-a-mimph

There was black smoke on the fells. Thick as long-boiled fat, and the stink of burning came through my closed windows. It rose from aback a hill, this sick, lost cloud. Made the sun safe to look at and lit the sky up beautiful, pink and orange, making a sunrise you don't see over land, and I was filled with a right terror you'd not believe and the calmness that comes with that.

It was silent and far away, the fire, and the more I looked, the more it filled up the air and then the fields, and the more I couldn't stop looking.

There was a woman running down the hill. A barefoot woman, a bare-legged woman, in a nightgown. No, a coat, that was it, a long waterproof, held closed with one hand. Could see her trying to yell. Our Helen.

I pulled on my boots, got out the house, and rode to meet her on my quad bike. The sky had flipped, and all the soot and smoke was pulling low, sticking to the ground with a roof of blazing air fitted atop the fells, and any noise she made, any whimper, any shout, sounded louder and clearer and waited long till it could be heard. She stopped when she saw me. Rested at the corner of a field, at a gate, using the slats to keep from falling. When I got there, she reached through and grabbed two fists of my shirt, leaving black where she touched. She tried climbing over, pulling back the bolt, but stopped tired. "What's happened?" I asked her.

"He's burning it all down. Talked about it for years."

"Is anyone else in the house?"

"Just him. The dogs ran to the hills."

"Did he get out?"

"I couldn't see."

"Might still be time to stop him."

"Can't ask you to do that."

I got back on the bike. "Get to my house. Get someone out here."

I opened the throttle across two more fields and ripped out the top of a hill. From on high, I could already feel heat on my face. The smoke covered everything, and the way it swirled—curling back on itself again and again in great shelves of soot that wedged the sky open. The tall barn was the only building I could see burning. Built on the low side of the drylot with a hundred years of Curdale stone in its walls, taken from the becks and streams, stacked with every colour of fell rock, green and grey and black, square boulders at its corners and great slabs to frame the doors, it stood uneven as the ground and from its cracks it glowed. Each hole bigger than a knife prick had a plume of white smoke streaming out, hundreds of them, like a string net hoisted high above, and the shutters cooked and fell while the metal hinges all hung on. Flames spilled from the blown-out windows, curving about their ledges, feeling for what else they could catch. Up and up. All of it going to the roof, which spat and shrank.

I drove into the flat pasture leading to the compound and dumped the bike. Looked about at the sheds and outhouse. Looked at the storage tanks full of water or molasses and the green single-skin barrel of paraffin. That was safe for now. I walked into the lot. "William." My voice blackened. "You bastard. Where are you?"

I heard something from the old horse shed, a clang, a shout. Went to it and kept low to the ground, pulled my shirt over my head, huffed at my armpits. A thumping at the walls, wooden slats buckling, and the top of the stable door was opened with smoke streaming out in a thin layer. Got closer and the breeze from inside hit me like a belting oven, and it was all blackness. I wrapped my hand up with my shirtsleeve and unbolted the lower half of the door. Got on my knees, near flat on my belly to keep from supping the air. Couldn't see a thing. It wasn't darkness, though there was no light—it was the soot that was blinding. I went in farther, and felt about, grabbing handfuls of straw and the hot ends of tools. "William?" I heard that shout again. Creakier now. An animal noise. One of the Jacobs had got in, horns scratching, back and forth against the wood, and she'd one leg caught in a tangle of chicken wire. I reached out and held her ankle, waggling, pulling. Still on my belly. Sprang her loose and she kicked me in the side on her way out. I followed after—inching to where it felt cooler. Staggered upward out the door, on one knee, and whatever was burning in that barn had sprung, filled my lungs hot, stirred the flames to twice their height. Dust rose in whirls from off the ground and the roof unbunged in a skyscraper of ash, a wild well that spurt and spurt and filled the air with cinders that split themselves about me as flapping bats.

I went to the main house. Door swinging on a wind I couldn't feel and I couldn't see flames but there were fumes. I stepped in the hall and my eyes stung That sweet smell again. Wood spirit. Cooking spirit. The walls were wet with it and the slate floor slippery and the carpets soaked. "Get out here now," I shouted. "Or I'll kill you." Breathed through my fingers and looked in the toilet and the kitchen. It got harder to breathe and harder to think, the drunkest

I've ever been. Turned about, not sure which room I was looking in or who I was looking for. I only knew I was looking for something. Went to yell for William again and said my own name, then my dad's, then Helen's. Soon as I left one room, I'd to figure out why I'd come into the next. "Get out, you silly prick. Still got time." I went in the telly room and felt sure he'd be sat in his chair like always. In the hall, I looked up, sunlight from the stair window was full of smoke, little puffs, and I saw William's hand stretched out on the landing. Climbed to him with my back rubbing against the wall. He was out but his nose and lips were twitching like a sleeping dog's. Saw a tear of flames in the corner of the bedroom aback him, white like one great spark, so I shut that door and dragged him to the front room, bumping every step. Smart thing to do would've been to drag him all the way out of that farm. To keep going till I could wash him clean in Halig Beck. Smart thing would've been staying with Helen.

Laid him on the rug, rushed about for a bucket, filled it from the kitchen sink, then ran back and dumped it on his head. "There's still time," I told him. He twitched. I pounded on his chest and shook his chin, and he opened his eyes. "You'll be all right," I said. Tried to get him to drink but he turned his mouth.

"Steve?" he said.

"Have a drink."

He took a sip.

"We need to go," I said, and drank some of his water.

"I can't breathe."

"Wasn't that the plan?"

"Is Helen safe?"

The heat softened his face, and it swelled as though time hadn't taken the fat from his cheeks. He was a young man again and he looked rested. Pleased. I wanted to squeeze him like you do a lamb or a baby. Squeeze him so I didn't have to hear him say her name. "She will be," I told him.

"Out the back." His head turned toward the kitchen. "Be easier."

"Easier for who?"

The light had gone from the room, window by window as the smog outside pressed against them. The fire struggled with the doors and stairs but you've no idea how hot it got. Wax from both my ears was melting, dripping down my collar. Your thoughts are made of air, and I can scarce remember what happened. "I can't carry you anymore," I told him. Not sure it was true.

"You can't?"

"You want us to both die in this house?"

He coughed, and I could see how weak he was. "Why'd you come, Steve?"

"I don't know."

His nose started running, streaming to his neck, and his breaths came so quick they turned to a throttle. I got on my knees and placed his head in my lap. Cleared his face with my wet hands. He stared in my eyes as I wrapped him in that coat, bundled him and put his arms at his sides. Took a clump of wool from the fleece rug he lay on, a big tuft, and I placed it in his right hand, closed his fingers about it. Same thing I'd seen them do to my granddad's body—so God would know why he was busy on Sundays. I stood and headed for the kitchen. Moving quick so I couldn't change my mind. Heard him say one last thing. "You think you can do what I couldn't?"

I found a tablecloth and wrapped it about my head, left a slit for my eyes and ran outside. There was nowt to see aback or ahead of me. The house faced south, faced the barn, so I pushed against the smoke—hoping that was forwards. I felt grass under my hands, then mud, and the wind cleared enough for me to see the fells. I got on my feet and went to a mound of earth that I'd to dig into with my fingers, slithered up and lay on that mound, hugging it. There was a brick in my head, that's how it felt, I could see it as though in front of my eyes, and it stayed where my thoughts sat, and it would get fuzzy and I'd feel like bowking. Pain throbbing in my fingers and down to my privates. I tumbled down the other side of the hill and fell on my back in a small dale. The smoke crept over me till that was all I could see again, and an evil sleepiness came over me.

I don't remember the blue and white lights flicking overhead or being pulled out, only that I was moving again and that was fine by me. My skin was purple as a dead ram's bollocks, and I was full of tubes and wires. Paramedic asked me, "Was there anyone else?"

I shook my lying head. No.

Helen gripped my hand and held it twice as tight to make like I was able to grip back. She lay in bed next to me, resting atop the covers. I'd been drinking pure air in a straw down my throat for days and I didn't feel so bad till I stood up. I'd been given so much oxygen, I was floating inside myself, dragging my body, felt like a puppy with a tree trunk. Helen scarce left my side but that morning she told me, "I'm leaving." No feeling to it. "Soon as you're able to work again."

"What do you mean?"

"I mean, I've been waiting years to be off. Didn't know that's what I was doing, but it was. William, he called it my worrying."

"You've no need to go," I said, hearing my voice wheeze. "Plenty of room here."

"There's always been plenty of room, Steve. We live on a mountain."

"What more do you want?"

"If I had a good answer to that, I would've left ten years ago."

"It can be different now."

"You'll make it better? Make it work?"

"Course I will," I said, "You belong here."

"That sounds like a threat."

"I've seen you out there. Been with you. It's when you're at your best."

She let go of my hand and sat up on the bed facing away.

"Where you going to go?" I said.

"I'll stay with my sister."

"In bloody Stoke?"

"In bloody Stoke."

"You'll start plucking your own feathers out. You don't know what it's like."

She'd not been in my room in Yow House before. Not till I was bedridden from smoke. First time she'd looked at what I'd done with it—the clean-pride walls, the net curtains, the chest of drawers I left empty for her. "They found his body today," she told me. "William's. They identified it. Thought it was a sheep at first. One that'd got caught in the fire."

"Why would a sheep be in the house?"

"He wasn't in the house."

"Where was he?"

"They said he'd crawled all the way to the front gate before the paraffin tank blew up."

"That bloody idiot."

"Didn't you check the house?"

"As much as I could."

"Why'd you think he'd be in it?"

"It's where he lived."

"You said you couldn't find him."

I meant to answer—kept thinking what I could say. Wanted to tell her I loved her. Instead, we sat in silence till she got up and tucked her shirt neat in her skirt. Looked in my eyes and said, "I used to think you were different from William."

"So did I," I told her.

"Did you reckon we'd just live here, together?"

"I wanted you to have the choice."

"Well, at least you made it an easy one."

It was even easier for her to piss off with nowt to pack.

Medder-a-mimph

Working the land, you don't die like other folk. Nowt you did was made to last out the year, and all that's left behind is your tools. There's no ceremony for what comes next—some new-comer picks up the spade you dropped, then keeps at it same as you did, keeps at it so long as they're alive. I've lived twice the life William did, and I'm still going with this sodding thing. Fewer and fewer who can say that. We're old men, no shoulders left to stand on, ears went before our voices did, held crooks so long they turned to walking sticks, grew more skin or lost some bones and each year we turn our sleeves back another fold like children in our coats. Our retirement is death and I've saved up enough of that to go out filthy rich.

Some younger folks come in, we call them that, young, means they've grey hair instead of white. Each tries their hand at smallholding—shy grazing flock on the acid flats, growing hardy crops in seagull shit, spit-shining tractors with six cylinders they'll never use. Nowt grows back under the next spring's sun and each new farmer's gone so effing quick, you'd have more luck learning the names of daffodils.

I've stayed in Yow House all these years. I'll not call it living, I'll not call it my home, and you'll not know it for the place it was. The ground's paved a hundred foot in all directions, the hills stomped into a granite shelf, a retaining wall set in a cliff face, stone walls fenced off to make a wet yard, stuck a storehouse against the kitchen wall, stuck a ribbed hay shed against the storehouse, a barn that rises above the big roof, a metal tower rising above that, stuffed fuller than my head with lovely shite, shod a thin road to the lanes of Bewrith. It all grows about me without sense. The buildings, the gates, the paths, the machines, in a root ball like twelve men lived here, twelve men tending five thousand head of sheep, but there's the one man with half his senses.

I keep a mountain herd and leave them on those shelves of rock. On borrowed hills. Gave up thinking they follow me just because I walk up at their front. I'd have to know where I was going to lead them anywhere. I keep it nice, down in the grass, let the clover run and sleep the seeds among the oats, and ask each sheep to kindly join me for the spring. I couldn't tell you how many I've got. The flock, it grows and shrinks with no tide to steady it, and I see them fresh each time like my shirt off in the mirror. Fat hungry ewes I've not seen before, ewes I've known ten seasons gone off hitchhiking, a ram I met once as a lad come out in the shearing. I'm always counting, double, triple, more—spot a lamb leaping through the tall sedge and it comes out the other side all new, a gimmer, a springer, a toothless ewe.

I pollarded the whole flock myself, sold every Jacob once that fire died down. I'd had them by the house for an easy job and they stared and stared with nowt to stare at, could see them watching from my windows—while starkers in the hot-cold shower, making toast, one leg out the bedcovers. Them black striped eyes always reflecting night and their horns forever growing. Would smack on the glass. "Quit looking, you horrible bastards." And they'd not move, so off they went to auction.

Took me near four summers, but I made Caldhithe back into what it should be, a hill farm—no cider, hens, or ponies, no offcomers sleeping in the dry barn, no time for milking cows or lowland sheep, no Suffolks, Romneys, Ryelands, or mixed flocks, no Swaledales, Rough Fells, Balwens. What can't grow in the fells doesn't belong. What the sheep or me can't eat, I don't plant. Herdwicks is all I know, all I mean to. Herdwicks with their white heads asking for snow and backs built to mop up January.

For years after the mess, I kept thinking I saw our Helen about. Ambling down the lanes or in the village, working her old shop, walking through the fells with a hood up, at bloody Morrisons out Penrith way, trolley full of wine bottles. Any lass tall enough, any lass with brown hair that gets redder the more you look, lasses with their hands resting in their coat pockets or ones dressed for an evening in a city they wouldn't let me in. Never got close enough to check it wasn't her. And I'd get scared. You've heard of some of the big bastards I've met but it was them lasses that made me shudder. I'd think about her for the day and feel calmer for it and I suppose that's why I never checked.

Then I did see her. Just the one time—ten years after she'd gone. Stood on a mound that rose over old Caldhithe where the sunk roofbeams were turning back to trees. And I knew it was her, soon as looking, and there was no fear that time and no thinking. Walked up and stood by her side. "You still here, then?" she said.

"I'm still here," I told her.

She looked younger. Had gold hoops along her arms and in her ears. Looked smaller. Got blond in her hair that must've come from a different sun. She'd not the clothes on for mountain air, and she tucked herself beneath my arm and held my hand. Told me she lived on the east coast now, a fishing town in Suffolk. Collected sea pottery for a living. Married a new fella, and I gathered he was a fair bit younger than her. Didn't have to ask what I'd been up to—she knew by looking. "It suits you, this," she told me. "More than it suited me. More than William."

"You can always come back. Take over from me."

"I think if you came down from here, we'd all be in trouble."

"What's that mean?"

"When we've no sheep left, we'll be feeding them our children."

"If you hadn't been gone so long, I'd say you'd been spending too much time with me."

She kissed me on the forehead before she left, and since that day, I stopped seeing her so much in all the lasses that come through. That's how it is. I've been a thief. Not a very good one. And there's so many things you can't steal. Can't be given.

I'm still here. All I can ever think to say. A lot of fellas will learn something fierce, get good at it, do it for a long while, so long it gets too familiar, so they forget it and find something else. Always a bigger mountain for climbing and if there's not, they get to building one. I'm not that way. If I get sick of sheep, days they're downed by cars or drop dead from worry, I check their ears are dry and eyes are clear, I check their tongues are unbit by midges, see their necks are wrapped in scarves of neat wool, no mites or ked or scab. If I get sick of their sprouting hides, rubbing themselves bald on the pruning rocks, their hair reeking of soaked hay, I look to our walls and check the copestones, squeezed together without gaps like horse teeth, not room enough to shove a daisy stem, check no stile has snapped its back in two, no windthrown trees seesawing on the boulders. If I get sick of the slanted gates and the lunky holes caving in, I get down to the grass and test my knees, I check the cat's tails, cocksfoots are rooting, dig out clogging pebbles with my penknife, cut up hawk-weed, sorrel, sandbur, violets, check the stems for black bean eggs or pea moth. If I get sick of the ryegrass bleaching, well, the soil's not so far off from that, and I check it's dark as tar, made to crumble, packed with life, four worms for every handful, nowt dead in soil save what we bury, want dirt so lively it crawls off my palm. And if I get sick of the clart and muck, when a mole's ripped through or the roots grow black, there's sky to look at and things above that.

There's folk who're always moving on. Saying they want to see the world beyond here. But they're not seeing it proper—they can't be, can't see a thing till you've seen all of it. It'll follow my life till it's over but that's my plan. Find out what Caldhithe's built on and where it ends. See it for what it is.

Gigget

It's been twenty years since William died but I've no head for numbers. Back then, each year felt like five or ten, and I lived so quick that all I've left is waiting. A year can be a lifetime—go ask a finished lamb. That was William's story, though I can't see for it my own, and there's only one last bit worth telling, from two harvests now gone.

It was winter in the fells. When the nights are so long darkness gets in short supply and there's none left to put shadows on the ground. Couldn't read the land or maybe it had nowt to say. The ewes were at The Nunnery, taking salt air for their lambs, and I needed to get the farm ready for the mid-year sun. I rode out to a wide slope of Niskr Crag with a pocketful of twine. Came to the turning of Caldhithe where the mountains meet the hills and the walls have been toppled so long the rocks have grass growing over them. It was time to build them back up. The fields were frozen, but the snow hadn't settled. No difference to me.

It's a mistake to stay still in weather that cold. Need to keep moving. If your skin shrinks too close it'll start fleshing itself. It's a mistake, and it's one I always make. I found a spot by a gap of fallen drystone where the wind broke on my back, and I sat as a rock myself. Pulled my hood tight so only my nose poked out. I'd a beard, a long, long beard, and I let it take over and the hair atop my lip had joined with the hair in my nose and I thought I'd soon have a hairy

279

tongue like a cat. Got to work. Setting the twine about an A-frame and tying it to stand tight in a gale. Rolling boulders with two hands while cross-legged, placing filling stones in layers that narrowed as they rose but never wobbled, smashing stones against bigger stones to make them fit.

All you can hear out there is the wind, louder than your thoughts, feel it on the back of your eyes, and if it ever died down, I think I'd make a tune with my lips to keep it going. But it never dies. The wind. Only thing that doesn't in the fells. In winter, the only thing that's not dead. It's always whistling, trying to rip your clothes off or whipping you from the floor like a sail, and when it can't move your body, it gets to work on your mind—fresh breeze waking you up and the cold telling you to lie down and sleep.

I've told you what I could hear but not what I couldn't—the sound of footsteps, crunching, breaking frost. Sound of someone walking up to me. My chest flinched like I'd swallowed a gunshot when I saw a fella looming over my shoulder. I fell sideways and my hood blew off and I looked at him. He was stood with the sun in his eyes and the mist at his back, and about his head was a hat made of light, a disc of rainbow colours, pouring from out his hair and his ears and his neck. He stepped closer, like the mist had carried him there, and all I could see was William. His back bent with the same crook and his legs carried him with the same gentleness and there was a lying honesty in his face. He was wrapped in black. Tall black boots over black britches and a black fleece with a collar that covered his throat and chin.

He kept walking, and I was leaning on my hands, losing sense of my fingers. I knew who it was. "All the way out here, Steve," he said. "Almost like you don't want to be found."

"Is that you, Danny?"

"You look bloody old."

"You're not so young yourself."

I'd always thought he'd grow to look like his mam's son but there was none of her except them blue eyes. "What you doing out here?" I said to him.

"Followed your tracks. Wanted a word."

"You could've waited at the house."

"I've waited long enough."

"Well, get yourself over here." I stood and warmed my hands with my breath. "Unless you've forgot how to build walls."

"I didn't come here to work."

"Work's all there is. There's no talking without work."

He got on his knees and started sorting the rocks, making piles of face stones and pinning stones, picking each one up, feeling the shape ready to lay it out. "I went to see our old house," he told me. "My old house."

"Of all the sights you could've come looking for."

"That's the one that belongs to me."

"This all belongs to you."

"Aye?"

"If it belongs to anyone," I said. "That why you're here? Come to get your farm?"

"Not sure yet." I got him to lift the big copestones in place atop the wall and started setting the length for the next gap I was filling. He looked into the valley. "You've got these walls looking straight, Steve. Could roll a marble all the way to the village on them. How much left to go?"

"There's always more to go."

281

"Is that true? Where do they end?" he asked. "Never thought of that before. Do they end?"

"You don't know where the walls of your own land end?"

"Do you?"

"Not far from here." I pointed like we could see owt. Pointed to the far edge of Niskr Crag. "Let's go see it." I took down the frame and my legs twitched awake. "You're thinking you're going to run the place. Best know where it is you'll be running."

"What about finishing this stretch of wall?"

"It can wait."

We walked, following that wall along its crinkled ridge, pushing through the white haze as the route went on and on, with boulders, fallen through stones, cracked slabs where stretches of wall had collapsed. "You speak to your mam much?" I asked him.

"I didn't for years." He kept touching something in his pocket. "Only more recent that I've been in touch."

"How she doing?"

"She's well. Too well. Makes you think how different things could've been."

"You shouldn't hold any of what happened against her."

"Who does that leave?"

"That's something for you to decide." I looked back at his face and stopped searching for his parents in it. "Y'know, it's good to see you."

"You're kinder than I remember."

"That disappointing?"

"Makes it harder to understand it all."

"There's no bloody kindness in owt I've done." Was feeling weaker with every word I said. "What did you want to talk about? You didn't come here to catch up."

"It's something my mam said. Something I didn't know about. She said when that fire happened at Caldhithe, you went in to save my dad."

"Tried to."

"I can't help thinking, y'know, I lost everything. Or near enough. And you got to live here."

"I've got joints with so much swelling I can hear them squishing when I walk. That's what I got."

"Yow House looks good."

"Aye, it's not so badly these days."

"Could you have saved him?"

"He needed more help than I could give." I pulled my hood tight as the strings would let me. "Let's go see where this wall ends."

If you knew the batter of the land like you'd laid it yourself, you could build a drystone wall higher than any ladder will reach and never worry about it tumbling. Built proper, they're only falling when they're pushed. They age like some cave cheese. Rinsed and rinsed, grow rinds, and grow together, joints scraped to fit as one brick. The rocks don't come alive but there's life to them. They bloom and knot till you can't see how anyone could've built them. The farther we followed them to their end, the more gnarled the walls became, the more hidden by moss and tufts of grey sheep grass, and they don't end as you might think, like a spun-out yarn, they twizzle off on a foreign ridge and close in another fella's pastures. I was taking Danny to this stone sheepfold that no one had a claim to and from it set off two more walls that cut through fells I'd never walked on. Other side of that sheepfold was a cleft of mountain, slopes of stubborn green, too steep to build on and too steep to see over. We leaned against that last stretch of Caldhithe. "Now you know," I said to him. He stepped closer and placed one hand on my shoulder, and in his other hand he held this perfect knife. Shone without any sun to catch. Didn't know they still made knives in Sheffield. "Danny," I said. "I've been here waiting for you to come back. I'll leave. It's all yours."

"What is?" He pushed me, not so rough like, but I ended up on the ground. "There's nowt bloody here."

"It's what you make of it," I told him. "What your dad made of it for you."

"You're meant to bury your dad's bones. Not inherit them."

"I asked you to come see him off."

"From what I've heard, you did a good enough job of that."

"I didn't start any fire."

"You never did, Steve. You never started owt, did you?" He turned to the fells. "Before I left, I saw these hills or these mountains, or whatever they are, saw them every day for eighteen years. And I still feel funny looking at them. My legs go wobbly like I might fall up one. Never felt badly when my dad died but these rocks make me want to bloody cry." He saw me sat quiet, listening. "He died to keep living here, but he never said why he wanted to. He never said it was because it's beautiful or owt like that, he said art was effing stupid, never cared if mam looked nice. I think he bloody hated them, the fells. Filled himself on pretty landscapes and still went hungry. But I know how he felt. I've tried getting off this mountain and I'm starting to think there's no way down." He held the knife so tight it rattled. "You think he'd want me to kill you?"

"William?" I said, keeping the lad's eyes. "He'd have wanted to do it himself."

He started rubbing his face like it needed to come off, swallowing down air, throat wobbling like some seabird, and he started to yell. I didn't back away. Didn't shield myself or wipe the hiss of spit from off my face. If he was going to kill me, he'd have to bloody do it.

We heard a baa. A bleating. That stopped him. So loud it cut through the wind and deep into my own mouth like I was making the sound. A bleat only a big animal could make. "What sheep's out here?" he said.

"I don't know. Shouldn't be any."

I looked about where the mist would let me, and I saw something on a cliff face not far away. There was a cave set into it, an overhang, a rip in the side of Niskr Crag with steps of jagged rock leading up. We heard it again, the bleat, coming from the opening.

"Let's go find this sheep," he said and put his knife in his pocket. "Get walking, Steve."

The older I get, the blurrier the world seems. We walked straight and I fell where the ground did. Could feel the air getting colder and wetter as it netted mist, trapping clouds to the floor. The wind would pull fog away and then dump twice what it took. I'd no idea the direction we were going but every time I caught a look of the cave it seemed closer.

Kept my hands stretched out in front of me and they came upon a cliff. "This way," Danny told me. The steps we climbed were set into a crack, one that got smaller and smaller and each ledge of rock got smaller with it. I was tired, and if I stopped still, my body twitched and my brain zapped, pictures flickered in my head of faces and colours and bodies. I was crawling on the steps and a moss grew on them that was right soft, left a smell on my hands like Earl Grey. I was near doing a roly-poly to get across each slab, and when I got to the last one, I lay on the ledge of earth outside the cave and stared. "Go in," he told me.

Up close it was a wide opening like the slit of a letterbox. Scarce room to stand, and the sunlight made the walls and roof all silver and there was no floor I could see. Rocks wedged side to side. Sharp and flat and flinted up to my boots. Formed crisscrossed piles like a hoard of treasure and they seemed to be made of different rock than the rest of the mountain.

The bleating came again from the back of the cave. Started loud and clear and didn't stop. It fell to a gurgle, hocking like a blocked sink, and swelled back loud to a baa, a scream. "Closer." I'd to duck lower to move forward and then there was only darkness. I scraped out with my foot and the air felt warmer and dryer and that tea smell came on stronger—grassy and oily. I put my hands out and I knew something was there, soft, softer than the moss had been, and I felt its shape. It was a mound. A mound of wool. Stacked up to my own height and swooped down to the ground on all sides so it made a carpet, and I couldn't tell where it ended. There was a strange warmth from deep inside, like a bed you've slept in, and the mound moved under my touch, and I kept feeling along till I gripped a ram's head in both hands, and I felt the cut scales of two horns, long as my arms.

Danny was aback me, and I heard him banging something to-gether, then a thin beam of light shone out his hands. I could see the wool was reddish brown except at its edges where it grew into grey. A drained grey, a grey that only comes from age, no other grey like it. The wool was in thick layers, more than I could count, and when I reached in, it was shit-beaten together, fused to the body beneath and harder to pull apart than bungee cords. About its head the hair looked frayed and chewed, and from each point of the roof dripped water and where it landed the fleece was green and growing lichen. A flea skipped across my hand and there was more life on the back of that animal than in all the fells about us. Mites and tics and mouse droppings. A clump that rose out its side, a big growth, leathery and full of circles—must've been a wasp's nest at some point. I only knew the animal still lived from its wheezing. Each breath it took lasted three of mine. I lifted back the wool from its brow, thinking it blinded by its hair, but them eyes. Whiter than the rest of its head, ready to burst, and they didn't follow us or the torchlight. It moved its muzzle to meet my hand, sniffed, and went to baa. When I looked into its toothless gob, I was looking into the deepest part of the cave, and it seemed them four stomachs were the cause of every storm and gale on Caldhithe.

At my side, I felt Danny reach for my hand and he placed the torch in it. Curled my fingers about it for me. "Move." I stroked the ram's ears and pressed my forehead to his. "It's time to move, old man." I fell to my knees and held the torch up. Danny placed his hands on the ram's head and on its neck, tracing along its back and feeling cancers and hardened notches. He took out his knife and started hacking away at the wool, cutting it from out of the walls, shunting the ram till it could move. I saw its legs, worn to the knees, and as Danny moved it, more wool unwound and pulled up from the ground and dragged like a gown. He was half carrying it, letting it take all the weight off its legs, and he brought it to the opening of the cave, resting it down on a smooth slab of rock.

"You're all right, lad," he said. "You're all right."

He grabbed the fleece and started cutting closer to the body, slicing off tufts and throwing the trimmings to the wind. Soon found he didn't need the knife. Ripped its hair out easy with his hands, till all its head was free to shake.

After that day, every bird in Caldhithe made nests of ruddy wool.

He turned the ram to its other side, looking at the view from Niskr Crag, and began stroking its neck with both hands. Feeling out the long breath running from its heart to its jaw. Began shaving, smoothing up its throat, tensing that tube of life. He held his knife in his mouth as he stood aside its shoulders, then cut its neck so deep and sharp he scored the rock and left a wedge like soda bread—its windpipe halved and throbbed, blood shot high then streamed and smacked against three walls. Rusty took one last leap and turned the floor to bedrock with his gushing neck. Danny laid his knife above its head and left me there alone as the mountain soaked deep and red.

About the Author

Scott Preston is from Windermere in the English Lake District. He is a graduate of the University of Manchester's writing program and received a PhD in creative writing from King's College London. *The Borrowed Hills* is his first novel.

About the Typeface

In 1722, the English punchcutter William Caslon released the first few sizes of his typeface, which became popular throughout Europe, and eventually the American colonies. Benjamin Franklin was known to favor Caslon, and it was used for the first printings of the Declaration of Indepence and the Constitution.

Carol Twombly revived Caslon for Adobe in 1990, and added new features like small caps, ligatures, and fractions. Adobe Caslon Pro is widely used in book publishing today thanks to its readability and practicality.